THE TEMPER OF A WITCH

"You whey-faced son of a bitch!" The teapot exploded against the wall, just behind where the wizard's head had been, showering him with hot tea and porcelain fragments. "You lying, double-crossing *hypocrite*." Wizenbeak ducked the creamer, which splattered his black robes with its contents, and deftly caught the cup which followed it.

"What seems to be the problem, Your Majesty?" He inquired, catching a second cup, and one of the two saucers.

"I gave you a simple assignment," said the Princess Marjia. She was a pretty young girl of about ten, wearing a pink-and-white dress which enhanced her light brown hair and blue eyes. "One short list of some people I wanted dead. And what do you do? You make a great big deal of hanging one Witchfinder and let the rest off the hook!

"Intolerable!"

By Alexis A. Gilliland
Published by Ballantine Books:

WIZENBEAK
THE SHADOW SHAIA

LONG SHOT FOR ROSINANTE
THE PIRATES OF ROSINANTE
THE REVOLUTION FROM ROSINANTE

THE END OF THE EMPIRE

THE
SHADOW
SHAIA

Alexis A. Gilliland

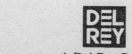

A Del Rey Book

BALLANTINE BOOKS • NEW YORK

A Civil War, Seen from Afar

Part I. The Hunting Lodge

KIRNDAL enjoyed blood sports and regarded hunting from horseback as the moral equivalent of war, having nine-tenths of the excitement and only a quarter of the danger. Today he returned to the hunting lodge in an excellent mood, having arrived as the hounds were killing the stag they had been pursuing. Liveried servants proffered trays of meat pasties and glasses of fortified red wine at which the king and his courtiers paused momentarily en route to the map room.

"A rebellion against our cousin Kahun?" he said, popping a sweetmeat in his mouth. "How droll, how utterly amusing! Tell us the details, Count Osmet."

"Such details as I have, Your Majesty," the count replied, "I will relate with pleasure. There was, in the north of Guhland, a wizard who . . . doubtless with good reason . . . feared being put to the stake by Fadel's pack of witchfinders. His name was Wizenbeak, and he may have had a connection with the late Prince Gatsack, though this is uncertain. In any event, he appears to have commanded a small force, perhaps a platoon of mercenaries."

"Hardly enough to make a respectable showing as bandits," remarked Kirndal.

"Indeed yes, Your Majesty," replied Osmet. "However, he had established a base in the wastes of the Semeryan—" He studied the map beside him for a moment. "—perhaps an inch or two above the top of the frame, about—" He pointed. "—*there*. Just above this little flyspeck which is the village of Autmerida, sitting at the edge of the map, if not the world." A liveried servant passed among them with glasses of strong, sweet wine. Count Osmet took a glass, a sip, and continued.

"So. We are used to thinking of Guhland as ardently, entirely

Syncretist, Your Majesty. In the south, this is true, but in the north, there is a strong Orthodox presence. And one fine day Fadel the Witchfinder-General sends out deputy witchfinders to the county seats all over Guhland, including even the wretched flyspeck of Autmerida.''

Kirndal held up his hand for a second. ''Why did our cousin let this imbecile Fadel do such a thing? Without the witch-burnings, his succession to power should have been as easy as eating boiled asparagus.''

''I can answer that if I may,'' Archdeacon Gyasi said. ''At Your Majesty's suggestion I have recently made a study of Guh-land's current politics.''

There was an interruption as one of the king's house dogs, a spaniel, slipped its collar and came bounding over to its master. It pushed its face forth to be petted, lolling its tongue in syco-phantic satisfaction, a model for courtiers to emulate. Kirndal indulged his pet for a moment, then motioned for the groom to take it away.

''Where were we?'' he asked. ''Oh, yes. Guhlish politics. So?''

''Witchfinder Fadel levied the charge of witchcraft against Queen Shaia and brought her down, to Kahun's direct benefit; and Fadel charged Nasar-Namatu with witchcraft and burned him at the stake, to Kahun's direct benefit. As a reward, this Fadel was raised to high position and given mastery of the Tar-elian Order. So, Your Majesty, we have a newly anointed king beholden to a powerful and very dangerous minister. When Fa-del asked . . . or demanded . . . to send witchfinders through-out the country, Kahun acceded to his request.''

Kirndal took a sip of wine. ''That would be very like our cousin,'' he conceded. ''Letting this Fadel oppress his people monstrously, then, 'Oh, how could this have happened?!' and necessitate hanging the minister who served him so faithfully. Earning the undying and doubtless well-deserved gratitude of his nation, thereby.'' He waved a beringed hand languidly, ''Go on, Count.''

''So, Your Majesty, the deputy witchfinder arrives in Aut-merida, and this poor wizard thinks: 'What to do, what to do?' And he comes into town with his men, seizes the witchfinder, kills or hires the mercenaries he had with him, and sits in the town hall writing out false monthly reports to the Witchfinder-General, telling how he has again met his quota to the cheers of the crowd!'' There was a general laugh. ''This goes on all winter, until finally somebody writes a letter complaining that her neighbor wasn't burned the way he was supposed to be, and Fadel investigates."

"The Inquisition has been quite selective in their burning, Your Majesty," Gyasi said. "Crazy old ladies and paupers might be either faith, but the only property owners put to the torch were Orthodox."

"Exactly so," Count Osmet said, "which, of course, went over very poorly in the strongly Orthodox north. Even the Syncretists in the north, who might have expected to profit by the seizure of Orthodox property, were eventually opposed to the burnings." He emptied his glass. "So this Wizenbeak fellow, upon being found out, figures he might as well be hanged for a sheep as a lamb and raises the standard of rebellion, going into the seven or eight nearest counties and killing the deputy witchfinders that had been diligently doing their jobs."

"The North of Guhland was always poor and spoiling for a fight," said Kirndal.

"Possibly so, Your Majesty," the count agreed. "The last word I had was that Witchfinder Fadel was marching north at the head of the Tarelian Order to put down the rebellion."

The king walked over to the map and studied it for a moment. "The Tarelians ought to be sufficient," he said at last, "more than sufficient. That wizard is as good as burned, but . . ." He hesitated a moment, then shook his head. "No, no. They'll catch him."

The master of the hunt led a dispatch rider, travel-stained and dusty from a long trip, into the map room. Kirndal took his dispatch case and sent him off to the kitchen for a meal. Opening the case, he broke the wax seal on the neatly tied stack of wooden chips and began to read.

"Well," he said at last, "it appears that I was mistaken in my judgment of this matter. The Tarelian Order has been destroyed, '. . . as if by magic,' in the altiplano north of Autmerida." He turned to the next chip. "Fadel and a few of his officers managed to escape the debacle. Queen Shaia—wasn't she reported dead?—has turned up with her two children, proclaiming her son, Prince Dervian, the rightful king." He turned to the next chip. "Lasco Genzari and Count Braley appear to be leading the rebellion." He looked up. "Count Braley was fencing instructor to our cousin, Prince Gatsack. Fancied himself a strategist, as we recall. But Genzari?" No one was familiar with the name. Kirndal read through the other chips. "There seems to be no mention of wizards at all."

"Yes, Your Majesty," Archdeacon Gyasi said deferentially. "One is compelled to wonder, however, what exactly happened to the Tarelian Order in that far distant place."

"Destroyed as if by magic," the king mused. "Wizenbeak, eh? How very, very interesting." He shaped the end of his waxed mustache between thumb and forefinger. "Our cousin may have a problem. If so, *we* may have an opportunity." He walked over to another map and laid his hand on one corner of it. "This is Kalycas Province," he said. " 'Twas ours; 'tis theirs. Perhaps now is the time to take it back again."

Part II. In the Garden

They met in the gazebo at the near end of the formal garden behind the hunting lodge: Kirndal; Archdeacon Gyasi; Count Nulka, the ambassador to Guhland, recently recalled for consultation; Captain Bertino, his military chargé d'affaires; and the venerable Doctor Ras-Haleji, a well-respected wizard. The king sat contemplating the grooms rubbing down the horses in front of his stables.

"Your Majesty did not mind losing at the cockfight?" Count Nulka asked a bit anxiously.

Kirndal shook his head. "One always minds losing, but the cock . . . he raised his spur for one last blow even as he died. That was thrilling. He lost, but he never quit; and we are not unhappy with the bird. Indeed, we could wish that more of our human servants performed as well."

"We try, Your Majesty," said the ambassador, who had taken what was, for him, a substantial wager.

"Yes, yes." Kirndal snapped open a small golden case, moistened one finger with the scented wax contained therein, and applied it carefully to the ends of his mustache. "Time to get down to business, Count. What word from Guhland?"

"According to the first reports, Prince Kahun fell at Sifoty Field, Your Majesty. Unless, of course, he was eaten by a dragon. Captain Bertino, here, was an observer at the battle and can tell you in detail what happened."

"Later," the king said. "Continue, please."

"Yes, Your Majesty. Upon word of the death of Kahun, the civil war did not halt, exactly, but sort of suspended itself, King-Patriarch Kahun having made no arrangements for the succession to either of the great offices he held in the unanticipated event of his most untimely demise."

"Our late cousin had no heirs of the body," Kirndal agreed. "It could be that we, ourselves, might lay claim to the throne of Guhland, though such a course would be . . . to put it mildly . . . rash."

"The threat to make such a claim might be more productive than any attempt to execute it, Your Majesty," Gyasi said.

"Better not even to talk about it," the ambassador said. "In any event, Prince Dervian, nephew of the late Kahun, and titular leader of the rebellion, appears likely to be crowned king with his mother Shaia as regent. The problem for the Kahunists is that each of the several great houses most potent in his support find themselves with equally feeble or equally valid claims to the kingship, and since none of them will yield pride of place . . ." He shrugged.

"What a pity," Kirndal said. "Shaia will play them off one against the others and take the whole lot. Didn't you explain that to them?"

"Yes, Your Majesty." The ambassador looked rueful. "Each great duke would fight like a tiger to be king, but each of them considers Prince Dervian a lesser evil than any of his rivals."

"Or the King of Lagualia," Gyasi added.

"Probably so," Kirndal conceded, shifting his weight on the wooden bench. "What about the succession to the patriarchy?"

"When we left Cymdulock, the Congregation of Clerisiarchs was unable to muster a sufficient number of votes to lawfully abolish the position, and they were deadlocked between the Mambrinistas, who supported the new Witchfinder-General, Archdeacon Rehbeinji—"

"Who's he?" Kirndal asked brusquely.

"The successor to the late Fadel, Your Majesty. He is indeed the champion of the whole idea of witchfinders as a means of dealing with magic."

"Yes, yes. Go on."

"He was opposed by an ad hoc coalition, led by Archdeacon Gorabani, who had been Prince Kahun's chief lieutenant in the Congregation. We have since had word that Gorabani was given the patriarch's hat."

"So we heard," the king said. "How did they stand on the question of continuing the civil war?"

"The Mambrinistas, having done the most to injure the new regime, were most in favor of fighting to the last drop of blood," the ambassador said. "They might have prevailed, except that one of the gates of Cymdulock was betrayed to enemy cavalry patrols before the arrival of the main army."

A cough. "Indeed," he cleared his throat. "Why such bitter opposition to the queen mother?"

"She had been unpopular before," the count said, "because she had seemingly gained sufficient power over King Grathnys to prevent him from settling the succession on one of his two sons—her stepsons—Prince Kahun and Prince Gatsack. For a time, it was common gossip among the wizards in Cymdulock that Kahun believed his father had become a ghola, a walking corpse under the control of his stepmother, and that Kahun had spent large sums of money seeking a spell that would let the dead rest in peace."

"We recall your mentioning this foolishness in your dispatches," Kirndal said, nodding. "Was this the origin of the epithet 'Witch-Queen' hurled against Shaia?"

From the back of the hunting lodge came the sound of furious barking. A black cat was sitting in the kitchen window, washing its face, utterly contemptuous of the opinions of the dogs below. The huntsmen quickly quieted the excitement in the pack, and a kitchen wench shooed the cat off the windowsill and closed the window.

He repeated the question. "Was that where the slur 'Witch-Queen' came from?"

"If it wasn't exactly the origin, it was at any rate about this time that term came into common usage," the other replied. "The subsequent introduction of the witchfinder suggests that Prince Kahun was patiently laying the groundwork for the assault which cleared his path to the throne."

"Perhaps," the king agreed doubtfully, "though we had never counted patience as one of our cousin's virtues."

"Quite so, Your Majesty," the ambassador replied, picking a single grape from the bunch he held and eating it. "After the debacle in the altiplano, when the revolt in the north sprang into full bloom, King-Patriarch Kahun hung the wretched Fadel, gathered an army, and marched north to put down the rebellion himself, falling at Sifoty Field."

"So he did," the king said. "You were there, Captain. What happened?"

"We marched north, Your Majesty, and the rebel commanders picked their ground to make a stand at Sifoty Field. The loyalist plan of battle was to drive a pontoon bridge across the millpond that was covering Genzari's weak left flank—our left as we faced him, sir—forcing him to commit his reserves, at which time Kahun would signal for the main attack on the right.''

"You mention Genzari, Captain. Was he in overall command?''

"Yes sir. He was Queen Shaia's personal commander.''

"So we had heard.'' Kirndal fingered his mustache. "What do you know about him?''

"His disposition of men on Sifoty Field seemed perfectly sound, sir; maybe not brilliant, but good enough.'' The captain rubbed his chin, thinking. "When his opportunity came, through luck or sorcery or whatever, he struck at the right moment and he didn't hesitate, though he waited to commit his cavalry.''

"Interesting.'' Kirndal nodded, as if filing away an important tidbit of information. "The man is sound, but possibly reluctant to commit himself to deliver the decisive stroke. Why did he hesitate with the cavalry? Usually that spearheads the attack.''

"Yes sir. The reason he held back the cavalry—I've been thinking about it, sir—was that there was this noisy kite overhead that was scaring . . . that was stampeding the horses. Genzari must have waited until it crashed, so his cavalry would stay under control.''

"Ah,'' the king said, "we have heard a great deal of self-serving garbage about sorcery winning the battle. This noisy kite was not sorcery?''

"No sir. See, the Tarelians had supposedly been beaten by sorcery, only what it was, see, was the surprise use of troll-bats. Fadel wasn't prepared . . . the joke was that the only thing he knew to do with witches was to burn them. When the troll-bats made an attack in the rear, why, he and his officers panicked, and most of the men were lost in the desert. So Kahun was prepared for Wizenbeak and his troll-bats. His army, sir, they had all sorts of lures and poisons, you could smell the ground kimjii root downwind for miles and miles.'' The captain rested his elbows on his knees and leaned forward. "But there *was* some sort of sorcery, sir. This big old kite, what it was was a mess of three-sided pyramids, 'tetrahedrons,' Doc here called them, making one great big tetrahedron, all green and white, with the wizard in the middle.''

"Right. Why do you feel there was sorcery, then?''

"Well, sir, it went up on this little old string, it did, only there wasn't no wind. No wind at all, sir. The air that morning was flat, still, absolutely dead calm; and the kite, it just went on up with its big green tail hanging limp beneath it."

"Go on," Kirndal said, fascinated in spite of himself.

"It was looking us over, spying out our positions, sir, tugging at the string that held it in place, and bing! all of a sudden the string cut loose, and the kite came drifting over our lines . . . over Kahun's army, sir. Some of the soldiers thought it was a dragon. When it got closer it must have smelled the kimjii root, because it began to make the most godawful racket you ever heard, swooping and lurching overhead with no wind at all to keep it up. But it wasn't a dragon, sir, it was a kite with a man inside. I saw him myself from a distance of not more than twenty feet—I was on the ground trying to hold my mount steady, sir, and it just came by roaring and squealing something awful."

"Did you see any troll-bats?" Doctor Ras-Haleji asked.

"There was a couple of little animals, sir. They might have been troll-bats, and there might have been more of them that I didn't see."

"Go on," the enthralled king said, "what happened then?"

"Somewhere in there Kahun ordered his archers to shoot it down, sir. Everybody was shooting in the air, and our own arrows were falling on us, and then our own cavalry on the left stampeded into our center. That's when Genzari ordered the attack. Then the kite crashed in the trees, and *that's* when he must have sent in the cavalry. After the crash we got word that King-Patriarch Kahun was dead."

"You saw his body?"

"Yes sir. They had it on display on a cart. The sign on the cart said he hit his head on a tree branch while he was running away. He wasn't cut, but it looked like his neck was broke, so it could have happened like that."

"I can add a little to that," Doctor Ras-Haleji said. "The report is that King Kahun carried an extraordinarily potent countercharm against troll-bats in his saddlebags. The thing was, it exerted a powerful narcotic attraction for them, the narcotic being present in a swiftly lethal concentration. If Doctor Wizenbeak's kite was powered by troll-bats, they would have got wind of the countercharm and gone after it, chasing your unfortunate cousin to his untimely death."

"Yes sir," the captain said. "What I heard was that there were four or five dead troll-bats in Kahun's saddlebags, but I thought it was just garbage."

"Fascinating," Kirndal said. "And Genzari didn't pursue the leaderless enemy army?"

"No sir, they scattered in six different directions, and Genzari, he just headed straight down the road to Cymdulock, and don't nobody get in his way. With Kahun dead, sir, there wasn't no one to fight anymore."

"That seems to have been the case," the king agreed. "So, wizard. What else have you found out?"

"About the battle?" Doctor Ras-Haleji peered over his glasses at the king and smiled. "The kite *should* have flown with the wind, Your Majesty. A weather spell from Cymdulock is thought to have caused the dead air which Captain Bertino reports. One assumes that Doctor Wizenbeak had devised some means to communicate what he observed directly to the ground . . . a useful thing in a battle, I have no doubt. And with no wind, he must have improvised a means to get aloft with the remarkable consequences we have just heard."

"Interesting," Kirndal said. "Pay too much attention to your magic instead of what you're doing, you'll cut yourself in the foot every time. What do you know about this wizard?"

"Doctor Wizenbeak? I checked the book on him. He was born Jafzhi William Rebeak, of middle-class parents—the mother's family owned a glass factory, the father was an auditor in one of the banking houses. Very bright, our boy was bored in school, so he ran away and joined a circus, becoming a mountebank. His father disowned him. In time he received a small inheritance from his mother and used it to study magic with Doctor Raswisenji."

"How did he get his name?"

The wizard rubbed his nose. "Somewhere he had dropped Jafzhi, his father's name. And then on graduation he combined his family name with that of his teacher to become Doctor Wizenbeak. When the dean asked for a middle name to go on his diploma, he chose 'Weird.' Eventually he moved to Rosano and found work in a glass factory, handling troll-bats. His specialties are water wizardry and card tricks."

"Water wizardry, eh?" Kirndal scowled at Ras-Haleji. "You have anything more?"

"Doctor Raswisenji was a very learned man, Your Majesty, a student of the great Raspujin, my own master . . ."

Kirndal pushed up one bushy eyebrow with his forefinger and glared. "You try our patience, wizard," he growled. "Have you anything more recent?"

"No, Your Majesty," the wizard said. "After the glass factory burned down, the alumni society lost track of him."

"Right. He lost his job and stopped sending money, so as far as you all are concerned, he ceased to exist." The king turned his little gold case of scented wax over in his fingers, scowling. "Well, see what else you can find on him. Count Nulka?"

"Yes, Your Majesty?"

"You won't be going back to Cymdulock. You did a good job, no reflection on your work, understand?"

"Yes, Your Majesty," the ex-ambassador said.

"Archdeacon Gyasi, here, will assume the post," Kirndal said. "Two things to do. First, talk to patriarch—not Kahun, what's the fellow's name?"

"Gorabani, Your Majesty," said the new ambassador.

"Yes, yes. Talk to Patriarch Gorabani and see what sort of pretensions he has. Find out, well, you know . . . you talk with the man, it suggests questions. Talk with him. Talk with the Congregation of Clerisiarchs. Get a feel for what's going on in the Church. You understand?"

"Yes, Your Majesty."

"Good. We'll consider the matter of a possible schism when you return. Then you present your credentials to the new ruler. No hurry, wait until whoever it is has been formally invested. Let us know the date you'll be going in. You'll have carrier pigeons. Use them. You understand?"

"Yes, Your Majesty."

"Good. When you present your credentials, demand the return of Kalycas Province. You'll be leaving this evening, but we have the demand already written up for you."

Gyasi turned a little pale. "Present an ultimatum, Your Majesty?"

"Well, we are actually demanding the province on penalty of severing diplomatic relations," the king said. "Given the recent civil war in Guhland and the inexperience of our cousin, Prince Dervian—a mere child, after all—it was felt that a gentler approach would give the opposition more chance to blunder." He fingered his mustache, refining the curl at the end. "But in the real world, of course—away from the intellectuals who involve themselves with diplomacy—you couldn't tell the difference."

"Yes, Your Majesty," the archdeacon said a little wanly, "but why now?"

"Because we say: Now!" Kirndal scowled, then relented. "For your own information, Gyasi, in the aftermath of a civil war, a minor child ascending to the throne of Guhland under a hated regent appears to be a rare Lagualian opportunity.''

"But why the Archdeacon Gyasi, Your Majesty?'' asked the ex-ambassador as they left the gazebo.

"Because he has a perfect excuse to talk to the losing side in Guhland's civil war,'' Kirndal said. "He has been authorized to say nothing, he *will* say nothing, but men hear what they want to hear.'' He rubbed his hands together, his rings making a muted clinking. "More chances for Guhland to make mistakes.''

2

Guhland: The Civil War Remembered

It was early evening in Cymdulock. Archdeacon Obuskaia entered Saint Mambro's Church quietly and walked past the velvet rope that marked off the little side chapel for private use. The big man dropped a silver coin in the collection box and lit a candle that his sins might be forgiven. As he knelt to pray, a small dark figure stepped out of the shadows behind the buttress and knelt beside him.

"Good evening, Buska," Basir Orunjan said, softly. "You took your own sweet time getting here, didn't you?"

"Others have business, too, Basir," the big man replied. "You want to meet privily and at your own convenience, find yourself another fool."

"Gently, brother, gently. God has preserved you from the wrath of the Witch-Queen, at least temporarily. You'd heard that except for Rehbeinji you were the top of the list?"

"My enemies take excruciating pleasure in telling me so," Obuskaia said. "My friends console me with the thought that if Shaia knew what she was doing, it would have been me instead of him. So?"

"So it's time to start thinking about a counteroffensive. Have you any ideas?"

Obuskaia rolled his eyes heavenward. "No," he sighed. "Some of us have not yet recovered from the catastrophe which overwhelmed King-Patriarch Kahun. Did you have something in mind?"

"Yes, but I'll need your help."

"I'll help if I can. What are you going to do, persuade Patriarch Gorabani to make a fight of it?"

Orunjan chuckled. "Well, yes, of course. *Try* to persuade him, at any rate. You can pray that God gives him to see the light. More realistically, if we can get the Tarelian Order functioning again . . ."

"Why not reverse the decision at Sifoty Field?" the archdeacon said with a touch of sarcasm. "As long as you're making wishes, do it right."

"Now listen," Orunjan said urgently. "This is a gamble, but it offers us a chance to win big. If we proffer the Tarelian Order to the Crown, as a gift, with the Church funding it, just like always, and contrive to retain control . . ."

"Oh, Basir, be serious. How are you going to do that wonderful thing?"

"We're making Doctor Wizenbeak an archdeacon. Maybe he can find water in the desert, but he doesn't know his ass from his elbow when it comes to military affairs. Besides which, the Witch-Queen figures to be keeping him pretty busy, so he won't have the leisure to find out. We make *him* the master of the order and have Gorabani assign *me* as his special assistant."

"So you could put your own people in? Even a rustic like Wizenbeak wouldn't permit it."

"Not in the top slots, but at the company level." Basir leaned toward him, dark eyes shining. "We'd sit tight, build our strength, and bide our time, so when the opportunity arises, the mighty arm of the Church is once more ready to smite the ungodly!"

"You're thinking of re-creating the Tarelians and then using the witchgold to expand them suddenly in a crisis?" That just might work, thought Obuskaia. A war chest, secret or no, needs to be lavished on an army, which means the army has to be in place before you start spending money on it. And the Tarelians had been *formidable*!

"Exactly! Comes the day, we throw out the top officers and stand revealed in our true colors as we hire every mercenary in the country!"

"You are mad, Basir, mad!" Obuskaia said, "but I rather like the idea. What's the first step?"

"Someone has to make the proposal in the Congregation," Orunjan said. "That way, when the patriarch asks me about it, I can modify and amend someone else's baby, instead of trying to persuade him to go along with me the whole nine yards."

Ah, indeed. Well, I could get Anezkva to propose the idea, thought Obuskaia, so it isn't too obviously a Mambrinista project. But what excuse could we offer the Congregation? He smiled suddenly. We *will* be paying reparations, I have no doubt.

We can offer to reestablish the Tarelians, under Wizenbeak, as part of them. The Congregation would buy *that*, even the Reformers. And the reparation schedule is something Gorabani can work out with the Witch-Queen, if she takes us up on it. And if she does, maybe Orunjan can pull it off. Maybe. What would we be losing? We'd be voluntarily paying something right now, instead of having it extracted under protest later.

"I'll see what can be done, Basir," he said at last, "but I can't promise a thing."

She had never sought the throne of Guhland, but in the war against Kahun her resemblance to the dead Shaia, and the impersonation it had made possible, had been the key to victory. With Kahun dead, that victory now seemed the most transient of happy illusions, solving one set of problems only to replace them with another. If she wished to secure the throne for Prince Dervian, seemingly the only honorable solution to her situation, it would be impossibly difficult to strip off the mask of Shaia, recently Witch-Queen of Guhland. Her life, and the lives of her friends, depended equally upon her success as an impostor and as a ruler.

She was a peasant girl from the north, educated far above her station, far below her intelligence. Physically she was lean, sharp-featured, and tough as old harness leather. Dr. Wizenbeak had rescued her from a witchfinder's dungeon the day before she was to be put to the stake and had taken her oath to serve as his apprentice. Under his somewhat casual tutelage, she had learned a little about magic and a great deal about troll-bats and the art of government, subjects to which she had been almost inadvertently exposed. She was in her early twenties, with black hair, still short from being shaved in the witchfinder's dungeon, and brown eyes. As a matter of policy, she wore no makeup at all.

Her garb was deceptive: a mauve silk gown with full sleeves, a great shawl of black lace over her shoulders, a black velvet cap of maintenance trimmed with pearls. About her neck she wore a necklace of amethysts set in white gold, with matching bracelet and ring. At a distance she looked much older than she was. The black hair and smooth, slightly olive skin was attributed to Shaia's dark arts, a natural beauty taken for an artifact, to thus become a source of gossip for women, wariness for men. Publicly, she maintained that she was dressing down so as not to distract attention from Prince Dervian. Privately, she had dressed to look more nearly the age of the True Shaia, whose body had been torn apart by the sectarian mob that sacked the Royal Palace.

"Janko" Jankura, apprentice to Dr. Wizenbeak, the False Shaia, Regent-Elect of Guhland, sat at the head of the table in one of the small rooms near her suite in the Citadel. Even with the skylight cleaned, the room was cheerless and dark, the consequence of a blocked chimney that made the fireplace unusable. It was a temporary expedient of the most marginal character. For her Privy Council Chamber she would have to seek out a more congenial location elsewhere.

At her left sat Lasco Genzari, the former mercenary who had risen to be general of her army. He sat immobile, his deeply lined face and grizzled hair conveying that certain solidity, dependability, or weight of character called *gravitas*. His lack of imagination was offset by his hard-won knowledge of his profession. On the field of battle, you could depend on him to make no unforced errors.

Beside him, Count Braley, Prince Gatsack's fencing master and strategist, who had continued the struggle against Kahun after his master's death at Mewis Field. Brilliance, audacity, and discipline all were overshadowed by his physical good looks. His devotion to the art of the sword, he said, had led to certain indifference to women, which had, in turn, inspired the calumny that he preferred boys. For obvious reasons, no one had ever put the question to him directly.

At her right, Dr. Wizenbeak took his seat. A long nose, supporting rectangular emerald spectacles in gold wire frames, topped his long beard and flowing mustaches, mostly white. The voluminous black robe of a lay preacher, lumpy with pockets, lay open over the green and white shirt of a water wizard. He was lean and brown and agile, hands gnarled with age, but still dexterous.

A cut crystal bowl of oranges and plums sat in the center of the table, and a decanter of good red wine with inverted glasses sat on a linen napkin that covered a silver serving tray. A carpet on the floor and gilt-frame mirrors on the wood-paneled walls tried to impart a touch of graciousness to the otherwise cramped and dreary room.

Jankura turned to Wizenbeak, who had not been late although the last to arrive. "You saw Patriarch Gorabani today?"

The wizard nodded. "Yes," he said softly. "He confirmed the offer he'd made yesterday." He snapped open his diptych, peering at it to read what had been inscribed on the wax surface.

"One, I am now formally an Archdeacon of the Syncretist Church, to be vested at my earliest convenience." From an inner pocket he produced a scroll of parchment and laid it on the table.

"A bit strange for a wizard, don't you think?" Braley asked.

"Hunh. Gorabani himself is a wizard," Wizenbeak replied, without looking up. "And some of the Reformers know more magic and less religion than I do. No big deal." He turned back to the diptych. "Two, he is prepared to make some sort of settlement on the witchgold. He will send over a negotiator . . ." He peered at the wax surface. "Someone named Kurjima. I'd guess he wants to be able to settle without saying that he was the one who sold out to us. Three." He coughed. "Three is strange. Since I am now an archdeacon, and therefore a good old boy, Gorabani offered me the position of master of the Tarelian Order."

"Instead of abolishing the order as we had demanded?" Jankura asked.

"An offer of Church funding goes along with it," the wizard said, "money we'd have a hard time raising on our own."

Jankura nodded. "Go on."

"Fourth and last, he wants us to stop the persecution of the Mambrinistas, who are, after all, his fellow clerisiarchs."

"And yours," Jankura said, touching the scroll with one long finger.

"Yes, Your Majesty," the wizard agreed. "I have, however, retained my prejudice against burning people, so in spite of my advancement to the Congregation of Clerisiarchs, I do not consider the Mambrinistas my fellow anythings. Gorabani has made us an offer which we are bound to consider."

"He was going to appoint you Grand Master of the Tarelian Order?" Jankura asked, twisting the large amethyst ring on her forefinger. The Tarelians had been the mighty arm of the Church Militant, badly broken in the civil war, and presently disbanded.

"Irrevocably," Wizenbeak said, sitting back in his chair. "I am to be master for life, in writing, and by proclamation. Also, to help in rebuilding the order, I have been offered a levy on the revenues of the Church." He pushed the diptych across the table to her.

"How very generous," Jankura said sarcastically, looking over the numbers. "This is our own money they're offering us. By rights we should be getting it as reparations."

The wizard shrugged. "Yes, of course. That and more, eventually. This is now, which is something else."

"Suppose we just seized their properties for the treasury?"

"You'll have to do it between now and the coronation, Your Majesty," Lasco Genzari replied, "because that's when our own levies start marching back north."

"And, of course, Patriarch Gorabani has sworn to oppose such a step," the wizard added. He smiled apologetically. "Nevertheless, if you think it can be done, go right ahead."

Count Braley shook his head and rested his elbows on the table. "It's doable," he said at last. "I think if our backs were to the wall, we might be able to pull it off, but I don't fancy the odds. This is money in the bank."

"You don't think we could do better trying to pry loose some of the Church lands?"

"Ah, no, Your Majesty," Braley said softly. "Reparations are one thing, land reform is something else."

"What about Lagualia?" Genzari asked. "If we take on the Church over land reform, we're like two water birds fighting over a fish, with Lagualia as the fisherman that will seize the prize."

"Doctor Wizenbeak?"

"Land reform is nothing but trouble. The beneficiaries won't fight for you, and the landlords—the Church, in this case—will fight against you to the bitter end. Which they're inclined to do anyway. Besides, Genzari is right."

Jankura nodded. "I have to agree. So what's the down side of Gorabani gifting us with the Tarelians?"

There was a pause. Finally Count Braley turned over two wine glasses, filling one for Jankura and the other for himself. "Doctor Wizenbeak's health," he said, raising the cup, "Your Majesty."

"What do you mean?"

"Archdeacon Wizenbeak here rebuilds the Tarelians up to their old form, right?" Jankura nodded. "The Tarelians are figured in our order of battle, right?"

"I see what you're getting at," Genzari said. "When the good doctor dies, the Tarelians revert to Church control."

"Exactly," Count Braley said. "Stick a knife in old Wizenbeak—you should pardon the expression, doctor—and the balance of power shifts dramatically." He took a swallow of wine. "Whenever *they* decide."

"Do you then think we should not accept Gorabani's offer?" Jankura asked.

Braley's overly handsome face assumed a rueful expression. "You asked me what the down side was," he said at last. "I don't know that we can do any better."

"Lasco?"

Genzari fingered his closely clipped mustache. "Take it, Your Majesty," he said. "The Tarelians were one hell of an outfit, and I'd just as soon have them on our side."

"Doctor Wizenbeak?"

"Take it. I can ask Patriarch Gorabani to consult Your Majesty about any future appointments." He might even consent to do so, thought the wizard. "In any event, it appears to be a problem for the future."

"I see," Jankura said. "At one stroke we let the Mambrinistas slip through our fingers and permit the Church to rearm itself." She took a sip of the wine Braley had poured her. "A good day's work, gentlemen."

"Your Majesty has a better policy to offer?" Genzari asked politely.

They sat in the ad hoc Privy Council Chamber, Jankura, Genzari, and the clerisiarch Danya Kurjima, special assistant to the patriarch.

"The Church is, of *course*, repairing the Royal Palace," Kurjima said patiently. Patriarch Gorabani had selected him to conduct negotiations with Queen Shaia and, after the introductory session, left him to fend for himself, with the admonition that what he did was subject to review. "While the riots were entirely the responsibility of Prince Kahun, our people were caught up in the swirl of emotion and may have acted unwisely. Any damage we did, we will repair. But a new roof? We didn't touch your old roof!"

"The operational word is old," Jankura replied from the other side of the table. "The current roof was rebuilt after the great fire one hundred thirty years ago. Oak timber framing with chestnut planks covered by lead sheet." She had spent some time discussing the matter with the chief of maintenance and as a result had a number of arcane details at her fingertips. "We were planning to replace the roof. There was a suite of silver furniture in the Hall of Mirrors that would have taken care of a good part of it."

Deacon Kurjima looked pained. He was a slender man, about

sixty years of age, white-haired, with a face that suggested wisdom.

"You could build a lot of roof for eight hundred fifty pounds of silver," said Genzari. "Of course after the riot, it isn't there anymore, the silver."

"We have no idea what happened to the silver furniture . . ."

"Nor to the gold service for one hundred seventy-nine," Jankura said. "It was originally for two hundred, but there was a certain amount of pilferage over time. This time, our guests took everything."

Kurjima sighed. "The Church sincerely wishes to accommodate the wishes of the secular authorities, but it isn't easy. Hanging scores of deacons and lay preachers will hardly make us better disposed toward the justice of your claims."

Genzari fingered his closely clipped mustache. "We showed great restraint, Doctor Kurjima," he said. It would be more fun to put the screws to Gorabani, he thought, but I suppose that's why the patriarch delegated the assignment. "You should understand that we were, until the very last minute, going to have twelve empty nooses on the level between Rehbeinji and the others. To symbolize our determination to hang the Mambrinista archdeacons that have so far gone scatheless."

"That bloody deed would have ended any hope for accommodation between us," the deacon said gravely. "Even the threat would have chilled our tentatively warming relationship."

"Some of us, and I will mention no names," Lasco Genzari said, "but his initials are William Weird Wizenbeak, feel that such an accommodation is impossible, and that the only safe course is to break the power of the Church in secular affairs."

"God would never permit it! The power of the Church is rooted in the hearts of the people of Guhland!"

Jankura laughed. "*Tell* us what God will not permit, Doctor Kurjima! The Congregation of Clerisiarchs which rules the Church is as rotten as the palace roof!" She sat back in her chair and folded her hands in her lap. "Now it happens that while I have the greatest respect for Doctor Wizenbeak, it isn't always practical to do what he wants. One cannot reform the Church and also have the peace needed to recover from the civil war at the same time. My inclination is to choose peace, and let the Church repair its own roof."

Kurjima studied her for a moment. She was wearing mauve and silver, quiet but tasteful—appropriate for the queen mother. Still, her hair was black, showing none of the gray that ought to be there, and her face was unlined, tangible evidence that she was using witchcraft to dust the age from her appearance. On the other hand, it was well done. "Your Majesty is most kind," he said.

"Naturally, we'd need some sort of indication that the Church was interested in living in peace with us."

"What we had in mind, initially," Genzari said, opening his diptych, "was the repayment of the property seized from the so-called witches your people burned so enthusiastically."

"The witchgold?" Kurjima asked. "There are some problems, there. Records were destroyed or not properly kept, and much of the reputed bullion has simply disappeared, like your suite of silver furniture."

"I'm talking real estate," Genzari said. "Land. The practice was for the witchfinder to seize title after the owner was burned, selling it at bargain prices to his friends, with the money going to the Church. We propose to return title to the heirs of the decedent—that's lawyer talk for 'burned witch'—without compensation to the present owner. Their remedy would be to recover the sale price from the Church."

"That isn't entirely unreasonable," the deacon conceded. "What if no heirs can be found?"

"Then the title reverts to the Church that the owner belonged to prior to her demise," Jankura said. "In most cases this would be the Orthodox Church."

Kurjima made a few notes in his diptych. "That is not too bad, in principle," he said at last. "There is a potential problem in that the Orthodox do not have a ruling congregation as we do, but instead consist of independent congregations. They ensure doctrinal conformity . . ." He stopped and smiled gently. "Orthodoxy has been my special study," he said, by way of apology for his digression. "With regards to your proposal, it seems both moral and ethical." He snapped his diptych shut. "We shall consider the matter in the Congregation and let you know whether or not it is acceptable."

"That's very kind of you," Jankura said. "If it isn't acceptable, of course, I would have to admit that Doctor Wizenbeak was right."

"And if Wizenbeak was right," Genzari said pleasantly, "we would be obliged to hang us some archdeacons!"

"I understand. Yes. I shall discuss the matter with Patriarch Gorabani, and if you haven't heard from us in a day or two, consider it the silence of assent."

"It's a pleasure to do business with you, Doctor Kurjima,"

Jankura said, keeping a perfectly straight face. "What about a new roof for the palace?"

The deacon looked pained. "The Church will put on the new roof for you," he said, making a note, "but why chestnut planking?"

"It keeps the spiders off," Jankura said.

Above the reading room in Syncretisty Hall, the late King-Patriarch Kahun had remodeled an attic into a suite of offices. Upon receiving the patriarch's hat, Gorabani had simply moved into the master office, putting Danya Kurjima and Basir Orunjan in the lesser one. There hadn't been time to make any changes. A bust of Kahun had been removed. The life-sized portrait, which wouldn't go through the door, was temporarily covered with a drop cloth. A pair of Kahun's slippers lay under the sofa waiting to be discovered.

"Are we planning to attend Archdeacon Rehbeinji's hanging, Your Holiness?" Basir Orunjan asked in minimally civil tones.

Patriarch Gorabani composed his black-gloved hands in front of him and considered the question. The newly minted patriarch was tall and lean in early middle age, a classically handsome face saved from prettiness by a strongly hooked nose. His close-cropped hair was dark brown, his eyes hazel, his complexion olive. He wore a clerisiarch's red robes, purfled along the edges with the white and gold embroidery that marked his rank. This, together with the great signet ring on his right forefinger and the massive gold chain of office hanging from his shoulders, denoted the wearer as patriarch of the Syncretistic Church.

"Rehbeinji is no longer an archdeacon," he observed at last, "nor a clerisiarch, nor even a member of the Church. He has been excommunicated therefrom for what we have described as 'crimes against humanity.' "

"Thrown to the wolves, you mean?"

"Don't be tiresome, Basir. You saw the list that Wizenbeak handed us. Do you doubt that the others on the list would have been taken if we had balked at Rehbeinji?"

"No, sir. But we should have fought! The Witch-Queen would drown in the blood of martyrs!"

"The Congregation of Clerisiarchs rejected that option when they elected us patriarch, Basir." Gorabani sat back in his carved wooden chair as his face relaxed toward the beginning of a smile. "Had *Rehbeinji* been elected . . . what was the little scurril that was making the rounds then? 'When martyrs' blood / Pours down the sewer drains / Ah, then, my friends / The future will be bright!' ''

"He had the majority, Rehbeinji did. *He* should have been elected instead of you!''

"Perhaps he had a majority of three or four votes, Basir, but not the two-thirds majority that was needed.''

"A contemptible quibble, Your Holiness, the sophistry of a bean counter! *You* were elected because you promised to protect him!''

Gorabani sighed. It was true, and he had tried, but Wizenbeak and Genzari had said 'Rehbeinji dies. Give him to us, or we shall take him. And if we must *take* Rehbeinji, we shall be none the worse for taking a dozen others.' So he had cast Rehbeinji out, hoping to save the rest.

"That's true,'' he said quietly, "but we promised to protect others, as well.''

Orunjan turned away from the window, hands clasped behind him. "It grieves me to say this, Your Holiness, but the Congregation should have elected him and hung you.''

"They had their chance. Rehbeinji *offered* them the opportunity to be martyred for the Church. In the end, that's why he lost. The appetite for martyrdom is easily sated.''

"No, Your Holiness,'' the little man said sourly, "the taste for martyrdom is easily lost, else we should be surfeited with saints.''

"Perhaps. But why reproach us because the Congregation doesn't share your zeal? Besides, do you wish to fight, or merely to die fighting? If you intend to prevail, the will alone is not sufficient. One must meet armies with armies.''

"Without the will, armies are useless,'' Orunjan replied. "Give the word, we can raise an army! We have the gold to do it, Your Holiness!''

"What would you do, hire the scattered losers from Mewis Field?'' Gorabani asked derisively. "Better to make the best peace possible in the circumstances.''

"You'd make peace with the Witch-Queen?! What other great strokes of policy have you hidden up your sleeve?''

Gorabani sat turning the great gold signet ring on his forefinger. "Basir,'' he said at last, "you have been *extremely* useful to us, and your past services are *greatly* appreciated, but you are no longer indispensable. Do you understand?''

Orunjan walked over to the gabled window and looked out across the square. "Yes, Your Holiness. I have spoken my mind, and you have decided you need a more pliant archdeacon to replace Rehbeinji. Though you'll find none better qualified.''

"That is not yet certain," Gorabani said, "but if we are to follow a policy of conciliation, we shall have need of conciliators.''

"You've changed, sir. There was a time when you were as bold as they came.''

"The times changed, old friend. We were bold in the service of Prince Kahun, taking the risks he wished taken the surest way we could find.'' The patriarch shook his head. "Since Mewis Field, a lot of things have changed. King-Patriarch Kahun is dead, and the Witch-Queen is wearing one of his hats, while I am wearing the other. We are no longer trying to do Kahun's bidding as expeditiously as possible.''

"What are you trying to do?''

"End the civil war, Basir.''

"Wonderful. And the property confiscated from the witches that were burned, is that to be returned to the 'rightful' heirs, also?''

A man will forgive the murder of his father, before he'll forgive the theft of his patrimony, mused the patriarch. Returning the witchgold is something the Church has got to do, eventually, but do we have to tell Basir today? He sighed. "There is ample precedent for refusing to do so, old friend.''

Wizenbeak sat in the sedan chair, absently rubbing the troll-bat's ears as he pondered his relationship with the troublesome animal. Branka was bright enough, he conceded, but he wasn't, what . . . committed? No. Dedicated? Not exactly. He weighed various analogies . . . taken young and kept separate from its fellows, a troll-bat develops an almost doglike devotion to its handler, producing a most felicitous bonding in the best cases. Branka, now, had been taken seasonably, but by Princess Marjia . . . who, of course, had been obliged to give him up.

Troll-bats were dangerous animals, even to experienced handlers, sometimes; and Jankura had very properly made Marjia get rid of the little monster. So Marjia had given Branka, her own personal troll-bat, to him to train up as best he might—for *her*. So naturally Branka, faced with divided loyalties, had become somewhat . . . catlike? Not exactly, he decided, more like a natural troll-bat—if such could be imagined, the animals not existing in a state of nature. A feral troll-bat? He felt his neck hairs bristle. Outside, someone shouted a command, and the sedan chair was lowered to the ground.

The wizard gently eased Branka back into his pocket and pushed the curtain back. It was raining, and they were in front of Syncretisty Hall, with a liveried servant holding an umbrella for him. The seat of the Congregation of Clerisiarchs, he thought wryly. A few weeks ago they wanted to put a torch to *my* seat, and now it's welcome to the club. He sighed and climbed carefully out of the sedan chair. Reasons of state are the devil. Without them, they wouldn't have asked, and I wouldn't be accepting, and we'd both be happier.

Inside the front doors, the servant with the umbrella turned him over to a small, sallow-faced clerisiarch with dark eyes.

"Doctor Wizenbeak? We've been expecting you. I'm Basir Orunjan, special assistant to the patriarch." He did not offer to shake hands, nor did the wizard feel at all moved toward such a gesture.

"Your hospitality is overwhelming," Wizenbeak said with the faintest parody of a bow.

"I sincerely hope not," the reply. "Our intention was to be merely correct."

They walked through the reading room and past the library and lavatories, coming to the high-ceilinged room where the Congregation sat. Wizenbeak looked around. Shabby green carpet, choir stalls salvaged from some ruined church, a nondescript table and chairs in front of a gilt throne . . . somehow he'd imagined a far more impressive setting. Still, if he imagined the galleries above the choir stalls crammed with people, listening to the great debates of the past . . . one could very easily come to feel awe. The very stones reeked history.

"Who sits where?" he asked.

"The patriarch sits at the end," Orunjan replied, "the secretary, Archdeacon Darussis, sits at the table, and the sergeant-at-arms, Archdeacon Obuskaia, sits behind him."

"Hunh-hunh." The wizard nodded. "I meant, who sits in the benches? Where are the Mambrinistas?"

"On our left, usually," Orunjan replied. "The Mambrinistas used to sit on the right of the throne, and up front—"

"You just said left, didn't you?"

"*Our* left, Doctor Wizenbeak. The patriarch's right, as he faces the chamber. Patriarch Gorabani has used his discretionary powers to decimate them—in part to provide funding for the

Tarelian Order—and the survivors now sit a bit further removed. Follow me.''

They walked down the green-carpeted center aisle, past the long table, and up to the throne itself, which, the wizard noted, was rather crude in the execution. Basir Orunjan slid back a green velvet curtain to reveal an open doorway to the right of the throne as they faced it.

The left cloakroom was long and narrow, furnished with leather-cushioned benches, and dark wooden chairs of assorted provenance. Archdeacon Darussis, Patriarch Gorabani, and three other clerisiarchs were sitting by the corner windows.

"Good afternoon, Doctor Wizenbeak," Darussis said, rising and extending his hand. "You know the patriarch, I believe. Archdeacon Obuskaia, one of our leading Mambrinistas." Obuskaia nodded curtly and remained seated, a bald, tough, ugly man of imposing size. The wizard thought he looked somewhat like a bear, a natural choice to be sergeant-at-arms.

"Doctor Kurjima, who is, like Doctor Orunjan, a special assistant to the Patriarch."

Kurjima stood up, as befitted Archdeacon Wizenbeak's superior rank and shook hands.

"And, of course, Archdeacon Anezkva," Darussis concluded, "our expert on theological jurisprudence." Anezkva was perhaps thirty, with prominent blue eyes and a high forehead. A scholar, decided the wizard, shunning the bruising contact with ideas in their wild state . . . but "theological jurisprudence" was a bruising idea.

"Excuse me," the wizard said. "Theological jurisprudence sounds like refereeing scholastic disputes. What do you do?"

"The Church retains jurisdiction over its own people," said Anezkva, rising languidly to his feet. "Imposing a higher standard of discipline on them than the secular authorities, we naturally find it necessary to try infractions in our own courts."

More concessions to demand, thought the wizard, but not now. "An interesting arrangement," he remarked quietly.

Anezkva smiled without warmth and proffered a patently limp hand, palm down.

As Wizenbeak took it, Branka climbed out from under his master's beard and walked down the arm that the wizard had extended. Anezkva's hand remained limp, his smile remained fixed, but it was obvious that he knew of troll-bats, and equally obvious that he didn't like them. Wizenbeak shook the limp hand firmly, afraid to startle Branka with an unexpected move, and on the third stroke Branka sat on his wrist, wrapping his own long, webbed fingers over the handshake. Aneskva's smile vanished as his unwilling hand applied a pressure that matched Wizenbeak's own. Then Branka sprang nimbly to his master's shoulder, as Archdeacon Anezkva sprang nimbly backwards, rubbing his hand.

After a second, seeing that Anezkva was unhurt, Gorabani laughed. The young archdeacon flushed, but said nothing.

"My apologies," Wizenbeak said. "Little Branka is still in the process of learning the ways of humans."

"No matter," Kurjima said. "We'll put him on the right. They aren't housebroken, either."

The patriarch permitted himself a smile, then got down to business. Reaching into his pocket, he produced the signet ring of the Tarelian Order, a carved bloodstone, set in red gold.

"This ring is the official seal of the Tarelian Order," Gorabani said. "The presentation ceremony is normally hedged about with all sorts of qualifiers, outlining the duties and responsibilities of the master of the order." He smiled. "The fact is, most of the recent masters have died a violent death, so that in giving you the title for life, we may not be doing you any favors. You set your hand to *this* plow, death alone will release you." There was a pause, and the wizard felt a cold wind blowing through his bones. For a pro forma ritual oath, this one had a lot of bite.

"Archdeacon Wizenbeak," the patriarch intoned, "will you accept the irrevocable responsibility for the Tarelian Order?"

"I will," the wizard said, thinking about his predecessors in office. Nasar-Namatu had been burned at the stake for opposing Kahun, and Fadel had been hung for overly enthusiastic obedience. He extended his hand, and Patriarch Gorabani placed the bloodstone signet ring on his right forefinger.

"You're the sixth to wear that ring," Orunjan said, producing a second wooden box, this one bound with brass fittings and closed with a catch. "Here are the deeds to the properties that will support it, all made out to the Tarelian Order. You wish to check them?"

"Later," Wizenbeak replied, placing his dress skullcap in one of his pockets. "Give them to me," he said, reaching for the box, "and I'll let you know if I come up short."

"That won't be necessary, Archdeacon Wizenbeak," Gorabani said pleasantly, "Basir comes with the deeds."

"What?"

"Doctor Basir Orunjan comes with the deeds," Gorabani

repeated. "We have assigned him as your permanent liaison with the Congregation, and with our office." He smiled and composed his gloved hands in front of him. "In your capacity as master of the Tarelian Order, of course."

3

A Civil War Seen Close By

CYMDULOCK Harbor. The band played a medley of popular songs and Count Darji-Damuso's honor guard of light horse formed up at dockside.

"They look pretty good, don't they?" asked the dashing young count complacently.

"If you say so," Dr. Wizenbeak replied, shifting his weight on his mount. He rode sidesaddle on a big blue mule, wearing the black robe of a lay preacher or wizard, with an archdeacon's gold chain of office, and an archdeacon's embroidered skullcap. "I must confess an ignorance of military matters that is little short of absolute. The band, however . . ." He shrugged and rocked one hand held palm downward, indicating an even balance between good and awful.

"Considering the warning you people gave us, even the band sounds pretty good, Master Wizenbeak," the count said. "We've had them rehearsing the Coronation March to the exclusion of everything else, when we get this special detail—blap!—with maybe an hour's notice."

"We didn't have all that much notice ourselves," the wizard said. "The word comes in that the Lagualian ambassador is arriving, so we should go meet the son of a bitch with 'full military honors.' It was either your lot or hire some street musicians."

"No matter," the count said. "The important thing is to look good to impress the ambassador. Lucky for you this fellow arrives before we return to the north."

Of course, sometimes notice doesn't help much, the wizard thought. You and your men are going to be heading back home after the coronation, with proper replacements nowhere in sight, in spite of the fact that we knew that you wouldn't stay around before you ever came. He sighed.

On board the docked ship, the ambassador's party formed up at the gangplank, and the bosun whistled them ashore. As they set foot on the soil of Guhland, the band began to play the Lagualian National Anthem. The handlers led horses to the ambassador and his staff, and once they were mounted Wizenbeak and Count Darji-Damuso rode over to meet Archdeacon Gyasi, the Lagualian ambassador.

"How d'ye do, Mister Ambassador," the wizard said genially. "I'm the ranking official sent down to greet you, Doctor Wizenbeak, and this is Count Darji-Damuso, whose troops so kindly provided the honor guard."

"Archdeacon Gyasi, ambassador from King Kirndal of Lagualia," was the reply. "I'm pleased to meet you." Gyasi studied the wizard's chain and skullcap for a moment. "Are you by any chance an archdeacon?"

Wizenbeak grinned. "Since the day before yesterday," he replied. "A messenger brought the stuff over this morning."

The Lagualian nodded. "Patriarch Gorabani just ordered an archdeacon created out of the whole cloth?"

"He didn't have much choice in the matter, Mister Ambassador," the wizard replied. "It was more a matter of political necessity than theological rectitude. You lose a war, funny things happen."

"Come on," Darji-Damuso said. "Let's review the honor guard and get it over with."

They rode past the northern light cavalry as the band played a very fair rendition of the Lagualian National Anthem, then headed for the Lagualian Embassy.

"I'm new at this business, Doctor Wizenbeak," Gyasi said, sitting astride the gentlest of white mares. "When do I present my credentials to Queen Shaia?"

"Good question," the wizard said. "The technical split-hair answer is never. Right now, Shaia is what I am told is the 'Queen Revenant,' the legal monarch displaced and returned to the throne." He pushed his glasses back on his long nose. "What we intend to do is crown Prince Dervian, so that Shaia will be the queen mother, and also regent."

"I see," said Gyasi. "In which case, would it be better, do you think, to defer presenting my credentials until after the coronation?"

"Hunh-hunh," Wizenbeak grunted. "It would at least spare

the protocol officer some vexing problems. Plus, we're moving toward the coronation as fast as possible, so it shouldn't be all that long.''

Their route took them past the Royal Palace, which had been sacked when Kahun took power and was now undergoing extensive renovation. The outside walls were fitted with scaffolding, and from the scaffold were hanging about one hundred men, mostly in black. One, gaudy in red and gold, hung in solitary splendor two whole floors above the rest.

"My God," Gyasi said, "what's that?"

"Witchfinders," Wizenbeak replied. "The Queen Revenant doesn't much like them. The one on top is Archdeacon Rehbeinji, the late Witchfinder-General."

"She'd hang an *archdeacon*?"

"As you see, Archdeacon. Of course, *they* would have burned her at the stake, so we must make proper allowances. I don't imagine she'd be so harsh on a properly accredited diplomat, such as yourself."

"Ah, yes, yes, of course." The ambassador wiped his forehead, though the day was cool. "But why so many?"

"We thought it best to get it behind us," Wizenbeak said. "A prince, upon taking power, should take steps to secure it. And unpopular steps, which must still be taken, had best be done all at once." A shrug. "As you see."

"Yes." A long pause. "It must be very gratifying to put the problem of witchfinders behind you."

The wizard looked over at the ambassador. He'll hear it eventually, anyway, he decided, I might as well tell him now. "That happens not to be the case," he said gently. "The residue of the witch burnings is that the property of the unfortunate 'witches' went to the Church. Gold and silver simply vanished, real estate was sold at bargain rates to the friends of the Church, or more accurately, the friends of the witchfinders. We cannot restore the dead, but we have an obligation to compensate their heirs."

"That should be simple enough," Gyasi said. "The Church erred, the Church should pay."

"You won't get an argument on the subject from me," Wizenbeak said.

Syncretisty Hall, Cymdulock. The seat of the Congregation of Clerisiarchs, the ruling body of the Syncretist Church in Guhland, sits on Dyers Lane just off Cathedral Street, near Saint Mambro's Church. On the ground floor, in the Stag's Head Dining Room, Archdeacon Gyasi sat down with Patriarch Gorabani and his special assistant, Basir Orunjan. Gyasi looked around the room. Walnut paneling, polished hardwood floors, a marble-mantled fireplace with a carved boar's head—but no stag's head, not even a picture of one. Best not to ask, he decided. A servant poured coffee from a long-handled copper pot into the tiny cups before them.

"As you saw," said Basir Orunjan, a small man with dark, intense eyes, "we have some of the finest art in Guhland, if not the world, collected over the past few centuries from the renovations of the various Church buildings around the country. That wonderful freestanding spiral staircase in the library . . . two hundred and twenty years old and it was built with no nails at all! Isn't that remarkable?"

Gyasi touched his cup gently, assuring himself it was still too hot to drink. "Quite remarkable," he said. "In Lagualia, I fear the Philistines would replace it with marble."

The patriarch smiled. "A point, Basir. Our guest has scored on you. However, we expect the good archdeacon didn't come to Cymdulock to admire our murals or lovely statues." He turned to Gyasi. "What is it that you want?"

"What any ambassador wants, Father." The form of address was ambiguous without being insulting. "Information. Kahun is dead. Why do you retain the office of patriarch which he rescued from the dustbin of history?"

"It's a long story," Gorabani said, holding his tiny coffee cup in gloved hands. "The short answer is that when King-Patriarch Kahun fell at Sifoty Field, there was no question that either the kingship or the patriarchy was going to remain vacant. The only question was, who would wear what hat?"

"Why didn't you simply abolish the office?"

"It wasn't easy to create," Orunjan said with a touch of regret, "and in the time we had, it wasn't possible to abolish, even if the Congregation had been agreed on abolition."

"Which they weren't, of course," Gorabani added. "The Congregation was split on everything, especially on whether to resist the Witch-Queen and defend Cymdulock, which would have meant a siege, which we weren't prepared for. But mainly everybody in the Congregation was pushing and shoving to put his own man in as the new patriarch."

"And you succeeded? Whom did you beat?"

"The Mambrinistas, who couldn't muster a two-thirds majority for any of their candidates, and the Witch-Queen's candidate, who hadn't yet arrived from Sifoty Field.''

Gyasi took out his diptych and stylus and made a note in the soft wax. "Who are the Mambrinistas? Not their names, what do they stand for?"

"Mambrino was the great witchburner," Basir Orunjan said. "A long ways back he purged the country of witches and wizards and magic, and they made him a saint. When Kahun raised Fadel as Witchfinder, a whole lot of free-floating discontent got organized, and 'Mambrinistas' was what they called themselves.''

"Return to the virtues of the good old days," Gorabani added, composing his gloved hands in front of him in an attitude of prayer. "Plus they included some people, like the good Doctor Buska, who are the heads of banking houses.''

"A lot of money to be made burning witches," Orunjan remarked, taking a sip of coffee, "which was why it was so hard to keep in check.''

"Right. And the Witch-Queen's . . . I assume you mean Shaia?''

"We do not speak That Woman's name," said the little man with an unexpected spray of venom.

"Perfectly understandable," Gyasi said mildly. "There is a Lagualian folk saying: 'Those whom we injure, we cannot forgive.' We'd heard she was dead.''

"We thought we were rid of her," the patriarch replied, "but she came back like the proverbial cat. Not from the dead, I hope. That would have unsettling theological implications.''

Gyasi checked his diptych. "I should imagine so. Who was her candidate for the patriarchy?"

"A water wizard named Doctor Wizenbeak," replied Orunjan. "Being a lay preacher with political connections, we made him an archdeacon just like—" He raised his hand and snapped his fingers. "—that!"

"Had he arrived sooner on the scene," Gorabani added, "he might have been made patriarch. As it was, the Congregation's fear and loathing of this detestable creature was just barely sufficient to elect ourself in his place.''

Gyasi made a note. "Yes. One final question, Father. Do you claim obedience from the Lagualian clerisy?''

Patriarch Gorabani laughed. "Oh, hell," he said, "I can't even command the obedience of the archdeacons *here*!''

"I may have phrased that badly," Gyasi said, sitting back in his chair. "The Syncretist Church is, in theory, universal. Are you, as patriarch, the newly anointed head of the Church, also, in theory, universal?"

Gorabani finished his coffee and set the cup down. "Good question," he said at last. "Kahun thought so, I imagine. What do you think, Basir?"

Orunjan sat telling his prayer beads for a moment. "Form a commission to study the matter, Your Holiness," he said at last. "In a few years they can turn in a definitive report."

"We shall consider the question," the patriarch said, composing his velvet-gloved hands before him. "Possibly a commission to study the matter *would* be appropriate, even as Basir suggested." He stood up, adjusting his robes. "In the meantime, we are engaged elsewhere. Our assistant, Basir Orunjan here, remains at your disposal for the time being."

Jankura looked up from a stack of chips she was reading. "You met the Lagualian ambassador?"

"With full military honors," Wizenbeak replied, pushing his glasses back on his nose.

"Did he say anything, make any request?"

"King Kirndal evidently wants him to ask specifically whether or not Gorabani considers himself patriarch of the Lagualian archdeacons, who had no hand in selecting him—which may be why an archdeacon was chosen to be the ambassador."

Jankura nodded. "Maybe so. We'd be happier if the coincidence of the Lagualian ambassador having business with the losing side of the civil war and the prospective invasion of the Eastern Marches didn't coincide so neatly."

"I don't see what can be done about it, Your Majesty."

"Probably nothing," she said. "When is he coming to present his credentials?"

"After the coronation, he told me," the wizard replied.

They stood in the nave of the great Cymdulock Cathedral, the clerisiarch Basir Orunjan, sallow of skin, his dark eyes hooded, standing beside the taller Archdeacon Gyasi, newly arrived ambassador from Lagualia. The air smelled of fresh-cut wood from the scaffolding and wet plaster, as last minute renovations for the coronation went forward.

"A scandal, Your Excellency," said Orunjan. "Kahun commissioned the great Sipatu, himself, to paint the chapel ceiling, over there, and in three weeks, by divine inspiration and the toil of his hands, he produced a half-size cartoon of the victorious Kahun ascending into Heaven, which was acclaimed by the Academy and accepted." His amber and jet prayer beads clicked noisily as they passed through his fingers, reflecting a certain measure of inner distress. "He had already translated the drawing to the ceiling itself and was beginning to block in the clouds and light colors of a spectacular masterpiece—perhaps the best thing Sipatu had ever done—when That Woman took power! No consideration for aesthetic values at all, the Philistines simply went in and painted the ceiling sky-blue!"

"There may have been political motives," Gyasi said mildly.

Orunjan simply grunted. "Philistines," he said. "They made no attempt to preserve a great piece of art, which, I will concede, memorialized the political opposition. But they didn't even offer Sipatu a kill fee." Then, seeing the other's puzzled look, "A kill fee is what you pay an artist when you choose to end a project through no fault of his own after he has invested time in it."

"Indeed," Gyasi said. "We shall write down Her Majesty Shaia as a Philistine and an oppressor of artists, as well. What else can you tell me about her?"

The amber and jet prayer beads clicked softly for a moment. "What's to tell?" Orunjan said at last. "She will rule as regent for her son, Prince Dervian. Her court, which tells much about the ruler at its center, seems utterly lacking in quality. No poets, no artists, no musicians; only Duke Falenda, who survived the overthrow, has any pretense at class." The prayer beads clicked. "Her general-in-chief is the mercenary commander, Lasco Genzari, of whom the best one can say is that he fought well in losing causes."

"There have been enough of those in the past thirty years," Gyasi agreed, taking out his diptych. "Perhaps his luck has changed."

"Perhaps, perhaps not," the little man said. "The game is not yet finished. Also she has the terribly handsome Count Braley, who was Prince Gatsack's fencing instructor and strategist, though it is hard to credit so pretty a face with real intelligence."

"There seems to be no question of his fencing ability, at any rate," Gyasi said. "Has there been any hint of a scandal between Braley and Shaia?"

"No, no, no, unfortunately! He is rumored to prefer young men. Which may be why he hasn't been given charge of the education of Prince Dervian. The prince is being instructed by a tall police officer who by some mischance or inadvertency stood loyal to the royal children when Kahun took power. An uncultured nobody, I can't even think of his name.''

"Who else is in her inner circle?''

"Doctor William Weird Wizenbeak, water wizard. A mountebank turned old fool, but he has the royal ear, this magus.'' The prayer beads clicked softly for a while. "He has been made an archdeacon, an honor which, for all my learning, has escaped me, and if certain conditions are met, he may . . .'' Orunjan stopped and sighed. "Excuse me. Doctor Wizenbeak has at least as much class as the rest of Shaia's advisors. He has her ear on demand, it is said, no small thing, surely; and he is the tutor of Princess Marjia, for what that may be worth.''

The Lagualian ambassador made a note in his diptych. "You seem somewhat hostile to these people,'' he observed.

"The Witch-Queen is locked in a struggle to the death with the Syncretist Church, Excellency. The Church helped Kahun bring her down, which she has not forgotten and we cannot afford to forget. What did you say? 'Those we injure, we cannot forgive?' That's about the case here.''

"I see little evidence of such a struggle,'' Gyasi said. "A single archdeacon—who was her implacable enemy—was charged with treason and hung. But no, I'd look for the Church and the regent to live together in peace and harmony. Why not?''

"Maybe that's how it would be in Lagualia,'' the little man sneered. "Your clerisy has no balls! But in Guhland—'' The prayer beads clicked grimly for a moment. "—we give no quarter.''

"Admirable,'' the ambassador said, making a note. "And how does the wizard get on with the princess?''

"Court gossip says very well.'' Basir sniffed. "Marjia was behaving a bit of a brat until Wizenbeak took her in hand, but now everything seems to be sweetness and light.''

Inside the Civil War

THE Citadel, Cymdulock. A massive castle, built on the heights dominating the city. Formerly given in fief to Duke Fadel, it was temporarily occupied by Queen-Mother Shaia and her court while the Royal Palace, sacked in the Kahunist Rebellion, underwent restoration. Strong, safe, and secure, the Citadel was also somewhat Spartan, a residence more suitable for a tyrant than any ruler happy in her subjects' love.

"You whey-faced son of a bitch!" The teapot exploded against the dressed stone wall of Princess Marjia's bedroom, just behind where the wizard's head had been, showering him with hot tea and porcelain fragments. "You lying, conniving, double-crossing *hypocrite*!" Wizenbeak ducked the creamer, which crashed against the wall, splattering his black robes with its contents, and deftly caught the cup that followed it.

"What seems to be the problem, Your Majesty?" he said, catching a second cup, and one of two saucers.

"I gave you a simple assignment," Princess Marjia said from the other side of the coffee table at the foot of her bed, "a short list of names of some people I wanted dead. And what did you do? You make a great big deal out of hanging Witchfinder Rehbeinji and let the rest off the hook! Intolerable! That's what it is, you muck-pissing idiot, *intolerable*!"

"When we rode past the palace, there were maybe a hundred witchfinders hanging on the scaffolding. I wouldn't call that letting the rest off the hook."

"Horseshit!" the princess snapped. "You hung a bunch of nobodies! Petty bureaucrats and clerks! I told you who I wanted on the list!"

"The list was very useful," the wizard said, pushing his emerald glasses back up his nose with the hand that held one cup and the saucer. Branka, his troll-bat, crawled out of his pocket to see what all the excitement was about.

"I didn't make out the list to be useful!" screamed Marjia. "I made it out because I wanted those witch-burning, whoreson Mambrinista sons of bitches DEAD! They are exploiters of the ignorant, flayers of the innocent, corrupters of the faith, and I want to KILL them!" Princess Marjia was a pretty young girl of about ten, wearing a pink and white dress that enhanced her light brown hair and blue eyes.

"Yes, Your Majesty." Wizenbeak took out his handkerchief and wiped a drop of spittle off his face. "But it did help. Once the clerisy saw we knew what we were talking about, they were ever so much easier to deal with. Besides, you yourself suggested using it as a bargaining tactic, to take Rehbeinji first and pick up the rest later."

The little girl made a visible effort to calm herself. "Yes," she said. "So I did. But the way events are breaking, if we don't hang the bastards before the coronation, they won't get hung! Now *do* it!" Her voice rose to a scream of rage and frustration. "DO IT NOW!"

"Be reasonable, Your Majesty," Wizenbeak pleaded, as the troll-bat climbed up on top of his head. "After hanging the last Witchfinder-General, the patriarch has graciously consented to abolish the office—"

"You are trimming and compromising with my vengeance," the little girl said grimly, "and I won't have it! You have the authority and the duty, the by God *obligation*, to carry out my orders, and I *demand* that you do so!"

The wizard sat down in the window seat of her bedroom, pushing the cups and saucer behind him. "I am truly sorry, Your Majesty, but I do *not* have the authority. Jankura, acting as queen mother, takes advice from five or six people, me included. But she makes up her own mind and she's starting to take her own course, and it was her decision to try to reach an accommodation with Syncretisty Hall."

"She is *your* assistant, sworn to obey *you* as her master, is she not?"

"Yes, she is," he said. "But that was then and this is now. The fact is, I have *never* tried to enforce the oath she took, and probably couldn't if I wanted to."

"Make me no excuses, Doctor Wizenbeak," Princess Marjia said. "You hold her oathbound; I hold *you* oathbound. Now you can go in there and enforce it because I damn well insist on it! I demand it! Do you understand?''

Theoretically she's right, thought the wizard, but as a practical matter, her judgment leaves something to be desired. In this, as in her past policies, she tends toward a certain literal-mindedness, a certain inflexibility . . . He pulled at his long nose. ''I understand,'' he replied wearily. ''I took oath to the True Shaia—your own, sweet self, before the mob sacked the Royal Palace—and I have faithfully presented your views to the council. Your wishes have been made known, your opinions have been heard, but I don't have the power to impose them by fiat.''

''You have the power,'' she said grimly, ''and I am telling you to use it!''

''Your Majesty,'' Wizenbeak said, gently pushing the troll-bat away from his face, ''I have given you what service I cóuld, to the best of my poor ability. But I took oath to Queen Shaia. You are neither Shaia, nor a queen!''

''I *am* the True Shaia!'' the little girl shouted, stamping her foot.

''Look at yourself in the mirror, Princess. What you'll see looking back at you is Princess Marjia, Shaia's daughter, in whom the soul, the spirit, the—the *ghost* of Shaia now resides. One is not oathbound to a ghost!''

''You senile old fool! You stinking old fart! I am not a ghost! I am here! I am alive in this room! And *you*, by God, have sworn to obey me!'' Tears had started to run down her rage-flushed cheeks, ''God damn you, God damn you, obey or *die*!''

Well, decided Wizenbeak resignedly, it would have come to this sooner or later. One cannot go on serving two masters forever, after all. He plucked his troll-bat, Branka, the tiny monkey-faced creature, from his shoulder and contemplated him for a moment. Now whose little troll-bat are *you*? he wondered. Or do I mean, whose little troll-bat are you, *now*? Receiving no answer, the wizard held the little monster over his heart. The troll-bat twisted around, soft velvet against his gnarled fingers, to look across the room at the furious little girl.

''Branka is your familiar, Princess,'' the wizard said gently, ''and he'll take your orders. Better, perhaps, than he'll take my own. A word to him, and I die. But as God is my witness, I cannot obey!''

Basir Orunjan studied the sludge in the bottom of his coffee cup. Even though it was mostly sugar, it was bitter to the taste.

Lagualian coffee, he conceded, unlike the Lagualian clerisy, had a certain authority.

"As long as we're in Syncretisty Hall," he said, "why don't I show you around?"

"My pleasure," said Ambassador Gyasi, rising from the table.

They went upstairs to the library, with its racks of unglazed scroll jars lining the wall, each marked with a little chip of wood tied on with a colored ribbon. On the north side of the library was the reading room, with tall bay windows curving gently outward, mirrors set between them, and French doors opening out upon a narrow balcony. The floor was piled thick with richly woven carpets, and around the room were scattered scholars' desks and benches.

"The Reformers wanted to remove some of the desks and replace them with soft leather chairs," said Orunjan, "the sort you invented in Lagualia. You couldn't read without falling asleep . . . but you know that, of course. We blocked the silly notion."

"Who's 'we,' " Gyasi asked. "The Mambrinistas?"

"Including the Mambrinistas," the little man said, "but also the Conservatives, the Independents, and the Greens—all factions on the right."

"The Greens?"

"An anti-magic faction entertaining the romantic notion that witches ought to have the same rights as sheep stealers," Basir Orunjan replied. "An open trial, a confrontation with their accuser, that sort of thing."

"Seems reasonable," Gyasi said. "Why not?"

"Eh . . . in principal it isn't a bad idea," Orunjan conceded, "but in practice . . . well, in practice the confrontation is so distressing to the accuser that, for humane reasons, we don't require it. The question is: Do you want to be rid of witches, or don't you?" He glanced sideways at the tall Lagualian as if to gauge his reaction. "This is all very recent. Under King-Patriarch Kahun their doctrinal differences never amounted to a hill of beans, but now . . ." He shrugged. "Too many egotists are asserting themselves against our new patriarch."

"What was Gorabani previously?"

"Kahun's dog," Orunjan said sourly. "And a skilled user of magic. So he made his way to the top over better men, such as Archdeacon Obuskaia, because he was willing to let the patriarchy fall into the hands of an out-and-out . . . well, that's water over the dam.''

They walked back through the library, past the lavatories—"functional but devoid of any artistic merit,'' as Orunjan put it—to the hall where the Congregation met to conduct business.

"The green carpeting is to soothe the spirit,'' he said. ''The magnificently carved and polychromed choir stalls on either side were salvaged from the renovation of Saint Bulaph's at Rosano—'' His dark eyes glanced sideways at the Ambassador. ''—where Philistines would have no doubt put in marble.''

"A matter of taste,'' Gyasi said mildly. ''They seem very pretty.''

"Pretty, hell! They're *magnificent*!'' the little man growled. ''The clerk sits at the table between the aisles, and the patriarch presides over the lot from that utterly tasteless gilt throne at the far end.''

Gyasi looked around the long room with its lofty, beamed ceiling. ''There are no seats in the choir stalls?''

"Folding half seats,'' Orunjan replied. ''You appear to remain standing, but can actually take some weight off your feet. It encourages the virtue of brevity among the speakers. Follow me, we'll check out one of the cloakrooms.''

They went halfway down the aisle and through a door barely five feet high that split the front two rows of stalls, turning to the right of the throne. Behind the choir stalls was a long, narrow room, furnished with wooden benches and lockers, a few racks of manuscript jars, and a few scholars' tables. The stained-glass clerestory windows provided an easy, diffuse illumination, but globe lamps hung from wall brackets. Two clerisiarchs looked up from a table at the far end of the room.

"Well, hello there, Basir,'' Archdeacon Obuskaia said. ''Come on over.'' He was a big man, tall and broad, thick and muscular, with powerful hairy hands and a massive bald head. His was properly the top name on Shaia's short list of Mamprinistas to be deleted.

With him was Archdeacon Anezkva, stoop-shouldered, with stringy brown hair and prominent pale blue eyes. His nose was long and pointed, and his handshake, as Gyasi discovered, was seriously limp. One looked at him and dismissed him—a serious error, for if he was a poor lover, he was a good hater. He had failed to make Shaia's short list, possibly because he hadn't been pointed in her direction.

They chatted for a while, in a pleasant sort of way, about

horses, the weather, and the merits of various schools of art. Then the conversation drifted to politics.

"Why do you insist on referring to the queen mother as the Witch Queen?" the Lagualian ambassador asked.

"Hah!" Orunjan barked. "Would you prefer '*That Woman*'?"

"We call a spade a spade," Obuskaia said. "It was her ruthless mixing of magic with politics that led to the current revival of witch-burning!"

"Ah, indeed," Gyasi said mildly. "I hadn't realized the practice was Shaia's own fault. In Lagualia we imagined it was Prince Kahun's choice of weapons against her."

"The Witch-Queen is an evil woman," Anezkva said, "and a bad ruler besides." Well, he thought, we come to the point at last. It is one thing to think that a Lagualian invasion would be welcome because it would unseat the Witch-Queen; it is quite another to blurt it out to the Lagualian ambassador, who may be deliberating that very choice. He licked his lips with a dry tongue. "Some of us would welcome a foreign invasion, if it would bring down the Witch-Queen!"

It would be unseemly to whip out my diptych and start taking notes, thought Gyasi, but this isn't something I'm going to forget to put into my dispatches. "Gently, gently, brothers," he said softly, "someone unfamiliar with your righteous indignation might construe your remarks as treason."

Obuskaia's eyebrows went up. Terminal rashness, he thought uneasily, the good doctor is overbold if not utterly foolhardy—and we're in it together, whether I like it or not. "If this be treason," he growled, "make the most of it! It isn't as if we were putting ourselves into deeper shit than we're already in."

Princess Marjia's lips formed the word of command and then stopped as Shaia's cool intellect began to appraise the situation. A dramatic gesture—even a melodramatic one—most unlike the old fool. Fish or cut bait, he was telling her, but what would happen? Would Branka obey? Either he would, or he would not. And if he would not, the wizard stood free of his oath. What were the odds? That had to be the wrong question. With Wizenbeak, if he bets he can make the Jack of Spades jump out of the deck and spit cider in your ear, you take the bet, you get an earful of cider. Forget the odds. With the old fart dead, would her position be improved? No. He was her only connection to the grown-up world. Like it or not, oath or no oath, she was heavily dependent on him. She couldn't afford to kill him, not when he couldn't be replaced.

And she couldn't afford not to kill him if she made the attempt. She bit her lip in frustration.

"Why won't you kill the Mambrinistas for me?" she asked in a small voice.

Dr. Wizenbeak let his breath out slowly. He would go on living, then. Two to one Branka would disobey her command to kill him, three to one Shaia would work it out as she had. Not bad odds, but terrifying when your life was on the line . . . The cream-colored woodwork and the yellow comforter on the bed were suddenly alive with vibrant color as the glorious warm sunlight poured through the window.

"Because Jankura wants to end the civil war," the wizard replied. "She feels that binding up the wounds of the country ought to take precedence over settling old scores."

"She wants to be a statesman," the little girl said. "If we don't deal with the Mambrinistas now, we'll have to deal with them later. We should have rounded them up the day we marched into Cymdulock. 'A prince should commit all necessary evils at the beginning of his reign so as to get them behind him.' "

"That's water over the dam," Wizenbeak said. "Besides, I'd just as soon not have her trying to go by the book." He cupped Branka in one hand and, when the little animal yawned, he gently returned the troll-bat to its inside pocket. "How much later?"

Marjia climbed onto the bed, her legs dangling a few inches off the flagstone floor, and bit her thumbnail, a gesture characteristic of Shaia. The nail was too short, and the lips too soft, and the thumb slid into the mouth with an easy familiarity. The princess did a double take and removed the thumb, staring at it for a moment in irritation.

"I don't know," she said at last, "a few years, maybe."

"By then it'll be Prince Dervian's problem," the wizard said. "King Dervian, when the regency ends. If the False Shaia is willing to let him solve his own problems, why aren't you?"

"I know more than she does," the little girl said sadly. "I sacrificed everything to put my son on Guhland's throne and I want him to stay there."

"Times change," Wizenbeak replied. "That's your dumb brother you're talking about, isn't it?"

* * *

The garden beneath Princess Marjia's bedchamber was an irregular triangle of ground, hemmed in by the windowed walls of the Citadel. Yellow and white climbing roses on the short southern wall sought out the sun in the abbreviated sky. Some carefully trimmed boxwoods, a small lily pond with a few darting carp, and shade-tolerant crab apple trees kept the roses company. A neatly graveled path looped around the pond to a sundial that was in the shade most of the morning and much of the afternoon. A solitary dragonfly darted back and forth over the lilies.

Wizenbeak, carrying out his duties as royal tutor for the princess, sat on one of the weathered wooden benches watching his charge play on the lawn. Her nanny had dressed her in a charming print dress, with a red velvet bow in her hair and a matching sash, which Marjia had described as "doll-baby cute." She was playing with Branka, or maybe *at* him. The troll-bat seemed not to be taking instruction particularly well.

"So the damned chain weighed in at nearly five pounds," the wizard continued. "And Orunjan says: 'You've got to wear it. It's tradition. All the archdeacons do.' So I'm wearing it." He pulled it out and let it clunk back against his chest. "Do you know how much junk I have in my pockets? I don't need another five pounds around my neck!"

"It'll build your muscles," the little girl said, frowning at the nonchalant troll-bat. Then she looked over at him. "Actually, you only need the pectoral nabla as a token of rank, to display a highly coveted honor. All that bullion is for looking important when you dress up. To impress fools. For slopping around in your usual slovenly manner, have a seamstress embroider the chain. Gold thread on a black ribbon. You can wear that and put the gold in a vault for a time like the coronation when you *want* to impress 'em."

"Electrum, actually," the wizard mused. "Nine parts gold, four parts silver, one part copper. I could find some use for it, probably, if I ever got back to building apparatus."

"The yellow rose," Marjia said, addressing the troll-bat, "*that* yellow rose. Bring it to me!" Branka made an amazing leap, pivoting in the air to pluck the exactly right rose off the trellis, and with the rose in his teeth he swooped back to his young mistress—until the last second, when he shot straight up over her head and exploded the rose. Yellow petals fluttered down on the little princess as Branka landed lightly on Wizenbeak's beard.

Marjia brushed a petal from her face. "What was it you were running on about before?" She sighed. "Orunjan wanted to do something with the Tarelians?"

"Spend money," Wizenbeak said. "The deal we got, as opposed to what we thought we were getting, is that we have a line of credit. We can spend it—that is, I can spend it, with Orunjan's approval—on the Tarelian Order only."

"And if you don't spend it?"

"The Church gets it back," he replied. "To some extent, the measure of a clerisiarch in the Congregation is how much money they have." He shifted his weight on the wooden bench. "Orunjan wants to put together a unit to march in the parade at the coronation."

"That's the day after tomorrow," Marjia said softly. "Who's he going to recruit on that sort of notice?"

Wizenbeak shrugged. "Ex-Kahunists, I imagine, or maybe ex-Tarelians. With the fighting ended, the mercenaries' halls should be full of them."

Marjia picked a rose petal off her skirt, rolled it into a tiny yellow ball, and flicked it into the lily pond, where a fish inspected it and let it drift.

"You don't need to hurry, Doctor Wizenbeak," she said at last. "Hire the men you want, not the ones Orunjan pushes on you."

"Hunh-hunh," he said, wondering how this might be done. "Whom do we want, and where can I find them?"

"Details." The princess sniffed, dismissing the questions with an airy wave of the hand. "I no longer command you, for all your professions of loyalty, but my advice is: don't hire any Tarelians until you interview them."

"What shall I ask them, Your Majesty?"

"How would I know?" Marjia replied. "I can't even make Branka pick me a flower. Think of something, wizard."

5

Coronation Days

WIZENBEAK, summoned into the presence, found himself cooling his heels in one of the gilt and mirrored antechambers of the Palace-in-the-Citadel with Count Braley. After Branka decided to take a nap rather than to continue practicing a simple "oblige the nice wizard" routine, Wizenbeak sat back in his chair, folded his gnarled hands across his scrawny middle, and studied the count's image in one of the mirrors. He *does* use eye shadow, the wizard decided, but tastefully . . . which ought to count for something.

"Well, Count," he said after a few minutes, "what's new?"

Braley, who was sufficiently handsome not to need eye shadow had the problem concerned him, looked up from the box of wooden chips he was reading and automatically adjusted the long sword and the shorter companion sword thrust into his sash. "Wars and rumors of wars," he said easily. "Fortunately nothing figures to break before Prince Dervian's coronation."

"Which is two days off," the wizard observed, dangling the nabla on the massive gold chain he was wearing. "Anything solid?"

Braley shook his head. "Smoke and rumors, mostly. The action, such as it is, seems to center around the Eastern Marches, the old Kalycas Province bordering Lagualia."

"That's Kahunist country," Wizenbeak said reflectively. "They don't like us, but they don't much like Lagualia, either."

"Right," Braley agreed, "so it's hard to tell if we're looking at a rebellion, a secession, a simple invasion, or the winter of some son of a bitch's discontent."

The mirrored door swung open on gilt bronze hinges and the chamberlain, a woman, waved them in.

Jankura was standing on a low stool as a bevy of seamstresses worked at fitting her coronation gown. The colors were muted, pale gray silk for the overdress and train, with a profusion of taupe lace and a ruffled white chemise.

"My apologies, gentlemen," she said, "but this has to be done by tonight, and I let you in as soon as I was decent."

"The coronation is the day after tomorrow, Your Majesty," the wizard observed tartly, a trifle vexed at having been kept waiting. "Does it really have to be done tonight?"

"Yes and yes," Jankura replied. "My schedule tomorrow is intolerably full; preserve me from many more days like it. Also, these ladies have to sew on the seed pearls and garnets, for which they must have the finished gown."

"I thought you were planning to feature Prince Dervian."

"I am. He's wearing black tights, red knee boots with golden tassels and four-inch heels, a white tunic, and the Royal Swords thrust into a simple soldier's sash—well, it's unbleached silk, actually, but the same pattern—add on the Royal Crown and Coronation Robe and he looks dramatic as hell."

"That sounds good," Wizenbeak said, "but why the seed pearls and garnets, then?"

"For the women. The men, they'll see Dervian, the swords, the crown, and that's it. Long live the king! The women will ponder and study over the costume. Gray, white, and taupe to show I'm staying in the background, but enough decoration to be believable. The seed pearls emphasize the baroque pearls in the crown; the garnets are just for pretty." She paused for a moment, raising her arms to accommodate one of the seamstresses. "You, Doctor Wizenbeak, are wearing that archdeacon's nabla like a cowbell!"

"Eh . . . say what, Your Majesty?"

"Jiji!" One of the seamstresses looked up. "Go over and set that chain properly." The young woman, her mouth full of pins, stuck her scissors in her apron and went over to the wizard, pulling the massive gold chain out on his shoulders and further down on his back.

"A little more in back," said Jankura. "That's good."

Jiji marked the edge of the shoulders and the center of the back with pins and stepped back. The wizard moved, and the chain slid back to where it had been. The seamstress looked through a wicker basket filled with stuff and came up with three rolls of black ribbon. She compared them with the wizard's black robe, found the best match, snipped off three lengths, and sewed them in place while the conversation went on.

"Excuse me, Doctor," Jankura said, "but hashing around with a coronation gown will do that to you. What was the situation with the Kahunist clerisiarchs?"

"King-Patriarch Kahun appointed five, and Patriarch Gorabani removed four of them. That's all. The claim that he decimated the Mambrinistas in the process is just blowing smoke."

"Right. Who was the survivor?"

"Young Viluji."

"Ah, yes. We wouldn't want to annoy the Vilujis, would we?" She nodded to herself. "What happens to the vacancies?"

Wizenbeak looked blank for a moment. "Oh? Nothing. Well, I may count as filling one of them, but the patriarch puts the others in his pocket, and the Congregation just gets a little smaller."

"He hasn't actually removed any Mambrinistas, then?"

"There have been some defections in the Congregation, people crossing the aisle, that sort of thing; but no, Gorabani hasn't removed anyone that was there when Kahun became patriarch." The wizard smoothed his beard. "For that matter, Kahun never removed anybody, unless he was going to kill them. The Congregation was afraid of Kahun, but they won't put up with anything from Gorabani."

"I see." She nodded; so the Mambrinistas had crawled back into the woodwork. "When he gets around to making some appointments, are we to be consulted?" That had been a sticking point.

"He agreed to give us advance notice, Your Majesty. Informally." The wizard sighed. "Otherwise, we could have had his formal refusal to do anything of the sort."

"Watch those pins!" Jankura snapped. "No consultation? Well, that's probably the best we can do. We threaten to intervene in their internal politics, and the threat—as you have frequently told me—is often more effective than its execution. What about the Tarelians?"

"I have been gifted with an assistant who wants to march a contingent of the reconstituted Tarelian Order in the coronation parade. Something I would prefer to put off."

"How big a contingent?" Braley asked.

"He said just the officers . . ."

"That actually sounds like a good idea," Braley said. "The Tarelian Order still has a formidable reputation, despite the fiasco in the altiplano campaign. Why do you want to delay?"

"Because if I'm going to head up the stupid order, I'd like to pick my *own* officers," Wizenbeak said. "I'd like to interview them before I sign them on, Your Majesty."

"Go right ahead, then," Jankura said. "What have we got from the east, Count Braley?"

"The raiding across the Lagualian border has dropped off, Your Majesty," he said. "A week after Sifoty Field, it had stopped completely on the Lagualian side. Our own people, crossing from the Eastern Marches to, uh, recover stray cattle, report signs of mobilization."

"And that box you have is the signs?" She nodded to herself. Braley had fed her the key question. "Why did the raiding drop off, do you think?"

"The Lagualian Marchlanders have been pressed into service," he replied.

Jankura sighed. Historically, it was a portent of war; first the raiding stopped, then came the rumble of a distant drum. Braley and Genzari had both taken pains to see that she understood the significance of the omens Braley had been seeking . . . had found. What to do about it?

"Indeed, Count Braley. And why would Lagualia pick this time to go to war with us?"

It's been almost twenty years since the last one, he thought, so they're due, but she wants to know: why now, why me? He glanced at Wizenbeak, who was having the tape sewn on his robe tied into neat bows to hold his chain of office in place. No help. A courtier would find a way to withhold the bad news or let someone else deliver it. A strategist survived by persuading his employer to face unpleasant reality. He adjusted his sword sash.

"The war may have been triggered by the succession, Your Majesty," Count Braley said, seeking to present the most palatable face of the truth. "The Lagualians must assume that Prince Dervian will be a weak ruler."

"You're probably right," Jankura said at last. "*They're* probably right, too. I wouldn't let my son lead the charge, and what sort of ruler is it whose mother won't let him ride into battle?" In a country of ardent witch-burners, she thought, who wants to die for the Witch-Queen? Or the Witch-Anything, for that matter. "The Lagualian ambassador is to present his credentials after the coronation. We'll find out then, I expect." What to do?

Branka, oppressed by the weight of the readjusted chain, climbed out of his pocket and perched on Wizenbeak's shoulder.

"Isn't he a darling," Jankura said, extending her hand. "Come here, baby." The troll-bat made a graceful leap to settle on her wrist with the lightness of a feather—and, in fact, the wizard's muscles were still supporting his weight. The seamstresses stepped back a little to watch. They didn't know troll-bats firsthand, but they knew stories used to frighten children.

"Now, Branka," she crooned, "my arm, sit on *my* arm." The troll-bat transferred his weight; he didn't move, but all of a sudden she was supporting him.

After a moment of mutual contemplation, Branka dived over the wicker sewing basket to pick up a spool of red thread, made a ballistic arch through the chandelier, and landed back on the wizard's shoulder. The troll-bat inspected the spool of thread and finally dropped it into Wizenbeak's hand.

"That's very interesting," Jankura said. "My Mischka won't take instruction from strangers and won't draw upon anyone's muscle but my own."

"Branka's smart," the wizard agreed, "but inclined to be independent. When he thinks he knows something, he won't practice it."

She nodded. "Then it's up to you to figure out how to make the drill interesting, isn't it, Doctor Wizenbeak?"

"Yes, Your Majesty."

"Good. I think it may also be best if there were a Tarelian presence at the Coronation Parade." Maybe it will give the Lagualian ambassador something to think about. "Interview them to your heart's content, but I want them in the line of march. You understand?"

Wizenbeak sighed; an order was an order. "Yes, Your Majesty."

The sedan chair deposited Archdeacon Wizenbeak at the edge of the parade field fronting the Citadel. Soldiers from his own personal household had set up a pavilion with his field desk and folding chair. In front of the pavilion, several clerks were sitting at cloth-covered tables, ready to put the names on the rolls. I didn't even select my own personal bodyguard, thought the wizard, Genzari did it for me. How the devil am I going to select the officer corps for the Tarelian Order? Especially when I don't trust my special assistant further than I could throw him.

Basir Orunjan came up to him, dark-eyed and smiling, and bowed deeply. Under his arm he carried two long boxes full of wooden chips. "All is in readiness, Master Wizenbeak," he said cheerfully. "The notice that we are recruiting for the Tarelian Order has gone out all over the city, just as you ordered, and the men have gathered here for your interview." He bowed again. "Some of them I interviewed myself in the past few days." He extended the boxes to the wizard, who took them and set them on top of his field desk. "Brave men, gallant soldiers, all of the most excellent character, I assure you. They will make fine officers."

"Yes, thank you," Wizenbeak said, looking over the field. There were, he decided, maybe three or four thousand men standing out there. If he interviewed one a minute from now until the parade started tomorrow he wouldn't be half done . . . and what sort of an interview can you do in a minute? He pushed his emerald spectacles up his nose to get a better view of the men he would be hiring. Perhaps he should call up the names Basir had compiled and reject the villains. The *obvious* villains.

"We have a good turnout," Orunjan said complacently.

"Yes." The mercenaries standing out there waiting to be hired were a motley crew, but there were sure a lot of them. The wizard sighed. "Sergeant," he called out, "have the ex-Tarelians form up in front."

The Tarelian Order had been headed by Archdeacon Nasar-Namatu, who had led them to the victory over Prince Gatsack at Mewis Field; and then by Fadel the Witchfinder, who brought the order to disaster in the Altiplano Campaign. Wizenbeak had been on the other side of the Altiplano Campaign, and one of the things he'd learned from interrogating prisoners was that Fadel had put in his own officers, right down to the company level.

About half the field seemed to be ex-Tarelians. Well and good. "Now then, Sergeant, I want the veterans of Mewis Field *only* on the far right, the veterans of the Altiplano Campaign *only* on the far left, with the rest in the middle."

Fadel's officer corps had been true believers, but not necessarily competent soldiers, the witchfinder having been much concerned to secure political control of the Tarelians. Of Nasar-Namatu's officers, some of them, the most senior, had been burned as witches beside Nasar-Namatu, himself. Others had been demoted or expelled from the order.

There were about a hundred men on the far left, perhaps forty on the far right. Well, thought the wizard, we are at last beginning to deal with manageable numbers. He had the sergeant line the forty up and march them in front of the pavilion. At close range they looked bad; worn and ragged clothes could be discounted, but some of them looked pallid, as if they had recently been released from prison, and some sported a scruffy growth of beard. Worse, the group as a whole conveyed a sense of fragility, of infirmity. Still, all of them had turned out for a chance to rejoin their old outfit and all of them were wearing the sword sash with the two swords thrust into it.

What would be the best way to do this, Wizenbeak wondered, sitting in his folding chair. As he slipped on his emerald glasses and gently eased Branka out of the troll-bat's soft, warm pocket, a nineteen-syllable mantra, whose literal meaning was that the geese fly south in autumn despite the beauty of the leaves, floated to the surface of his mind.

After Branka was fully awake and holding on to the wizard's hands, Wizenbeak recited the mantra. In the days of his youth, he had rashly dabbled in the blacker arts, hoping to become a lawyer or even a judge, and the first letter of each word in the mantra was a mnemonic for a spell that he had then learned by rote. The purpose of the spell was to ascertain the relative guilt in a group of conspirators. Never mind that the mantra was of severely limited use, and never mind that there were counter-spells; to pass the course you had to learn the professor's one professional achievement. Reciting the mantra brought the words of the spell to mind, and as he spoke them, wearing his emerald glasses, holding his troll-bat, he felt the spell bite. His glasses became slightly fogged, and as Branka stirred uneasily, all but about a dozen of the twoscore men he was watching faded into a hazy obscurity. Of the dozen, all of whom he could see with the utmost clarity, four had glowing auras about them. Well, thought Wizenbeak with satisfaction, forty is whittled down to four.

He removed his emerald glasses and let Branka go back to his pocket. Now that the four had been marked out for him, he saw that they appeared worthy of note. He stood up and walked over to the Tarelians, closely followed by the sergeant, diptych at the ready.

"I want *those* men," the wizard said, pointing them out with a gnarled finger. "Get their names and send them over in order of their seniority."

The third man was named Pardus Murado. He was five foot seven, 145 pounds, dark hair graying at the temples with a gray stubble on his chin. His fingernails had black bruises growing out toward the ends.

"Your comrades speak highly of you," Wizenbeak said. "What did you do?"

"I was in charge of training for the Blue Regiment, and at Mewis Field I led the Blues after it started snowing."

"And why were you stripped of rank?"

"I stood by Nasar-Namatu," Murado said softly. "I was arrested shortly after they took him." He held out his hands. "Fadel tried to make me 'confess' to purge my soul of evil."

"Fadel himself?"

"Yes, sir. Doctor Fadel was very interested in securing control of the order."

Wizenbeak sighed. "As am I, it would seem. After Kahun hung Witchfinder Fadel, Gorabani became head of the order. Why didn't you go with him?"

"I was still in jail. Besides . . ." Murado felt his beard. "Besides, after the Altiplano Campaign the order was in pretty bad shape, you understand? So when Gorabani took over, he decided to rebuild us from the ground up, reorganizing, he called it."

"Right," the wizard said. "Three reorganizations equal the full catastrophe, so you had Fadel's reorganization, the Altiplano Campaign, and Gorabani's reorganization, one right after the other?"

"Yes, sir. But the Congregation wouldn't give Gorabani the money, so the order was effectively in limbo. Just before you people swept into Cymdulock, they closed the barracks and the mess halls. The guards went away, and one of the trustees let us out of confinement."

"Hunh." The wizard pulled at his long nose. "Look, Mister Murado, I was on the other side and I haven't really caught up on all the internal politics that went on with you people." He fingered his chain of office for a moment. "My problem is to put the Tarelian Order back into shape as a fighting force. My other problem is I don't want it fighting *us*."

Murado adjusted the swords in his sash. "Us?" he said mildly. "Who's us?"

"Prince Dervian, the . . ." Wizenbeak hesitated a moment,

wondering about the propriety of "Witch-Queen" and deciding against it, "queen mother. I want the Tarelians to be the mighty arm of the Church Militant, but I don't want them cutting up the secular authorities. You understand?"

"Yes. We helped bring down the Witch-Queen, and now that she's back, you don't want it to happen again." He smiled, showing a chipped front tooth. "Do you really want to restore the Tarelian Order?"

"No, but I have my orders."

Murado laughed. "Hey, as head of the order, you have the authority to name your own deputy, right?" The wizard nodded. "So name Prince Dervian. The officers swear an oath to you, and an oath to him. Can we trust you not to use the Tarelians to flatten out the Church?"

"Of course," Wizenbeak said. After he interviewed the fourth man, he called Murado back.

"If I made Prince Dervian my deputy, would *you* take oath to him?"

"If I were an officer, yes." No hesitation at all, which meant that he was telling the truth unless he had anticipated the question and was lying. He having brought up the idea in the first place . . . the wizard gave up wallowing in the ramifications of the idea and once again pulled at his nose.

"Murado is a strange name," he said at last, "where did it come from?"

"I was born in Muradoji, near Rosano," the Tarelian replied, "and when I enlisted, the paymaster dropped the end. I liked it, so I kept it that way."

"The name suits you, yes." There was a long pause. "The other three spoke very highly of you. Would you take command of the Tarelian Order for me and Prince Dervian?"

"You want me to be your captain-general?" Murado seemed surprised, thoughtful. Then, "Could I select my own subordinates?"

"Yes and yes, subject to my approval. They would have to be willing to take oath to Prince Dervian, eventually."

"I accept." He extended his hand, and the wizard shook it. "When do I begin?"

"The coronation parade is tomorrow and I want the Tarelians marching in it. Begin now."

As General Pardus Murado and his comrades swept across the field, Wizenbeak picked up the boxes of names that Basir

Orunjan had so carefully selected and looked through them. Murado wasn't there.

Wizenbeak smiled contentedly. His active intervention was no longer required, but his wizardly sense of process told him that things would work better if he watched.

It turned out to be a long evening and a longer night. The first rosy-hued streaks of dawn were hardly visible over the dark and sleeping city the next day as Wizenbeak and a couple of bodyguards wandered down the whitewashed stone corridor toward his suite of rooms in the Citadel. As they turned the corner, they met a courier walking away from their door.

"Doctor Wizenbeak, oh, excuse me, Doctor Wizenbeak," the courier said as they brushed past him. "The queen mother wishes you to join her at breakfast, and you weren't in your room. Your batman said he hadn't seen you."

"Because I hadn't been home, I imagine," the wizard replied. He yawned and pushed his emerald glasses back to the bridge of his nose to hide his bloodshot eyes. Jankura wanted him at breakfast, so of course he had to go. His mind was awake, only his brain was moving with great difficulty. He needed to . . . what? Take a bath, put on a fresh shirt, go to bed, not necessarily in that order. He looked at his bodyguards. They weren't all that fresh, either—he could use a change of bodyguards, too.

"Come with me, please," the courier said, "I'll take you there."

Forget the bath, forget bed, yes, but the shirt . . . Wizenbeak yawned again. "Excuse me," he said. "If I might go to my room to put on a shirt, my appearance at the royal breakfast would be more seemly." He started down the hall.

"Please, Doctor Wizenbeak," the courier said, "the shirt you have on now will be perfectly fine."

The wizard opened his lumpish black robe to reveal his excessively ugly long underwear. "I'm not *wearing* a shirt," he said, testily. "Now, bear with me, young fellow, and we'll be right along."

In his room, his batman swiftly helped him don a fresh shirt. It had the green and white stripes denoting a water wizard, and the conventional three buttons at the collar. The tail that fell below the knees might be regarded as old fashioned, though, if not totally unsophisticated. In the next rooms, his two bodyguards went off duty, as the corporal assigned two more to take their place. When they made their command appearance, they ought to be looking good, thought the wizard with pallid satisfaction.

Somewhere it had been written that it was better to look good than to *feel* good. What stupidity! For politicians, maybe. Somewhere, long ago, some defunct general had been stuffed and mounted on his horse to lead his army to victory. He looked good, but he must have felt like death warmed over . . . and politicians everywhere thought that was the way to be. How come you never had a general stuffed and mounted for a victory parade? Too many jerks to share the credit with, of course. They'd give you a fine funeral, instead. Well, the Tarelians would look good in the parade today, that much had been done. They ought to be feeling pretty good, too, at least the ones that got hired.

Breakfast was in the new provisional Privy Council Chamber, otherwise the plant room, just off the queen mother's suite. Originally a battle platform, it had been engulfed by later additions to the Citadel. Now, with battlements and machicolations removed, the semicircular platform supported a timber-framed greenhouse, filled with kitchen herbs and potted citrus trees. Facing south, the room overlooked the same triangular garden that Princess Marjia played in. A dumbwaiter came up from the kitchen below; in the afternoon, the sun and the heat from cooking made the room uncomfortably warm, but now it was fresh and green and pleasant.

In the center of the room was a rectangular table covered with a white tablecloth, two chairs on each side, a taller chair with arms at the end. Well, thought Wizenbeak, I told her to insist on her royal perks. She learns fast, Jankura does. He took his seat at the table, next to Lasco Genzari. Facing him were Count Braley and Duke Falenda, a rather large man, with a smooth, haughty face.

"D'you know the duke, Wizenbeak?" Braley asked. "He's taken over as our Chancellor of the Exchequer."

"We've met," Wizenbeak said, recalling the circumstances of their last meeting. Falenda had known the True Shaia, possibly intimately, and as one of the few survivors of her immediate circle, he had to be kept on board. Accommodated, yes. Deferred to, no. Wizenbeak reached into a pocket of his robe and produced a deck of cards. Fanning them with one dexterous gesture, he extended them to the duke. "I'm an archdeacon now,

Duke," he said with a grin. "So it's perfectly all right for you to take a card, isn't it?"

Falenda remembered, also. The wizard had risen in the world, and he—he had done well to survive. He smiled politely and took the card. "Ah, Doctor Wizenbeak," he said by way of acknowledging past rudeness, "sometimes one is not in the mood for card tricks."

"I understand," the wizard said, squaring the deck. "Look at your card and slip it back into the deck." Falenda studied his card and did as he was told. Wizenbeak shuffled the deck once, put it on the table, and turned up the top card, the Queen of Spades.

"Your card, I believe?" he said politely, returning the deck to his pocket.

"Why, yes," Falenda replied. "That's quite impressive, actually. How did you do it?"

"If you knew, you wouldn't be impressed," Wizenbeak said. "You might even think me a mountebank or vulgar card mechanic." He pushed his glasses up on his nose, as Jankura entered behind him. "How do you perform your *fiscal* wizardry?"

"Her Majesty," Count Braley said, rising. All stood, and when Jankura had taken her place at the head of the table, she made a peremptory hand gesture, and they reseated themselves.

Breakfast was scrambled eggs with bacon and sausage, fresh baked flatbread with unsalted butter, and a great pot of herb tea. Later, fresh fruit in clotted cream would be served.

"So," Jankura said, "besides ourselves we have Patriarch Gorabani and Prince Dervian on the reviewing stand, as well as General Tomias and Count Darji-Damuso from the northern tier of counties." She produced a stack of wooden chips with names on them. "Tradition calls for ten. We have one extra place and all sorts of people who would dearly love to fill it."

"The victors of Sifoty Field should be up there, of course," Genzari said. "On Dervian's right would be myself, Count Braley, General Tomias, and Count Darji-Damuso. On his left would be Your Majesty; Doctor Wizenbeak; Duke Falenda, who opened Cymdulock's gates to our light cavalry; and Patriarch Gorabani . . . who would be merely one of King-Patriarch Kahun's lackeys, save for our glorious victory. Why is the son of a bitch on the same platform with us?"

"So the people can see the Church accepting peace from our hand," Jankura said, using the royal we.

Genzari nodded. "All right. Gorabani is up there to help legitimize our regime. Do we really need a tenth?"

"It's traditional," Duke Falenda said, "eleven for a monarch, ten for the monarch with a regent. I would personally suggest putting the clerisiarchs together, so that I would stand between Your Majesty and Archdeacon Wizenbeak, here." He took a sip of tea. "Also, by graciously offering up the tenth place we could make us a firmer friend of someone who might prove useful."

"And infirmer friends of everyone else in that stack of chips," Braley said, giving his sash a tug to secure his companion sword. " 'Why should that so-and-so be up there when *we* aren't?' "

"A good point," Jankura said. "I'd like to have ten, but not if we make enemies. The way it is, everyone up there belongs there."

"Nine is quite as untraditional as, for instance, twelve, Your Majesty. And there are several names you really ought to consider," Falenda said blandly, reaching for Jankura's stack of chips. "Allow me, Your Majesty." Jankura looked annoyed, but she let him take the list of names.

Pushy, pushy, thought Wizenbeak, pushing back his glasses on his nose. "Your Majesty," he said, "may I suggest your own darling daughter, Princess Marjia, for the tenth person on the reviewing stand? The left side would then be Your Majesty; Princess Marjia; myself, her tutor; the Patriarch, my fellow clerisiarch; and the estimable Duke Falenda, here."

"It's going to be a long, boring time," Falenda said. "I doubt if an infant as young as Marjia could do it."

"She's ten years old," the wizard said, "and if you stand her on a platform so she can see and be seen, I expect she'll hold up better than you or me."

"Do you really think so?" Jankura asked, holding her teacup in both hands. "She was quite excited at getting her gown for the coronation, not so much at the clothes as at the idea of making a display."

That's right on the money, Janko, baby, thought the wizard, a real sharp insight. "I know Marjia," he said. "She'll be right at home on the reviewing stand. I guarantee it."

Duke Falenda started to say something, but Jankura cut him off. "That's how it will be, then," she said. The duke shut his mouth and glared at Wizenbeak for the space of two heartbeats.

"Well done," he said coldly.

The celebration, as distinct from the official ceremonies, had already started. Country folk and city dwellers alike were already camping out in the square before Cymdulock Cathedral to be sure of getting a view, and vendors of all sorts slowly made their way through the good-natured throng. The sky was blue, the barometer was rising, and the weather was heading for a perfect fall day.

Unarmed parade marshals walked up and down the square and the streets along the parade route, keeping the route of march open. About midmorning the military units started arriving, foot and horse, with bands and banners, followed finally by the royal carriages that bore the coronation party through the cheering crowd.

After the coronation party arrived, they assembled themselves in the designated staging area, the recently de-Kahunized chapel to the right rear of the altar where the coronation would take place. In front, at the north end of the cathedral, the great doors then were opened, and the nobility began arriving in twos and fews, to the edification and entertainment of the people. In back, from the smaller southern doors, came a stream of runners and messengers attending to last-minute details overlooked in the press.

Wizenbeak adjusted the vestments, which Orunjan had brought in to him, and tried to get a glimpse of himself through the crowd of people around the pier glass that had been brought in. A weary old fool in fancy dress peeped back at him. I'm sure I'd look wiser if I had a nap, he decided, as Branka inspected his strange garb. After breakfast, they had gone through a more-or-less dress rehearsal at the palace and then piled into badly sprung carriages to ride over the cobbled and pot-holed pavement. Sedan chairs would have been smoother and faster, but incomparably less grand.

"They just started the choral prelude," Orunjan said, looking at his diptych, in which he had inscribed the program. "Lamentably rehearsed, too, for such an important occasion."

"When do we go on?" the wizard asked.

"A quarter of an hour, maybe."

Wizenbeak stretched himself out on one of the polished wood

pews that nobody was using. "Rouse me then," he said, pulling his skullcap over his face. Branka studied his master, then rested his long, webbed fingers very carefully on the wizard's bald pate.

Fifteen minutes later, Genzari shook him awake. Wizenbeak sat up in a panic, he'd been sleeping for hours, he'd missed everything!

"It's time, old friend," Lasco Genzari said. "Now we go out just like we rehearsed." In the nave of the cathedral the organ thundered with sonorous majesty.

"Now, that's more like it," Orunjan said. "Ulinaji is a virtuoso of the first water." A pause, as the organist completed a phrase. "A bit heavy on the pedal, though."

Hunh, thought Wizenbeak in amazement, I feel pretty good. Maybe I look really wise, too. He smiled at himself in the mirror as he went by. Well, he decided, that'll have to do.

Coming to the bar, he turned away from the altar, and as he marched down the aisle what looked like the whole Congregation of Clerisiarchs fell in behind him, starting with Archdeacon Darussis. As he turned and went through the low gate an usher was holding for him, he saw the second pew of clerisiarchs starting to empty. They might be better dressed than he, he decided, but none of them looked particularly wiser, or even as wise. Then he was behind Gorabani who was behind the altar, standing next to Lasco Genzari who had led in the military.

"Face the audience," Genzari said, raising his voice to be heard over the organ. Wizenbeak turned and saw Jankura coming up the center aisle. Prince Dervian was on her right, Princess Marjia was on her left, carrying a cushion with the King's Seal, and the Regent's Seal. Well, decided the wizard, Jankura's pale and tasteful outfit looks better than I'd thought. She was wearing the taupe lace like a bridal veil, with Shaia's wedding crown of pearls and garnets set like a wreath in her short, dark hair. Prince Dervian wore red and black and white, with the swords of state thrust into his sash, an ermine lined robe of royal purple, and the crown of the heir apparent.

Upon reaching the foot of the altar the party stopped smartly. Not just the principals, but their entrained retinue, as well. Practicing in the palace, they had kept running into each other, until Genzari persuaded them to accept his hand signal. The organist came in a beat late with the fanfare of trumpets from the organ, but the short blessing repeated three times by the chorus was splendid. Then Dervian stepped up before the altar and knelt before Patriarch Gorabani. There was a deep-throated roar of approval that shook the cathedral.

Jankura waited for the ovation to die down, then knelt beside Prince Dervian. There was a spatter of polite applause, quickly ended. The patriarch picked up the Regent's Crown and turned to Jankura, who removed the wedding crown and threw back her veil.

Gorabani intoned the ritual of coronation one line at a time, and the chanter, a big, round man with a powerful bass voice, repeated it after him, going up a half note each time, the chorus humming behind him. At the conclusion of the regent's part, which was musically incomplete, the organ picked up the note and wrapped it in a pianissimo minor chord. Gorabani placed the Regent's Crown on Jankura's head and took both rings from the cushion Marjia held. One of them he placed on her right forefinger, the other he raised above his head, reciting the next line as he did so. The chanter repeated the line, dissolving the musical tension, and the chorus, in full voice, repeated it after him. Gorabani went through the monarch's part with the chanter, who shifted into a major key, and the chorus, and finally a reprise by chanter, chorus, and organ after he placed the King's Crown on Dervian's head.

It was splendid and powerful, and Wizenbeak was moved in spite of himself even though, or maybe because, much of the ceremony had been cut. Jankura had sat down with the various masters involved with the coronation and eliminated the ruffles and flourishes that had, over the centuries, embellished, encrusted, and empurpled the ceremony with such a profusion of detail that the central core was no longer effective theater. At one point, the Master of Protocol had resigned on the spot when she told him to "Keep it simple, stupid." She merely refused to accept his resignation and soothed his bruised feelings by telling him that only one person ought to be in charge of a theatrical event, and she was it.

As the cathedral was emptying, the regent's party of ten went down a side aisle that marshals had kept clear, up into the organ loft, and out onto the small balcony to the left of the main entrance of Cymdulock Cathedral. As they came out one at a time, first Duke Falenda on the left, then Count Darji-Damuso on the right, the crowd gave them each a cheer. A curious thing, thought Wizenbeak, blinking in the bright morning sunlight, the nobles on the inside gave Dervian an ovation, but were barely civil to

Jankura. His nose tickled and he sneezed, then sneezed again. His emerald glasses would have prevented it, but what had Jankura said? "You look strange enough without them." It might be true. What had he been thinking about? The nobility in the cathedral sitting on their hands when Jankura received the Regent's Crown, yes. Out here, Dervian got a big hand, but Jankura got a bigger one.

Then the army started to pass in review.

"I thought the coronation parade went very well," Princess Marjia said, feeding bread crumbs from the remnants of her lunch to the carp in the lily pond. "What were you saying to Gorabani when the Tarelians went strutting by?"

"Hunh," grunted the wizard, opening one eye. He was stretched out on the grass in the shade of a crab apple tree, half dozing while he digested his chicken salad. Overhead, Branka was in the branches playing tag with Jankura's troll-bat Mischka. "He asked me what the change in the Tarelian Gonfalon meant. So I gave him some cock-and-bull story about its symbolic essence, and he said I really ought to consult the College of Heraldry before making changes like that."

Marjia thought a moment. "What change?" she said at last. "They had the dragon's head, erased, vert upon argent, the same as always."

"Wrong, Your Majesty." Wizenbeak propped himself up on one elbow. "The dragon's head was green and white stripes." He opened his robe to pluck at his shirt. "This stuff. Not solid green. Getting ready for the parade about three this morning, we found we didn't have a gonfalon, and nobody knew where they could lay hands on one, so we took a white bed sheet and my shirt and improvised the sucker." He stretched and yawned. "Somebody did a real pretty job of sewing."

Sitting up, he crossed his legs on the grass, leaned back against the stone bench, and resumed the conversation that had been interrupted by lunch. "Somebody did an outstanding job of training Branka, too, Your Majesty."

Marjia was silent as a carp swallowed a crumb, making a soft splash that set ripples across the little lily pond. "Not me," she said at last. "Branka is different."

"Tell me something I don't know," the wizard said. "When you got him, were you able to establish any sort of bonding?"

"No." Another crumb was tossed onto the still water. "Maybe he was too old. That's what I thought at first. But he wasn't trained by the book. I worked on him, and she worked on him, and he wound up with you. He never had a chance to bond with one person when he was the age to bond. Jankura thinks maybe . . .'' She hesitated. ''It sounds silly, but she thinks Branka socialized with people instead of other troll-bats. She thinks bonding between troll-bat and human is very unhealthy for the troll-bat.''

''It can be a damned nuisance for the human, too,'' said Wizenbeak. ''But Gruchka . . . my little Gruchka . . . was with me for twenty-one years, almost, and he was never sick.''

''Oh, come on, Wizenbeak. I knew the little monster. It never hit me until Jankura brought it up, but, for a troll-bat, he had to be a little crazy—maybe more than a little. Troll-bats take on the characteristics of their masters, and vice versa, which is why glassmakers have a drinking problem.''

''What?'' Wizenbeak had been in the business of manufacturing mother-of-glass and he knew it to be the truth. The troll-bats had to be kept sober enough to keep them working at a tedious job and drunk enough so they wouldn't go crazy and tear the place apart. Their handlers felt the strain—the troll-bat's strain?—and drank heavily to ease it. The idea that grubby, cloddish commoners, hardly a step above peasants, might have the same kind of bond with their vulgar, drunken animals as *he* had had with Gruchka was upsetting. ''Hey, I could *rely* on Gruchka!''

''And he could rely on you, because the two of you had kind of grown together over the years. You were *his* human.''

''Maybe so,'' Wizenbeak said, looking up at the troll-bats playing overhead. ''Maybe so. I miss the little fella, anyway. But Branka . . . ?''

''You can rely on Branka, too, I think. The archdeacon with the limp handshake . . . Branka felt your aversion, also what caused it, and took direct action to correct it.''

''Sheer naïveté on Branka's part,'' said the wizard.

''Come on, Wizenbeak, that was a very sophisticated response to a very subtle signal.''

''Hunh,'' he grunted. ''That bothers me less than the nap I took at the cathedral. Gruchka couldn't have done it, wouldn't even have known how.''

''You said it stood you in good stead,'' Princess Marjia replied.

''It did. That's what bothers me. That's why I thought maybe you were trying to control me through Branka. If Branka can put me to sleep, what else can he do?''

"Good question, Doctor Wizenbeak," the princess said, resting her chin in one hand. "You've worked with the little beasts a lot longer than I have. How would *you* train one to do the quick-sleep trick?"

"Damned if I know," he conceded. "How did *you* do it?"

"I didn't. A direct answer to a direct question. I didn't." She sat on the other stone bench, her feet barely touching the pebbled walk. "What else he can do, I don't know that, either."

"Yes, Your Highness." The wizard stood up like a black scarecrow unfolding. "I have a meeting with the regent coming up, and it were best not to keep her waiting." Branka came when summoned; but, being wide awake, perched on his master's shoulder. Mischka started to come when Wizenbeak called to him, then balked. Marjia chirped something and Mischka came to her, resting on her wrist like a tiny hawk. When Marjia extended her hand to Wizenbeak, Mischka refused to move. Finally, and with great diffidence, the wizard reached out and took the reluctant troll-bat in his hand, setting him gently on the shoulder opposite Branka.

Jankura was seated in one of the tall windows, dictating to a secretary, when Wizenbeak entered the room. Mischka was off his shoulder like a shot, brushing the red velvet drapes and dropping into his mistress's lap. She stroked his ears with ringless fingers as she finished the letter she was working on.

"I hear you've put a bunch of conspirators in charge of the Tarelians, Master Wizenbeak," she said. Against the northern light the starkly cut gray silk dress served to emphasize her naturally high color. "What about it?"

"Quite true, Your Majesty," the wizard replied easily. "It seems there was a cabal of senior officers planning the assassination of Fadel the Witchfinder. Of these, several were burned at Fadel's order." He twisted a strand of whiskers around one gnarled finger, wondering if he had acted wisely. "The penalty for such a heinous crime is hanging, of course, but the Military Court refused to convict on the evidence presented. The rest were found guilty of lesser offenses and sent to prison. It was my decision to select one of them to head the Tarelian Order for me, instead of accepting the list of hirelings pushed on me by Orunjan."

"They broke their oath and you took them on again?"

Wizenbeak pushed his glasses back on his long nose. "Yes and no. Yes, they broke their oath, and no, I didn't take them on again. This is the first time I took on any of them."

"Don't chop logic with me, Doctor," Jankura said, "I don't like it." She took a deep breath. "Why were senior officers of the Tarelian Order trying to kill Fadel, anyway?"

"That was the charge against 'em. Pardus Murado, the man I selected to captain the order for me, claims they were only looking for a way to rescue Nasar-Namatu from shameful death when they were betrayed by Fadel's agents provocateurs." He pulled at his long nose. "Who put the flea in your ear about it, Your Majesty?"

"Patriarch Gorabani. He said he recognized Murado and the others at the parade, and 'was appalled that you would select men of such vile character to rule a religious order.' Can you make changes?"

"Yes, Your Majesty."

"Stop acting like a stiff-necked old fool," Jankura said a bit testily. "Do you think it would be a good idea?"

Wizenbeak sighed. "No. Gorabani gifted me with a secretary to handle the Tarelian's detail work, Basir Orunjan. He had his list of officer candidates all written out for me the morning I had to make my hires."

"You should have taken the time to interview them."

"Orunjan's boys, Your Majesty? The day before the coronation parade?" He pulled his nose again. "There wasn't time."

"Perhaps not," Jankura conceded. "You're satisfied with Murado?"

"So far," the wizard replied cautiously. "He put on a good parade at very short notice."

"Then we'll go with him," she said.

"Good, good. What about his suggestion that Prince Dervian be made honorary deputy head of the order, so that he and the other officers would take oath directly to the Crown?"

Jankura sat back in the window. "Let that ride for now," she replied at last. "It would annoy the hell out of the clerisy to no useful purpose." She caught her secretary's eye. "Make a note of that and ask me about it in a week or two. What else was I going to ask the good doctor, here?"

The secretary consulted his diptych. "About the list of wizards and the troll-bat."

"Oh yes." Jankura slid off the window seat and began to pace around the room. "There isn't time, you know," she said at last. "Since we returned to Cymdulock, we haven't been able to pay proper attention to little Mischka."

"I'm sure that will change," the wizard said. She shrugged, and as she looked at him they both thought of the last days of the True Shaia, when she was beset with military and political problems, and fatally distracted by her time-consuming search for solutions sorcerous. In practice, mused the wizard, the ideal of the Philosopher-King gave either a bad Philosopher or a bad King or both. Would it be the same with Witch-Queens?

She held the troll-bat against her breast with one hand and caressed his head with the other. "No, Master Wizenbeak. If I want time for Mischka, I'd have to make it, and Guhland would be the worse thereby."

That could well be true, thought the wizard uneasily, shifting his weight from one foot to the other. Was that why she had me take Mischka over to Marjia's lesson today? "A bored troll-bat can develop troublesome habits," he said at last.

Jankura nodded. "And the glassmaker's solution is to feed them kimjii root or whatever to put them into a drunken stupor. When I do that to Mischka, I get sleepy myself. Or at least I lose concentration."

"At Marjia's lesson today, he played very nicely with my little Branka," Wizenbeak said. "If you wish, I could give him a regular outing."

"That's very kind of you," Jankura said, running a hand over her short, dark hair. "But Mischka deserves a bit more than a walk in the park. I'd like you to take him and actively use him, engage his abilities . . ." She choked, and her eyes were bright with tears. "Permanently," was a whisper.

"Hunh," muttered the wizard, pulling at his long nose. If I say I'm busy, she's even busier. If I say I don't want to, she'll insist—and I can't refuse. "And maybe double 'hunh.' Your Majesty is giving up a very powerful tool."

"That's true," she said, wiping her eyes. "To the master of the hammer, every problem can be solved by pounding. Put him in a glazier's shop, he doesn't do well. If we need magic, the thing to do is hire a few magicians."

"Your Majesty, sorcery is a far more subtle matter than pounding a hammer—"

"Yes, yes," she agreed, anticipating his argument, "and 'tis a traditional tool of statecraft. Still, it failed me badly when I had to deal with my stepson Prince Kahun."

There's no arguing with that, decided Wizenbeak. Kahun broke the True Shaia like a dry stick, and Jankura is good but a long ways from being the adept Shaia was. "Surely you aren't turning away from sorcery?"

"No, no. But I'll not set my hand to it anymore."

"It would be a popular move," he conceded. "Will you make a formal declaration?"

"Feh. Who'd believe it? To my enemies I'll always be the Witch-Queen."

"I'm afraid you're right," he said. "If you aren't turning away from sorcery, though, you'll need some wizards besides me in the house."

"Then we'll hire them, Master Wizenbeak. No tyrant ever had trouble finding civil servants, even wizards." Jankura turned to her secretary. "Give Master Wizenbeak the list of applicants so he can screen it for us."

The secretary walked over to his desk and produced a thick stack of chips from one of the drawers.

The wizard took them and looked at Jankura. "What's this?"

"We let it be known, discreetly, that we were hiring magic users. These all came in the last three days."

"Hunh! I would have thought that Cymdulock would have been purged of witches by now."

"The herd has been thinned out a bit," Jankura said. "These were likely in hiding."

"Yes, Your Majesty," he said absently, sorting through the stack of applications. He finished with a small stack on one hand and a large stack in the other. "Here," he said handing the small stack to the secretary. "These are people I know personally, or by reputation, that I would consider hiring. The others—" He shrugged. "Mostly I don't know them. A few are real losers."

Jankura took the large stack and dropped it in the wastebasket. "We'll interview the ones you recommended." She looked at the secretary. "When have I got time?"

He consulted a large red diptych. "Tomorrow evening would be the earliest."

She sighed. "Right. Have them come in, the whole lot. I'll see them in the plant room."

The secretary made a note.

"We'll have a little party," Jankura said turning to Wizenbeak. "As you see, I'm not giving up magic, only troll-bats, only poor little Mischka, here."

Which is the best part of the sorcery you've mastered, Wizenbeak thought sadly. Well, there's no help for it. He held out his wrist. "Come here, Mischka," he said. Jankura whispered something to her troll-bat and the little monster flew gracelessly over to perch on the wizard's shoulder.

6

Blows Against the Witch-Queen!

"I YIELD to no man in my detestation of the Witch-Queen," Basir Orunjan said, filling his tiny cup with Lagualian coffee from the long-handled copper pot sitting over a warming candle. "But give the devil her due; aesthetically, the coronation was the best in living memory." The three of them were sitting at a small table in the corner of the Stag's Head Dining Room, one of the smaller refectories on the ground floor of Syncretisty Hall. Many years ago it had boasted a stag's head mounted over the fireplace, but this had been long since removed. On the marble fireplace mantle, however, was a bas-relief boar's head, and the confusion it caused to new members constituted a kind of mild hazing.

Archdeacon Obuskaia composed his large hands in front of him on top of the polished wood table. "It had the virtue of brevity," he agreed. "Let us hope, most prayerfully, that Shaia's reign shares that virtue."

"Shaia's regency," Archdeacon Anezkva said, examining the dark sludge in the bottom of his cup. It was mostly sugar, but bitter to the taste. "Shaia rules, Dervian reigns. Don't forget it, Buska."

"Such a distinction," the big man said. "We have done her an injury. Therefore we cannot forgive her . . . and she knows it. I, myself, was on her short list. She put it aside, but do you think she forgets?" He shook his massive bald head.

"She's pulling the country together after a civil war," Anezkva replied. "If she offered you an amnesty, would you accept it?"

"For myself, alone? No."

"Come on, Buska . . . for the Mambrinistas."

"Ah." Obuskaia took a sip of his coffee. "*If* she made such an offer, *then* I'd have to consult, confer, caucus . . . We might take it, we might not. If she wasn't trying to get back the witch-gold, I'd take it like a shot.'' The House of Obuskaia had handled a lot of post-burning real estate transactions.

''That's already gone into law,'' Anezkva said.

''Yes. Well, certainly I'd be more inclined to take up an amnesty offer if we had the Tarelians going for us.''

''If the Tarelians were going for us we'd still be fighting,'' Orunjan pointed out.

''Possibly so,'' Obuskaia conceded, setting his tiny cup on the polished wooden table. ''Which reminds me, Basir. How did your plan work?''

The little man took a sip of coffee and grimaced. ''You were there,'' he said at last. ''What you saw is what we have to live with.''

''Hey, Basir, I don't know these people—not the ones you selected, not the ones in the parade. What happened?''

''The esteemed Archdeacon Wizenbeak, duly appointed Master of the Tarelian Order, made a few magical passes and selected Pardus Murado as his captain-general. All right?''

''Murado?'' Anezkva's pale blue eyes looked startled. ''Who ordered *his* release?''

What an asshole, thought Orunjan, taking a sip of coffee. ''Nobody. I expect he got out in the tumult when the city fell. Do you want to rearrest him?''

Anezkva shook his head. ''It can't be done,'' he said, oblivious to Orunjan's sarcasm. ''But look, if we can't forgive Shaia because we've done her an injury, we can't forgive Murado, either.''

''Wrong, Doctor Anezkva. We can tell Murado, 'We were only obeying orders,' and it would be true.'' Obuskaia pushed his chair back against the paneled wall and folded his arms across his chest. ''At least I could. What did *you* do to him?''

The other archdeacon sat silent.

''Hey, if we can't rely on the Tarelians we need to know why!'' Obuskaia said. ''Why can't *you* forgive Murado?''

''I was the judge at his trial,'' Anezkva said reluctantly.

''Go on.''

''Fadel had fixed sentence before the trial ever began. I was just going through the motions.''

''So why should he be mad at *you*?''

Anezkva sighed. ''His wife of three months came to my

chambers to plead his case. A pretty lady. I was much taken with her.''

"You took her to bed?" Orunjan asked.

"For a time. Not long. A few little weeks. She wanted to get her husband released, and I told her, well, I made her think it could be done."

"Hey, Murado's out, right?" Obuskaia asked. "The wife wouldn't tell the husband she'd been stepping out on him, no matter what the reason. She *didn't* tell him, did she?" Anezkva sat silent, eyes downcast. "What else is there?!''

"She got wise, Marya did. She . . . she was very angry with me, and threatened to expose me." There was a long silence.

"Go on," said Orunjan. "What did you do to her?"

"I denounced her as witch. She was burned with the very last batch, the week after Sifoty Field."

Obuskaia sighed. "That was a bit excessive, I fear. And Murado knows about it?" The other nodded. "Yes. Well, when we approach him, we'll try to avoid mentioning your name."

"You don't think Murado is our enemy after the way he was treated?"

"Don't confuse yourself with the Church," the big archdeacon said. "He might well stand loyal in a crisis."

"We *have* a crisis," Basir Orunjan said sourly, "and Murado is selecting officers we threw out in the previous crisis. Good men who were loyal to the order and its master before they were loyal to the Church."

"Wizenbeak isn't Nasar-Namatu," Anezkva said. "The Tarelians wouldn't stand by him. Would they?"

"Each one took oath to Archdeacon Wizenbeak, and I, myself, heard talk of making Prince Dervian an honorary deputy master of the order so the officers could take oath to him, directly."

"Totally unacceptable," the smaller archdeacon said, thrusting out his chin. "We must adamantly resist this—this brazen usurpation, this institutional subversion, this—"

"Hey, we lost the war, remember?" Obuskaia pulled a mournful face. "Basir's plan was to smuggle in our own people so we could hang on to the Tarelians without Shaia noticing. It didn't work, so we have to try something else."

"Yes, yes," the other agreed, "but what?"

"Sit tight and pray."

"Oh, shut up, Buska! We do nothing, the situation gets worse and worse forever!"

"You have any ideas?"

"I have," Orunjan said, resting his elbows on the table. "Take out Wizenbeak. I know it's sooner than we wanted, but time isn't on our side anymore. The next head of the order—whoever it is—will want his own people in place." He shrugged. "Goodbye, Murado."

"Hey, if we need to get rid of Murado, why not kill him directly?" Obuskaia asked.

"You think maybe he was the only one that doesn't like us?" Orunjan replied. "Wizenbeak would find someone else to take his place, maybe someone a lot worse. No. Making Doctor Wizenbeak master of the order was a gamble that didn't pay off, so the thing to do is cut our losses."

"I don't know if that's such a good idea," Obuskaia said at last. "The old fool's an archdeacon, after all. You start killing us archdeacons promiscuously . . ." He left the sentence hanging in midair.

"He's one of Shaia's main advisers," the little man said. "Maybe *the* main adviser, the gray eminence, though it's too early to get a firm reading yet. Remove him, the regime starts to wobble, and maybe fall. The best case is that I'll take over as acting master of the order and have time to bring in my own people."

"What's the worst case? The order going to somebody like Genzari?" Obuskaia looked thoughtful. The worst case was that they would be caught and hanged, but they were likely to be hanged anyway. The temptation was to struggle on the way to execution and take whatever chances were needed.

"We wouldn't be any worse off," Anezkva remarked. "Let's do it!"

"Hey, hey, what's the tearing hurry?"

"We're better off *without* the Tarelians than to have them adverse to our interest," Anezkva replied, his blue eyes flashing.

"It would take care of Gorabani's craven attempts at accommodation," Obuskaia mused. "And we're already at risk, so it's not like we have all that much to lose." He shrugged. "You want to take a cut at Wizenbeak, Basir, you go right ahead."

Princess Marjia sat in her window, watching the slow, steady autumn rain. "At least you went to the coronation ball," she said. "After standing in the reception line and drinking one lousy cup of lousy punch, they made me go home. 'Time to go beddy-bye, Your Highness!' ''

Lying on the bed, a wet cloth folded over his forehead, Wizenbeak groaned. ''Royalty gets all the breaks,'' he muttered without opening his eyes.

''Why is the punch so bad, anyway?''

''Hunh. To encourage temperance, chastity, and sobriety. Serve a really good punch sometime and see what happens. Your Highness *knows* that.''

''I didn't remember the punch being so awful,'' she said.

''You now have the delicate tastebuds of youth,'' Wizenbeak reminded her. ''For me, it was bad, so for you it would naturally be intolerable. Even one cup. I, myself, lost count after I started drinking the stuff out of a stein.''

''It sounds like a great party.''

''You couldn't throw a cream puff without hitting someone important,'' the wizard said. ''The place was full of beautiful people, some of whom, imagining that I was a pillar of the regime, made me the most lascivious proposals.''

Princess Marjia giggled. ''Is that why you switched to a stein?''

''Hunh.'' There was a long silence. ''No. I was conducting a thaumaturgical experiment. If Branka could put me into a deep sleep when I was really needing it, could he cure a hangover the morning after?''

''Could he?''

''The little son of a bitch wouldn't have anything to do with me.''

There was a discreet knock on the bedroom door, and Marjia's nanny opened it on the chain.

''One of yer bodyguards, Doctor Wiz,'' she announced. ''He wants yer to come with him.''

''Hunh-hunh. What for?'' There was a brief conference at the door.

''Some ambassador is presenting his credentials to Her Majesty the Regent, an' she wants yer there.''

''Is it that late?'' Wizenbeak wiped his face with the cool side of the damp cloth and sat up very slowly. ''I'm coming in haste,'' he muttered, letting the cloth fall to the floor and putting on his glasses, ''maybe even great haste. C'mere Branka, C'mere Mischka.'' There was a stir on top of the canopy, but no trollbats appeared. He stood up. If a drunken troll-bat made Jankura feel queasy, maybe a hungover wizard would have an off-putting effect on his familiars.

Princess Marjia spoke a word of command, and both troll-bats leaped nimbly on her outstretched arm. She talked to them for a moment, and they reluctantly consented to crawl into the wizard's capacious pocket.

"I guess that's it for today, Your Majesty," he said, pushing his emerald glasses back in place. "Do read that scroll I brought you, and we'll talk about it tomorrow."

The throne room was a converted ballroom, a cube forty feet on a side, with wallcloth of watered beige silk, and a white ceiling elaborately decorated with plaster molding that radiated from around the four great crystal chandeliers. The room was unfurnished, except for a low dais on the north side nested between the ornate wrought-iron staircases descending from the musician's gallery. A fine carpet covered the dais, and upon it sat the Throne of Guhland, a high-backed oak chair stained almost black, profusely decorated with gilded figures carved of limewood. Jankura sat on the throne, surrounded by courtiers, and guards were posted at the foot of the stairs to keep people out of the gallery. Other guards were posted against the walls around the room.

Genzari, wearing his general's uniform, met Wizenbeak in the antechamber whose glass doors opened onto the south side of the throne room.

"What's going on, Lasco?" the wizard asked.

"The Lagualian ambassador is coming to present his credentials," Genzari said. "Her Majesty wanted you and me and Braley to be there. Among other people." He fingered Wizenbeak's chain of office. "What did you do?"

A long pause. "The gold chain was too heavy."

"So?"

"So I was tired of wearing the thing. I had a girl sew a cloth-of-gold chain on my robe. A little quilting, it looks more authentic than I do." He fingered the pendant, "The nabla *is* the real thing, though."

"Right. How do you feel?"

"Awful," the wizard said, taking off his glasses to rub his eyes.

"You look awful," Genzari agreed. "After last night, though, I guess you're entitled."

What did I do last night, wondered the wizard as he carefully replaced his emerald spectacles. Best not to ask . . . even my troll-bats won't talk to me.

Count Braley walked in, wearing a gorgeous red, gold, and green tunic over a plain black and tan hauberk, his two swords thrust into the sash at his waist. His hair was carefully coiffed, and he smelled of lilacs.

"My dear," he said, "Doctor Wizenbeak, you were *wonderful* at the coronation ball, simply wonderful!"

I have disgraced myself, decided Wizenbeak, pulling at his nose in a distracted effort to collect his wits. Unless maybe it's worse than that. "How kind of you to say so, Count Braley. What exactly was it that impressed you so?"

"The dance contest with young Archdeacon Viluji, of course. I thought you'd won when you crossed two knives on the table and did the Northlands Victory Fling without knocking over any glasses; but no, he matched you step for step!"

I don't remember any of this, thought Wizenbeak hopelessly, he must be making it up. I don't even *know* the Northlands Victory Fling.

"So then you crossed your arms and did the kazatsky," Genzari said, "and the guests were crowding around to watch and clapping in rhythm and cheering! My God, how they cheered!"

"And Viluji tried," Braley continued. "He picked up the beat and went down with you, one, two, three times, on the other table, and the fourth time he fell off!"

"At which time you up and did a backflip to dismount the table," Genzari concluded. "I wouldn't have suspected you capable of such athleticism. Nobody should remember the cream puff at all."

"Cream puff?" the wizard asked faintly.

"You hit Duke Falenda with a cream pie," Braley said, "but that was earlier. Her Majesty had made some social gaffe or other, and Falenda had the ill grace to remark on it. He'd had a few, too, and when I reproached him, he began to get loud. That's when you threw the pie at him."

Genzari fingered his mustache and almost smiled. "A splendid diversion in a sticky situation. The count and Falenda were glaring at each other, when splat! the cream whatever-it-was hits the side of his face and he draws his sword. Without thinking. So Braley here draws his, naturally, and they stand there for a second until Her Majesty says for them to put away their steel."

"I don't remember any of this stuff," Wizenbeak protested. Would they be making it up? Is the military mind capable of such flights of fantasy? No and no.

"So of course I sheathed my sword," Count Braley said. "And the good duke, being no fool, sheathed his, and there was this big wave of nervous laughter and that was the end of it."

The doors of the antechamber swung open to admit the Lagualian ambassador, Archdeacon Haidar Gyasi, and his entourage. A chamberlain approached Wizenbeak and the two generals.

"The three of you will stand at the right of the throne when the ambassador presents himself," the chamberlain said. "Ah, Master Wizenbeak, you should be wearing hauberk and swords, as befits the master of a military order. You look terribly informal for this momentous occasion."

The wizard pushed his emerald glasses back up his nose and reached into one of his pockets. "My archdeacon's beanie," he said, putting it on. "If you can find me a sash and swords, I'll wear those, too."

"I'll see what can be done," the chamberlain replied. "Meanwhile, you are to stand in order of military precedence. You understand?"

"Hunh." Wizenbeak started to shake his head and closed his eyes to contemplate the swirl of colors washing behind his eyelids. "Ah, not exactly," he said as the pain subsided.

"As leader of the newest of Her Majesty's forces, you'll be on the end, next to Count Braley. Now, please to follow, gentlemen."

They found themselves fronting the right side of a V at the foot of the throne upon which sat Janko Jankura, the False Shaia, Regent of Guhland, who wore gray silk with silver brocade and a long tunic of the finest black lace. At her throat was an enormous ruby, taken in battle from Kirndal II, King of Lagualia. Facing them on the other side were Duke Falenda, Duke Viluji, and Patriarch Gorabani, with the youthful Archdeacon Viluji standing in the rank behind, looking almost as wasted as Wizenbeak felt. Someone handed the master of the Tarelian Order an officer's sash and swords. His captain-general, Pardus Murado, helped him put them on properly, and, when all was in readiness, the chamberlain announced the Lagualian ambassador.

The dignified Archdeacon Gyasi marched to the foot of the

throne and handed the chamberlain a scroll of parchment tied with a scarlet tape and sealed with the State Seal of Lagualia. The chamberlain inspected the seal and offered it to Jankura, who looked at it and nodded. The chamberlain broke the seal and proclaimed in a loud and official voice that Doctor Haidar Gyasi, Archdeacon of the Syncretist Church, was, indeed, the Lagualian ambassador.

"We are pleased to meet you," Jankura said, fingering her ruby.

"It is my honor to be here," Gyasi replied, his blue eyes hooded and a bit cold. "As Ambassador of Lagualia and representative of His Majesty King Kirndal . . ." He recited His Majesty's titles at interminable length. At the end there was a stir.

"Duke of Kalycas?" Jankura asked. Kalycas was the name for Guhland's Eastern Marches.

"Duke of Kalycas," the ambassador replied, "a province wrongfully seized by King Grathnys, late consort to Your Majesty."

Again, there was a stir. "Consort" was a gratuitous denial of Shaia's legitimacy. Braley adjusted his sword sash.

"We have here set forth Lagualia's claim to Kalycas," Gyasi continued, laying a second scroll at the foot of the throne, "and bid the Lords and Regent of Guhland study the matter closely. If, after two days, you fail to recognize the righteousness of this claim by ceding the province of Kalycas to my master, King Kirndal, I must, with the greatest sadness, dissever diplomatic relations between our two countries and depart for home."

After the ambassador made his exit, Jankura invited the two wings to close around in front of the throne. She sat back, at eye level with the tallest of them, and folded her hands.

"Advise me, gentlemen," she said. "What is to be done about this ultimatum? Duke Falenda?"

"We have two days," Falenda replied cautiously. "Perhaps we should first consider the merit of Lagualia's claim. Also, Your Majesty, what we have is not an ultimatum, which is the threat to go to war if some demand is not met by a specific deadline, but the much softer demarche, albeit with a time limit. The only threat is to withdraw diplomatic recognition."

Jankura nodded. "Your scholarship is most impressive. Duke

Viluji?'' The duke was short, with bowed legs and gray hair, an elderly jockey beginning to get fat. He had remained neutral in the recent civil war and prospered thereby.

"The northern foot are already on the way home," Viluji said. "The northern horse are taking their leave today. However, it is unlikely that the north would willingly fight for Syncretist Kalycas in any event. If we find Lagualia's claim without merit, could we contest it on the field of battle? I seriously doubt it."

"The late civil war has left the treasury empty, Your Majesty," Falenda added. "We can ill afford a war with Lagualia."

"Your Holiness?"

"The Church will support Your Majesty's decision in this matter," Gorabani replied, "but we are reluctant to counsel war with the civil war so recently ended."

Jankura turned to the other side: "General Genzari?"

"You can't afford not to defend the Eastern Marches, Your Majesty. You are too newly come to power to cede a province without a fight. Lagualia's appetite would grow with eating."

"Count Braley?"

"I agree. The major castles—Kalycas itself, Ayondela, Sibetio, and Baran-Beldon—are manned and provisioned to withstand a protracted siege. If we show ourselves resolute, the Lagualian army will find itself biting on granite. If we temporize, our garrisons will make terms for themselves."

"Excuse me," Duke Falenda said, "but Kahun took a Caesar's half of the garrisons with him to the disaster at Sifoty Field."

"Casualties were light on both sides," Braley replied. "With Kahun dead, the soldiers returned to their stations."

"Master Wizenbeak?"

"Your Majesty has no good choices," he said after a moment. "Fighting you cannot win, and not fighting you cannot avoid losing. I would urge that we fight, simply because an active course offers the hope of an enemy's blunder, and because . . ." he stopped and pulled at his long nose.

"Go on," Jankura said softly.

"And . . ." The wizard pushed his emerald spectacles back up on his nose. ". . . Well, because it's *better* to go down fighting, Your Majesty."

"Thank you, Master Wizenbeak." She shifted on the carved and gilded throne. "Patriarch Gorabani. You are reluctant to counsel war, you said. What other counsel have you?"

Gorabani sighed. "Your Majesty, it seems premature to talk of war at this point. Lagualia's possibly just and reasonable demands lie at your feet, unread. I urge the matter be studied at greater length."

"You would suggest that I form a committee to study the matter in the time we have? With, perhaps, yourself as its head?"

The patriarch smiled. "A very wise decision, Your Majesty. I would be honored to serve you thus."

"No doubt," Jankura said, nodding. "Has the Duke Viluji anything to add besides the obvious fact that the northern army has gone home?"

"Yes, may it please Your Majesty," Viluji replied, coughing into a linen handkerchief. "You do not have enough reliably loyal soldiers to hold Cymdulock with one hand and fend off a Lagualian invasion of the Eastern Marches with the other. The first loss against Lagualia . . . the first *report* of such a loss, and your enemies at home will rise against you."

"And my friends will join them to save their skins?"

"We live in an era of opportunism, Your Majesty. I should be false to your interests were I to deny it."

"Well said, Viluji. One may rely on you to stay bought until it is inconvenient. Duke Falenda?"

"I served you, then Kahun, and now you again, Your Majesty. As did many others now in your service. Once men learn to survive by turning their coats, they cannot be trusted to fight to the death for you." Then Falenda's smooth face took on a mournful expression. "Deeply as I regret the loss of a province, I fear a war at this time would end the dynasty."

Jankura sat fingering her great ruby for a moment before she turned to Genzari. "Lasco?"

"Will Guhland be more secure after the Eastern Marches are in Lagualian hands, Your Majesty?" He fingered his closely clipped mustache for a moment. "I wouldn't think so. Nor will you. And I wouldn't think that your domestic enemies will find a foreign invasion the happiest opportunity to rise against you. Keep the faith with your people and their masters will hesitate to betray you."

"Count Braley?"

"Your Majesty is too weak to temporize. Only bold action— and the luck that attends the bold—will save us. I say fight!"

"Master Wizenbeak?"

"I would catechize Duke Falenda, if I might, Your Majesty." Jankura half nodded. "You have our permission."

"Thank you. The duke feels we should abandon Kalycas for the good of Guhland as a whole. This would be a wise policy if Lagualia wishes only to regain a province which has passed back and forth between our nations in times gone by." Wizenbeak turned to face Duke Falenda, who was standing at his side. "The first question is thus: Do you think that Lagualia wishes only to regain Kalycas?"

"Yes, of course."

"Very good, Your Grace. And how did Kalycas come to Guhland?"

"King Grathnys won it in a war twenty-odd years ago."

"Exactly so," the wizard said. "Who was then King of Lagualia?"

"Kirndal V, the present ruler."

"Who, at the age of seventeen had just ascended the throne, as you may recall," Wizenbeak said. "He is now forty, and a seasoned campaigner. The question, Your Grace, is: If Lagualia wants only to regain Kalycas Province, and King Kirndal wants to fight a war with us—with Guhland—what will happen?"

"Kirndal *is* Lagualia," Falenda said. "Why would he want to fight a war with Guhland?"

"To beat us, Your Grace," Wizenbeak replied, pushing his spectacles back in place. "To avenge the defeat Grathnys inflicted upon him when he was a boy. Can you doubt it? Don't answer that . . . answer what will happen."

"Kirndal is the king," Falenda said at last, "and if he wants a war, he will have one."

"Very good. Your Majesty, ceding Kalycas will not avert a war. That war is already upon us, King Kirndal avenging his defeat at the hands of King Grathnys by taking advantage of the weakness . . . the seeming weakness of Grathnys' son, Prince Dervian. Sooner or later we must fight, whether we wish it or not."

"We could form a committee, couldn't we, Your Holiness?" Jankura said with a perfectly straight face. "A committee to discuss the impending crisis?"

Gorabani shifted his weight. "Yes, Your Majesty," he said softly, "that would seem to be the wisest course."

"We fight," Jankura said. "In two days we shall give the Lagualian ambassador an answer to this—" She touched the scroll of parchment with her foot. "—insolent demand. Consider the question of means and advise me that morning at breakfast.''

There was a general murmur of assent. Wisely or not, a decision had been taken.

In the antechamber outside the throne room, the master of the Tarelian Order paused by the yellow marble staircase with his captain-general to remove the borrowed sash and swords.

''As master of the order, you really ought to be wearing the two swords,'' Murado said as he wrapped the raw silk sash around the two scabbards.

''They weigh more than the chain of office,'' Wizenbeak replied wearily. ''A man wears all the insignia they want to pile on, he couldn't move.''

''These are real swords, sir, not some token of rank.''

''It doesn't matter; I don't know how to use them,'' the wizard said, removing his diptych. ''Anyway, I have to report back to Her Majesty in two days,'' he went on, making a note with his stylus. ''I want a status report from you by tomorrow evening.''

''I was there, Master Wizenbeak. She wants to hear about means, so we'll tell her about means.''

''What all do you need?''

Pardus Murado took out his own diptych. ''The order's table of organization calls for twenty-eight thousand men; we have 3,187,'' he said without opening it. ''Do you want the equipment we're short of?''

''Put it in your report. You tell me now, I won't remember.'' Wizenbeak pulled at his long nose. ''What else?''

''Time, sir,'' Murado said. ''We need time to shake down into a unit.''

''How much time?''

''That depends on what you want done, sir. We could defend the walls of Cymdulock right now, I expect.'' Murado felt his jaw reflectively. ''A war with Lagualia, though . . . Training the men up to the proper Tarelian elan . . . that might take two, maybe three months. Attacking with genuine brisance isn't something that just happens, you know. The officers have to have confidence in the men, and the men have to trust the officers, and you have to know who all you're going with.''

''Put that in, too,'' Wizenbeak said at last. ''I imagine you can get anything you need except time, but it won't hurt to ask.'' He fingered the golden nabla pendant from his robe. ''Figure that the Tarelians are going to war and give me two lists. What you want, and what you absolutely can't do without. I'll do my best for the order, but I have to know what it is."

Murado slipped his diptych back in his pocket. "Yes sir. We're already working on some of it."

Princess Marjia sat on the stone bench in the little garden with the scrolled manuscript the wizard had given her earlier. Wizenbeak sat on the other bench, elbows on knees, hands clasped together, watching Branka as he stalked Mischka, who pretended not to see him. A recent frost had nipped the yellow roses, but one white rose, near the ground, remained in bloom. The leaves on the crab apple tree had turned to bronze and were starting to fall.

"So that's what happened with Lagualia," the wizard said. "Her Majesty handled things about as well as could be expected in the circumstances."

"She took your advice, at any rate," Marjia said. "Will you be able to get the Tarelians outfitted in time to do any good?"

"One does what one can," Wizenbeak replied. "After I leave here, Basir has arranged for us to see this hauberk maker—Goel & Sons, I think—about some contract dispute." There was a rustle of leaves as Branka pounced and missed, and the wizard's eye fell on the scroll.

"You read through Jitauno's manuscript?" He wasn't eager to talk about contract disputes.

"Eh." Marjia shrugged. "Yes, I did."

"What did you think of his argument?" the wizard asked.

"He's crazy," she said.

"Well, he holds a minority viewpoint, at any rate," Wizenbeak conceded. "But if you discount the speculation—"

"You mean, about the Human-Dragon Wars? His whole argument is . . . is . . . He started with his stupid conclusion and worked backward from there. He's—what do you call it—tendentious." Shaia's vocabulary sounds strange coming from Marjia's innocent young mouth, thought the wizard. Worse, she is becoming less fluent with time, as if she were losing it.

"We don't know where the dragons came from," he said reasonably, "and we never found out, though the world is a big, big place and by no means well explored. One day they just came flying over the horizon. Why shouldn't they be creations of the troll-bats?"

"Because troll-bats are too little and too stupid to do such a thing," the princess replied. "Why not the dragons creating the troll-bats, if you want a connection?"

Wizenbeak sighed. The few dragons in human captivity had died of starvation. The consensus of classical antiquity—who had been there, after all—held it to be because the dragons were too dumb to eat their own captured rations. "Do you really think troll-bats are stupid?"

"No-o-o," she conceded, "but Jitauno has them doing strange and wonderful things to support his silly ideas."

"Forget about the creation of dragons," Wizenbeak said, sitting back on his bench, "Jitauno argues that the troll-bat's social structure is dominated by the females. Can you buy that?"

"Power flows from females and juveniles to the alpha males," Marjia said. "No, I don't buy it."

"Power flows from troll-bat ground crews to keep the dragons aloft," Wizenbeak said, "so you think the dragons are running things? If we were talking about *money* flowing, who d'you think would be in charge?"

"Money is different."

"Look, Jitauno has this theory." Wizenbeak pulled at his long, silky mustache. "Most of the time, we keep our troll-bats doped up so we can work with them, so they'll do about what we want more or less when we want it. Everybody else is talking about the vulgar *troll-bat brattus inebriatus*; Jitauno is talking about troll-bats in the wild state."

"Troll-bats do not exist in the wild state," Marjia said dismissively.

"Wrong, Your Majesty. Troll-bats do not coexist with humans in the wild state. We trap them with kimjii root and other drugs because they are so damned dangerous and we put them to work making mother-of-glass and other magic for us because they are so damned useful. Imagine an island with no humans, all right?"

Princess Marjia nodded. "I see your point. The troll-bats would be doing fine . . ." She hesitated. ". . . until famine got them, or sickness."

"Or war," Wizenbeak said automatically. Then he heard what he had said, and the hairs on the back of his neck stood up. "Two trives of fully alert troll-bats . . ." He pulled at his long nose. "Anyway, Jitauno argues that the male troll-bat, the recipient of the power from the females of his trive, also relies on the females to do his thinking.''

"Interesting. She may be projecting her human prejudices on an innocent animal, though.''

"She? Oh, you mean Jitauno.'' The wizard nodded. ''If he was a woman, that might explain why he was ignored. But follow the argument: the females work together to support the males going against the trive's enemies. The males, for all the extra power at their disposal, are poor, weak vessels bumping up against the hard, hard outside world. Not surprisingly, they don't live very long. It's the old females that have the experience, the judgment; and Jitauno thinks they are the ones in charge. He cites evidence—''

"Anecdotes,'' Marjia said. "Granny tales from the dawn of time. He talks about a trive with hundreds of troll-bats. What was the biggest one you ever saw?''

"Hunh.'' The wizard pushed his emerald glasses back in place. "Usually, you get a trive with around fifty animals, you split them into separate groups. More than that, troll-bats get hard to handle.''

"Right. So fifty is tops.'' She hesitated a second and sighed. "Only it isn't, is it? Fifty is all we can husband conveniently. On Troll-Bat Island . . .'' She left the thought hanging.

"Good point,'' Wizenbeak said. "Anyway, the thing is, your male troll-bat is a natural follower, drawing power from the trive and doing what it tells him to.''

"That's pretty much the way they behave,'' the little girl agreed. "The troll-bat draws muscle power from his human and tries to figure out what to do with it.''

"Right. It takes forever to get a troll-bat to follow your orders, even though he really wants to. Only, with Mischka and Branka, we have something else.'' The wizard hesitated for a moment. "How shall I put this? I think you and me and Her Majesty form a kind of pseudo-trive with Mischka and Branka.''

"Neither one of them is ever going to be an alpha male,'' Marjia said. "Even if you find females for them. They've both been neutered.''

"Oh? That's interesting. I could never bring myself to put my little Gruchka under the knife. Maybe that explains their better manners.''

"Maybe it does,'' Marjia said. "It might help some humans I could think of, too. Anyway, suppose you do have this pseudo-trive—which, frankly, I doubt—what are you going to do about it?''

The nanny opened the top half of the kitchen door behind them and leaned out. ''Yer hour's up, Doctor Wiz,'' she said. ''We'll be seeing yer tomorrow.''

''I don't know,'' said the wizard, as he stood up. ''Theory is theory and praxis is praxis, as my old master used to say.'' He wished the troll-bats to come to him, and, to his amazement, they did, arriving on his shoulders with a flurry of autumn leaves.

7

Assassination, Theory vs. Praxis

"THIS is a very disreputable part of town," Basir Orunjan said, his jet and amber prayer beads chattering in his hands, as the wizard climbed out of his sedan chair. "Bars, brothels, and bath houses abound."

"So Goel & Sons is in the low-rent district," Wizenbeak replied. He looked around; across the way was the Boar's Head Tavern, and the Five Horse Shoes. If there were a brothel or a bath house in the area, he couldn't see it. The narrow, twisted streets were cobbled, with flagstone sidewalks on either side covering what would otherwise have been open sewers. Here and there a broken flagstone had been replaced with boards. The unkempt buildings were low and shabby, two stories of soot-stained brick, sometimes with an attic or loft under a slate roof. There were no basements. The neighborhood had grown up around the conflux of canals that served its industry, but with the low ground and high water table, basements tended to flood.

The wizard and his entourage were in front of the white-washed office of Goel & Sons. Their factory, which had windows, was to the right of a narrow alley; and their warehouse, which didn't, was on the other side of a short dead-end street that fronted on a canal. "Park the sedan chairs over by the loading dock," the wizard said, "and post a couple of guards here at the door. We'll be out directly."

Tako Goel, the middle brother, met them in his cluttered office with the Tarelian's Chief Inspector and offered his guests coffee. After declining a second cup, the wizard got down to business.

"What seems to be your problem?"

"I don't have problems," Tako Goel said, "the Tarelians have problems. You want hauberks, I make hauberks. I've been in the business all my life, impregnating cloth with glass." He pulled out the contract. "Here. You specify the weight of the canvas, the design on the canvas, the quality of the mother-of-glass, the concentration of the working solution, the pattern you want to cut, and 'cut to fit.' What else is there?"

"Seemingly very little," the wizard agreed, glancing at the Chief Inspector. "But I get the most awful reports about your performance."

"These half-wits from the Tarelian procurement office," Tako Goel said, "they want to tell me how to make the hauberks, one step at a time, like I was an idiot that didn't know nothing. You know what they want? They want me to do everything the exact same way as the last fellow that did the work for them! 'That's the way it's always been done,' they say."

"And how are you doing it?"

"My way. I underbid the other fellow by more than a third doing it my way. Put the design on the canvas, then cut the pattern to the measurements, then sew up the hauberk—"

"I am unfamiliar with the art," the wizard said. "What do you mean, 'put the design on the canvas?' "

"Oh." Tako Goel rubbed his bristly chin. "Come through the plant with me. I'll show you."

The first stop was a long room with a stack of canvas bolts and a couple of workers spreading the bolt out to its full nine yards on a table, while other workers put a long silk screen on top of it and applied the design.

"The design is usually hexagons or squares," Goel said, "and we put it on with a little beeswax dissolved in spirits. Why we do it is to keep that part of the canvas from getting impregnated with glass, so the hauberk stays flexible. The Tarelians use hexagons on the outer layer, and rectangles on the inner layer, so the wax lines don't match up. For better protection, you know?"

Around the corner, workers were spreading pieces of pattern on the canvas and marking the outlines with chalk. When they had finished with one piece of canvas, other workers would change tables with them and cut the cloth. The cut pieces were then put into baskets, and the tailors would come in to pick up a basket, which they would take into the next room to sew together.

"Here you see the tailors with the measurements," Goel said. "The cutters cut small, medium, or large. The tailors, they have the measurements on chips and they set the dummy accordingly, then sew to fit."

"Right," said the wizard. "So you sew up the canvas hauberks with these wax lines in them. Then what?"

"Then we put them on basket hangers . . ." Goel reached under a table and produced a nested stack of wicker hangers shaped like a human torso with the neck ending in a hook. "One of these here. And let them soak in a vat of mother-of-glass liquor."

In the next room they saw a wooden trough that came up about shoulder high. There was a long rod over it, and the rod was completely filled with basket hangers supporting hauberks. The dark-colored mother-of-glass solution smelled faintly aromatic.

"Three dippings, three drainings, to make sure you don't have voids or dry spots, and then we let it stand overnight so that the mother-of-glass starts to set before we put it in the steam room. You know why we steam them, don't you?"

"To set the glass, of course," Wizenbeak said.

"Right. That's right, Master Wizenbeak. And then we put the inner and outer hauberks together, and they fit each other, and they fit the man we cut them for, and the muck-pissing Tarelian inspectors won't accept them."

"Why not?"

"Because we're not their regular supplier, is why not. You get all sorts of little fiddling nit-picks is what you get!"

"Is this true?" Wizenbeak asked the Chief Inspector.

"We were maybe a bit overzealous," the man conceded, "but we aren't getting the quality we're used to, either."

"They fit all right?" A nod. "They'll serve in the field?"

A shrug. "They pass the dart test," the inspector said contemptuously.

"Then what's wrong with them?" the wizard asked.

"The canvas is stitched together with waxed cobbler's thread," was the reply. "The old hauberks were put together with copper rivets."

The wizard removed his glasses and rubbed his eyes. In the silence, the telling of Basir Orunjan's prayer beads sounded a bit agitated. "If it isn't in the contract, don't reject for it," he said at last. "All right?"

"Yes sir, Master Wizenbeak. But we're buying crap."

"You get what you pay for," the wizard said. "Will you pass the rejections or must I write a waiver for them?"

"I'll pass them," the Chief Inspector said, and that was the end of it.

As they stepped outside, a fight broke out in the Five Horse Shoes, and as Orunjan walked over to the loading platform to bring up the sedan chairs, a couple of whores tumbled through the bat-wing doors into the street. The two guards at the doorway were watching the women and didn't see a lean young man step out of the alleyway between the factory and the office. He held a knife, hilt down, blade against the underside of his forearm, and walked toward a space about a yard in front of Wizenbeak, the natural route for an innocent pedestrian. One of the guards glanced at him and saw that his eyes were on the fighting women.

As he stepped past the wizard, the man pivoted, reversing his grip on the knife, and thrust upward for the heart. Wizenbeak felt a blow that took his breath away and sank to one knee. The young man sprinted across the street to disappear down an alley beside the bar.

Putting his hand to his chest, Wizenbeak found the knife protruding. One of his guards ran into the alley after the assassin, the other drew his sword and stood over his fallen master. Mischka and Branka came out, blinking and stretching, suddenly roused from peaceful sleep. Basir Orunjan ran over with the rest of the squad. The two fighting women simply disappeared.

"Quick, quick!" Orunjan shouted. "Bring the sedan chair and get him inside!"

As the porters ran over with Wizenbeak's official sedan chair, the wizard stood up and, taking the hilt of the knife in his right hand, began to work it loose.

"Get him back to the palace! Now!" Orunjan shouted.

"That'll do, Basir," Wizenbeak growled. His black robe was open, and in his left hand he was holding something while his right hand pulled the knife loose. "So," he said, reaching into his freed up inner pocket to remove a deck of playing cards, the very finest, hand-painted silk, stiffened with glass, "a perfectly good deck of cards ruined!"

"What?" Orunjan turned around, genuinely shocked.

Wizenbeak displayed the knife and the cards, and slipped the blade back into the hole it had made. "An upward thrust," he said softly, holding the hilt so that the cards were parallel with his body. "A diversion, an upward thrust, and a clean getaway. Somebody did some planning on this one, didn't they, Basir? Who all did you tell about our intended visit down here?"

"Wh-ah-ah-ah," Orunjan faltered, when the guard who had chased the assassin down the alley returned.

"The son of a bitch got away clean, sir," he said.

"You did well to give chase," the wizard said. "That was quick thinking, quick action." He contemplated the knife thrust into his deck of cards. Now what? he wondered. Then the reaction began to hit him, and he removed the ruined deck and put it back in his pocket with shaking hands. The knife he placed in the sedan chair. An inch or two lower, he'd have been dog meat. The thing to do was go back to the palace and tell Her Majesty. He was having a hard enough time pretending to be calm, best not to try to think. Yes. But what to do?

"We shall return to the palace," Wizenbeak announced, noting with some satisfaction that his voice wasn't shaking. He would have spat, to show that his mouth wasn't dry with fear, if he had only been able to muster up some saliva. "Let's go!" He crawled into the sedan chair and pulled the curtain down. Maybe the ride back would help him recover his composure.

Rumor outran fact, as it often does. At Syncretisty Hall, Doctor Kurjima was sitting with Archdeacons Darussis and Anezkva in the reading room when Archdeacon Viluji ran in, skullcap pinned at a rakish angle in his thick blond hair, the crowning glory of a singularly flamboyant costume.

"I say, fellows," he exclaimed breathlessly, "the word is that somebody stuck a knife into old Wizenbeak! He's dead!"

"Pity," Anezkva said, composing his hands and rolling his blue eyes piously toward the ceiling. "I hope it isn't contagious."

"He was stabbed, assassinated! He didn't catch the pox or anything, for God's sake!"

"Oh?" Anezkva unfolded his hands. "Well, I hope that isn't contagious, either."

"Are you sure of this?" Darussis asked.

"I just heard it, just as I was coming in the door."

"Interesting if true," Kurjima remarked, shifting his weight on the stool. "It would put a whole new complexion on a lot of things."

"We'll have to appoint a new master of the Tarelian Order, of course," Anezkva said. "Probably we ought to consult with Her Majesty the Regent to make sure everything goes smoothly."

"That's the patriarch's problem," Darussis said. "We don't *have* to consult, you know, and he *might* not choose to do so."

Anezkva blinked his pale blue eyes. "Well, all right," he said, "I only thought—"

"Don't go giving away the altar plate to be nice to the barbarians," Darussis said. "There's a war coming up with Lagualia, and that gives us a lot of leverage to exploit this, this . . ."

"Unfortunate turn of events," Kurjima interposed smoothly. "We mourn whenever an archdeacon dies and we deplore it when one dies violently. Still and all, I expect we'll miss the good Doctor Wizenbeak a lot less than some." His long slender fingers caressed his finely lined face. "This might be an opportunity, or it might turn out to be an unmitigated disaster. Did you hear who did it, Viluji?"

"No." The other shook his head. "Just the bare-bones report."

"Of course. Well, the thing to do is sit tight until we find out what happened. And then we want to give the matter some thought. Shaia isn't going to take the murder of her minister lightly, you know. She just isn't."

"What can she do about it?" Viluji asked.

"Cede the Eastern Marches to Lagualia and purge the Church of Mambrinistas, for example." Kurjima showed his teeth in a humorless smile. "If it turns out that Wizenbeak was assassinated by Mambrinistas, she might have no other choice."

"But . . . but *that* would restart the civil war," Anezkva protested.

"If the Mambrinistas killed Wizenbeak, maybe the civil war has already *been* restarted," the Patriarch's special assistant said. "Do you think Her Majesty wouldn't try to win it?"

Archdeacon Obuskaia walked in and threw his cloak on one of the benches. "You heard the news?"

"We heard," Anezkva replied calmly. "Wizenbeak's been killed."

"Worse than that," the big man said. "Much worse. Someone tried to kill him and failed. He's alive and well over at the palace, and Basir Orunjan has been taken. He's being held for questioning!"

Anezkva's face turned ghastly white and he put both hands over his mouth.

Kurjima clasped his hands around one knee and hooked his heel into the top rung of his stool. "Have you perhaps any idea what your friend Orunjan might say, Buska?"

Obuskaia shook his head. "No," he said sadly. "After a while he'll say whatever they want, I suppose."

"Right, right. As the patriarch's assistant, they'd naturally expect him to be executing the patriarch's policy," Kurjima said sadly. "Of course, Basir was always a terribly uncompromising, unforgiving sort . . . I suppose that came from his background as an art critic. Who would have expected an aesthete to be so bloody-minded?"

"Now what are we going to do?" Darussis asked.

"Wait and see," Kurjima said. He had not missed Anezkva's reaction to the news. "If one has a guilty conscience, perhaps he should go into hiding. Otherwise . . ." He shrugged.

"Otherwise what?" Obuskaia said.

"Otherwise you trust that your innocence will be your armor."

"Haw!" Viluji laughed. "Innocence! To please King-Patriarch Kahun the Mambrinistas brought down the Witch-Queen and burned Nasar-Namatu, that most honorable master of the Tarelian Order, as a witch. She came back, the Witch-Queen did, and the Tarelian Order came back, but just because Obuskaia here didn't have a hand in trying to put the quietus on old Wizenbeak, that doesn't mean he's *innocent*!"

"I'm on Shaia's list," Obuskaia conceded. "Innocence isn't really going to do it for me."

"What are we going to do?" Anezkva quavered.

"Struggle to win," Viluji said, extending his arms and doing a slow dance step. "Expect defeat, you'll either freeze, or die of heat!"

8

Damage Control

THAT evening Patriarch Gorabani called a special meeting of the Congregation of Clerisiarchs.

"We have been at the Royal Palace," he said, "and after talking with Archdeacon Wizenbeak and others, must concede that Doctor Wizenbeak was, indeed, the target of an attempted assassination this afternoon. Her Majesty the regent has reacted and, in our view, overreacted to this isolated and confusing event by placing the Clerisiarch Basir Orunjan under arrest on the charge of treason. We have insisted that our colleague be accorded all the privileges of his rank, the advice of counsel, and the full protection of law, and to this Her Majesty has agreed, albeit reluctantly." Clearing his throat, he continued.

"In addition, she has informed us that Prince Dervian is to be named as deputy master of the Tarelian Order, and the officers required to take oath to His Majesty, so that if a future assassination is successful, the place of the Tarelians in the royal order of battle will not be affected. We told her that this was totally unacceptable, that this would result in an immediate rupture of the fragile ties between Church and Crown. That wicked woman merely scowled and said: 'What a pity.' Threats and persuasion alike were without avail. In the end, she agreed to let us in the Congregation consider the matter, so that . . . *if* we agree . . . she will seem to be acting with our assent."

"And if we do not agree?" someone called from the back.

"We asked her that very question," Gorabani said. "She said that the Tarelian officers had already consented to take oath to Prince Dervian, that they thought it was a good idea, and that she intended to see it done."

"Outrageous!" boomed a voice that sounded like Obuskaia's.

"Disgraceful misconduct!" rasped a voice not unlike Anczkva's.

"No appeasement," two or three voices said together, and both sides of the aisle were filled with an indignant murmur. Agreement seemed entirely out of the question, and the discussion centered on what actions ought to be taken if the Witch-Queen persisted in this malicious and provocative course of action.

Gorabani sat back in his gilded seat of office, keeping as much order as he deemed sufficient. He had already concluded that the Church had no satisfactory course of action in this case, but it was necessary for the individual clerisiarchs to work this out for themselves.

Sometime later, as various procedural wrangles were beginning to snarl up the never particularly orderly progress of the discussion, Archdeacon Wizenbeak and Pardus Murado entered at the back of the room. Murado wore the captain-general's uniform with swords. The wizard wore his black robe open over a general's parade hauberk, two swords in ornately decorated scabbards thrust through the embroidered sash at his waist, and his massive chain of office. Beard bristling, a troll-bat on either shoulder, he strode into the room.

"May it please Your Holiness," he said, "there is news from the palace."

"Will Archdeacon Anezkva yield the floor briefly to hear Archdeacon Wizenbeak's news?" Gorabani asked.

"For news," Anezkva said, "I'll yield. Albeit briefly."

"Thank you," Wizenbeak replied. "First, the regent has summoned the Lagualian ambassador and rejected his demand for the Eastern Marches, called Kalycas Province by some. This not an hour since. Second, the Tarelian Order, under my command, has been ordered to the Eastern Marches to repel the expected Lagualian invasion. Third, I have been instructed to ask this body to approve the appointment of Prince Dervian as deputy master of the Tarelian Order. Fourth—"

"No! No! Never! Never!" The clerisy was worked up to full voice, and it took a little time to quiet them down.

"Fourth," Wizenbeak continued, pushing his glasses back on his nose, "Basir Orunjan is no more, having put the quietus to himself in his prison cell. One of the black prayer beads he carried contained poison."

He paused, but the news was greeted with dead silence.

"Well," he said after a short pause, "a moment of silent

prayer for the late Doctor Orunjan is not out of order, certainly. I must advise you, however, that Her Majesty regards this suicide as proof positive of his complicity in a plot against the throne. Further, that this suicide leaves the rest of the plotters—some of whom are almost certainly in this very room—free to continue their treasonous mischief. I return the floor to Brother Anezkva.''

''We will *never* agree to Prince Dervian as deputy master!'' Anezkva shouted passionately and he was echoed with a satisfactorily vigorous response of ''never'' from the clerisy.

''May I address the point, Your Holiness?'' Wizenbeak said coldly.

''Will Archdeacon Anezkva yield the floor?'' Gorabani asked. Anezkva nodded.

''The regent has made war with Lagualia her policy,'' Wizenbeak said. ''The Tarelian Order, with support from Duke Falenda and Duke Viluji, is her chosen instrument to carry out the first steps of that policy. The selection of Prince Dervian as deputy master is, I fear, a political necessity; it will happen with or without your approval.'' He paused for a second to look around the room, but nobody said anything.

''So. If the clerisy persists in combining intransigence with weakness, it will lose what little influence it still retains and can blame only itself for such misfortunes as will most assuredly ensue!''

''Threats!'' Anezkva shouted. ''Threats against the clerisy uttered in the presence of the Congregation itself! I tell you, brothers . . .'' He paused for effect, and Pardus Murado stepped forward a half pace, coming out of Wizenbeak's shadow. Not much, but he caught the archdeacon's eye.

''Why, if it isn't Judge Anezkva,'' he whispered, hand resting on the hilt of his long sword. The Congregation couldn't hear him, there had been no threatening gesture, but Murado had made eye-contact with the archdeacon, and after a heartbeat Anezkva recognized him. The archdeacon's face turned pale, and his throat choked him so that he could no longer speak.

''Does Archdeacon Anezkva wish to continue his remarks?'' the patriarch asked after a polite interval.

The response being inaudible, the question was repeated. This time Anezkva shook his head and sat down.

The Congregation of Clerisiarchs, however, was still resolute against cooperation with the inevitable. Late that night, after an interminable rehashing of old arguments, they voted not to accept Prince Dervian as deputy master of the Tarelian Order under any circumstances whatsoever, the thunderous voice of the Congregation drowning out Wizenbeak's lonely dissent.

Immediately afterward, the patriarch recognized Archdeacon Darussis over a number of calls for adjournment. Darussis put forward the question: "If it were felt necessary to have a member of the royal family in that position, would Princess Marjia be acceptable?" Archdeacon Viluji seconded. The patriarch, ruling discussion out of order on a non-binding advisory motion, called for an immediate voice vote, upon which he ruled that the ayes had it. When there was no challenge or call for a show of hands—it being very late—the motion stood as passed, and the meeting adjourned. In the minutes, the motion set down in Kurjima's own spidery hand was: "The Congregation found Princess Marjia acceptable for the post of deputy master of the Tarelian Order."

9

Preparations to March

EARLY the next morning, the master of the Tarelian Order and his captain-general found Count Braley sitting in the regent's plant room, drinking black coffee and watching the cold rain drizzle out of a leaden sky. There was fresh napery on the table, china and crystal, and ornately inscribed place cards. The staff must be getting organized, thought Wizenbeak, easing himself into his chair.

"What's new?" Pardus Murado said by way of greeting.

Braley glanced at him and shrugged. "Duke Viluji has offered fifteen hundred light horse for the Lagualian War," he replied. "They'd be under the command of his nephew the archdeacon."

"That's nice," Murado agreed, as a liveried attendant poured him a cup of tea. He took out his diptych and made a note with his stylus. "Fifteen hundred men, how many horses?"

Braley laughed. "You heard already? About nine hundred."

"Hunh," Wizenbeak said, putting cream and sugar in his coffee. "Sounds like Viluji's light horse is light horses. What's Falenda kicking in?"

"The baggage train. Carts, mules, muleskinners, and a month's rations."

"What would that be?" the wizard asked.

"Oats, onions, and potatoes, I expect," Braley replied. "You won't get any meat out of Falenda."

Murado made another note. "Right. Can we get more mounts, then? We ought to have two horses per man, minimum."

"We'll see," the wizard said, covering a yawn. "Horseflesh can be damnably hard to come by."

Genzari walked in and sat down. "Good morning, gentlemen," he said as the servant poured him coffee.

"Can we get mounts?" Murado asked, looking up.

"For Viluji's light horse?" Genzari asked. "I understand there's a herd from Kalycas corralled outside Rosano. Horsebreeders don't like pasturing in a war zone for some reason."

"We'll send an agent to Rosano today."

Genzari nodded. "Good thinking, Captain Murado. How have you done with your recruiting?"

"The order stood at 5,988 last night," was the reply. "The new recruits are mostly Kahun's former House Guard."

"They were a pretty good outfit," Braley said. "You don't have them in their own units, do you?"

"No, no. We spread them around amongst our veteran Tarelians as Master Wizenbeak suggested. Though if there wasn't a war on . . ."

The chamberlain entered and came to attention. "Her Majesty the Regent." They all stood as Jankura entered with Duke Bedirny, a tall, gray-eyed man with an erect bearing that belied his years. After Jankura seated herself at the head of the table, the others sat down.

"The Duke Bedirny was with Kahun at Mewis and at Sifoty Field," she said. "Wishing to remain seized of his lands, and preferring Prince Dervian to the Lagualians, he has offered two thousand horse and forty-five hundred foot for the relief of the Eastern Marches if they are sent as a Royal Army."

"Excuse me, Your Majesty," Wizenbeak said, "but I'm not clear what is meant by a 'Royal Army.' "

Jankura glanced at Genzari, who replied. "A Royal Army bears the Royal Gonfalon, which is normally associated with the king or prince. For the Bedirny, here, such service in the present war, if rendered loyally, constitutes formal forgiveness for being on the wrong side in the last one."

"Exactly," Jankura replied. "Prince Dervian, as the deputy master of the Tarelian Order, will—with the able assistance of Master Wizenbeak—serve as the Royal Gonfalonier. He is a bit young to be leading charges, but other than that, should be entirely satisfactory."

Wizenbeak pushed his emerald glasses up on his forehead and rubbed his eyes with gnarled fingers. "Ah, excuse me, Your Majesty," he said, "we have a bit of a problem there."

"The clerisy doesn't like it?" Jankura said coldly.

"Your Majesty's gift for understatement is truly impressive," the wizard replied, and proceeded to tell her what had happened at the meeting when he had broached the topic.

"Afterward, Doctor Kurjima made a point of taking me aside to show me the minutes," Wizenbeak said. "What had been inscribed for the next meeting—'The Congregation finds Princess Marjia acceptable as deputy master of the Tarelians'—is not precisely what was passed and will very probably be rescinded at the next meeting."

"But they are on record as opposing Prince Dervian for the post?" Bedirny said.

"Yes. Except for me, the vote was unanimous."

"I have the utmost respect for the Congregation," Bedirny said, "and much as I wish to support Your Majesty against Lagualia, in this matter I must urge that you honor the Congregation's expressed wishes."

Which means that in a break between Syncretisty Hall and the Royal Palace, Bedirny will side with them, thought Jankura. Of course, he wants me to honor the Congregation's *expressed* wishes.

Breakfast was served at that point, a perfectly cooked soufflé, with a side order of creamed spinach, and rolled biscuits with butter and crab apple jelly.

"Captain Murado," Jankura said softly, "would you have any objection to taking oath to Princess Marjia as the deputy master of your order?"

"Ah, why no, Your Majesty, of course not."

"Would your officers?"

"No, no . . . at least I wouldn't think so," replied the captain-general. "If any of the mercenary scum refuse, I'll dismiss them, Your Majesty."

"Very good, Captain," Jankura replied with a faint smile, "though I would expect refusals in this matter to be a matter of conscience from the most dedicated religious cadres." She turned to the duke. "I am prepared to honor the expressed wishes of the Congregation, Your Grace," she said. "Will you serve in a Royal Army under the gonfalon borne by my daughter, Princess Marjia?"

"Yes, Your Majesty, if the Congregation abides by the motion Doctor Wizenbeak described."

"We shall make the announcement this very day," Jankura said. "The Royal Army will hardly be ready to leave before the Congregation meets again, and if they rescind their approval, you are freed from your oath to serve." Bedirny would have left anyway, she thought, oath or no oath, but this way I might still woo him back.

"I doubt if the Congregation will rescind their motion," Wizenbeak said politely. "What Kurjima put in was a bit of procedural maneuvering designed to prevent an open break with Your Majesty. If you take them at their word, the rescission of the motion becomes virtually a declaration of war. Neither Gorabani nor the clerisy would have the stomach for it."

"Then we shall attempt it, gentlemen," Jankura said, and the matter was decided.

10

The Tarelians Make Ready

WIZENBEAK and Marjia entered the fencing studio where the Tarelians trained during bad weather, a big barnlike room with a flagstone floor and racks of wooden practice swords lining the walls. Above the sword racks on the north wall were translucent windows of glass-impregnated muslin, providing a diffuse light. There was a low raised wooden platform at one end from which the instructors could observe and address the students. The royal escort posted themselves at the entrance, and the two of them walked over to the sand table set up at the edge of the platform. Count Braley was standing at ease, chatting with Captain-General Murado. A dozen Tarelian officers stood at rest, waiting for the arrival of the master of the order.

"You're sure you want Princess Marjia to stand in on the strategy session?" Count Braley asked as they came up.

Wizenbeak nodded. "She is, after all, the Royal Gonfalonier, on whose behalf I am acting," he said, stroking his whiskers with an easy gesture. "Besides which, these gentlemen have taken oath to her; it is fitting that she should take an interest in their well-being." Braley shrugged and Marjia stepped onto the platform for a better view.

"Very well, then." He rested one elegantly booted foot on the platform and leaned over the table toward her. "What you see here is a model of the Eastern Marches, Your Highness, the vertical scale greatly exaggerated so that we may understand it more easily—"

"Address Master Wizenbeak, please," Marjia said. "If I should have questions afterward, he, my teacher, will answer them."

"You know all that stuff about sand tables, old boy?" Wizenbeak nodded. He doubted that Braley was being deliberately offensive. The strategist was only trying to find the right tone for his audience.

The principal terrain features of the Eastern Marches were three ridgelines running north-east to south-west, like a pair of forked branches laid with the stems parallel. The Kalyswash flowed north, away from the sea, and hooked around through a gap in the central massif beside the fortress of Kalycas. From there it flowed down the Kalyswa Valley, being joined by smaller streams and finally by the south-flowing Sibetswash, where Sibetio Castle was built on the bluff at the junction of the two rivers. Where the ridges forked, on either side of the river, were broad passes. The castle of Baran-Beldon dominated the gap to the north and east, the castle of Ayondela sat in the gap to the south and west.

"Very good," Braley said. "What we are doing is sending an army about half the size of the Lagualian army into the area for a fall and winter campaign. The reason for doing this is to prevent King Kirndal from laying seige to all four strongholds at once."

"How long will they endure a seige?" Captain Murado asked.

"That depends. Maybe six weeks, maybe a couple or three months for Sibetio." Braley pondered the matter for a bit. "We figure to lose one fortress, maybe two, and we'll try to retake it, or them, in the spring campaign, when our main force has been raised and trained."

"Right," Wizenbeak said. "Genzari was quite emphatic that I was to avoid engagements with Kirndal."

"Unless you can defeat him in detail," Braley replied. "If you find the Lagualian army split four ways, and you can fight them one at a time—why, go to it."

"Right," Wizenbeak said. "How can I tell if the enemy is just a piece of the army or the main force?"

Braley and Murado laughed, the less senior officers merely smiled.

"Love will find a way," the wizard said. "Doubtless I'll know it when I see it."

"As good an answer as any," Braley agreed. "The other thing you're doing in there is giving old Kirndal supply problems. He figures to live off the land, we're going to make it harder for him."

"Why not raise a proper army and go after the Lagualian sons of bitches?" one of the Tarelian officers asked.

"Because," Marjia said unexpectedly, "the House of Grathnys can't risk turning its back on the clerisy and the great houses.''

"It's true," Braley agreed. "Also, time is not on our side. We, ourselves, have to risk being defeated in detail, because it is the least evil of the choices available to us.''

"Which is why Kirndal is invading in the late autumn of course.'' Murado nodded.

"Well then, why doesn't a smart young strategist like yourself head up the army?'' Wizenbeak asked.

"Because you, old boy, are the master of the Tarelian Order, which has to go because we absolutely don't dare leave it behind,'' Count Braley replied. "And Genzari wants me here in Cymdulock. Don't lose, y'hear? We'd be in real trouble if you lost.''

"I'll try not to lose,'' Wizenbeak said, pulling at his long nose. "I don't fancy topping a pyramid of heads.''

"Excellent,'' Braley said, glancing at the officers. "Proper motivation is extremely important, as I cannot emphasize too often. Now, when you find yourselves on the sand table—that is, in the territory which the sand table is modeling—you will be marching east from Rosano on the old military road. Which, as you will note, follows the ridgeline and not the river. That will bring you up here—'' He pointed at the far corner. "—about five miles from Sibetio, on the eastern side of the Kalyswash. That is the point at which you must determine your course of action.''

"We have already determined our course of action,'' the wizard said mildly.

"Yes, Master Wizenbeak. But in order to march where the enemy is not, you must know where he is. Let us imagine that the Lagualian army is laying seige to Ayondela, here. You march up the ridgeline to Baran-Beldon and send the light cavalry across the river to harass the Lagualian supply lines and keep an eye on old Kirndal.''

"Right,'' Murado said. "What if it's Baran-Beldon that's under seige?''

"Master Wizenbeak?'' Count Braley asked politely. "Would you like to handle the question, old boy?''

"Cross the river at Sibetio and march up on the other side,'' the wizard said. "Of course, he probably wouldn't lay seige to Baran-Beldon unless Kalycas had already fallen.''

"Or, unless he had the two points under seige simultaneously,'' Braley said. "A good answer.'' Which was not surprising, since they had previously rehearsed it. The discussion went on until the end of the hour, at which point Braley and the Tarelians took a ten-minute break as Wizenbeak and Marjia returned to the palace.

11

The Clerisy Reconsiders

THEY sat in a booth in the Stag's Head Dining Room, Obuskaia and Anezkva drinking Lagualian coffee, Patriarch Gorabani drinking the more traditional herb tea.

"Kurjima screwed up the minutes," Obuskaia said. "The final motion at that meeting was advisory, you said, that was why you wouldn't let me talk. And look what happens!"

"Princess Marjia winds up taking the oath from the Tarelians," Anezkva said, "first the officers, and then the men! You know what we have if you don't straighten up the minutes? The Royal Tarelians, is what! Run by the throne, paid for by the poor, suffering clerisy!"

Gorabani took a sip of tea. "So what do you propose to do about it, gentlemen?"

"Call a meeting to correct the minutes," Obuskaia said. "That's the first thing. Then run the motion by the Congregation for what it is. If they have any balls they'll rescind it."

"Oh, really?" The patriarch smiled. "First, of course, you'll want to rescind the assassination attempt on Doctor Wizenbeak. After that, they might go along with you."

The big archdeacon sighed. "It is of the highest importance that we not lose the Tarelians," he said. "The Congregation *must* have the chance to straighten up what is at best an honest mistake."

"What's done is done," Anezkva said, his blue eyes flashing, "but this has *not* been done! This is Kurjima playing games with the minutes! The smooth-talking son of a bitch has gone too far this time, by God, and I for one won't stand for it!"

"The war with Lagualia gives us leverage," Obuskaia argued with as much persuasiveness as he could muster. "It would be shameful not to use it."

The patriarch took a sip of tea and sat back, holding the cup in the air. "Leverage works both ways, gentlemen," he said softly. "The war with Lagualia also requires Her Majesty to take strong action on behalf of her country which it is impolitic to oppose. And, of course, we are embarrassed that our special assistant should have been involved in the attempt against Doctor Wizenbeak."

"You're going to let matters stand?" Anezkva was incredulous. "You're not even going to let the Congregation have its fair say?"

"Nobody except a few die-hard Mambrinistas wants to continue the civil war."

Anezkva slammed his hand on the table, rattling the china. "The Witch-Queen went down once, she'll go down again!"

"Dervian is the lawful heir to the throne," the patriarch said, "and we are oath-bound to support him. Also, Shaia is regent, not queen. It makes one hell of a difference, you know!"

Archdeacon Darussis came over, holding a black velvet dress glove in one hand, and Patriarch Gorabani motioned toward the vacant seat. Darussis bowed and smiled and, upon seating himself, returned the glove to Gorabani, who slipped it into his pocket. A servant brought over a carafe of coffee, which was decanted into a cup and set steaming before the chubby archdeacon, who picked up the cup in one hand and the saucer in the other.

"Well," he said amiably, "nice to see you all."

"Queen or regent, it doesn't make a finger's worth of difference!" Obuskaia growled, folding his burly arms and pushing his bulk back in the chair.

"A finger's worth of difference?" Gorabani said. "Maybe so, Buska." He raised the first two fingers of his right hand in the sign of benediction. He then folded down the middle finger, leaving the forefinger erect. "Regent," he said, as he restored the sign of benediction. Then he turned his hand so that the back faced Obuskaia and he folded down the forefinger. "Queen! One damn finger, Buska, but it makes all the difference in the world!"

"You make debater's points, but no converts," Anezkva said, his blue eyes flat and cold. "We *will* bring up the matter at the next meeting." He got up and Obuskaia, holding his cup in its saucer, followed him.

"Good day, Your Holiness," they said in unison.

The patriarch raised his hand in benediction, "May Heaven bless you both," said he, with the faintest of smiles.

"What was that all about?" Darussis asked.

"The assassination attempt may have cost us the Tarelian Order," Gorabani replied, "but those two . . . they don't want to hear it. What did you find out?"

"A little," the chubby archdeacon said, taking a sip from his saucer. "First, the hair you gave me did, indeed, belong to the woman who held your glove. I used the mercury pool and three mirrors as you suggested, and the answer was an unambiguous yes. A longer hair would have been nice."

"Or nail parings, or a menstrual cloth, I know. You have to go with what you've got."

"Yes, of course," Darussis looked annoyed. "As long as we had the mercury pool set up, I rearranged the mirrors for using Berura's Incantation. You get three related questions . . . Well, hell, you gave me the questions, you know all that."

"Yes, yes. You have to spend one of them to establish the color polarity. Go on."

"So I asked, 'Is she a virgin?' and the smoke reflected off the pool turned violet. So violet is no, and yes would be green. Then, 'Is she a widow?' and we get a muddy kind of blue-green, not the best of contrasts by any means, but probably a yes. He took a sip of coffee. "Finally, 'Is she a mother?' and we get the violet again."

"So the violet has to be no," the patriarch said.

"Absolutely. We have a widow who isn't a virgin and isn't a mother, which isn't a whole lot of help. By now the hair is starting to curl a little, which means it'll be dead and useless in a few minutes, so I can squeeze in maybe one more spell. I tried a simple malediction, the Adesinas Wartbringer with candles. Nothing fancy, no sacrifices, just to see what we got."

"It didn't bite."

"It didn't bite," Darussis agreed, "but the candles didn't go out, either."

Gorabani refilled his cup from the teapot and frowned in concentration. Adesinas' malediction with candles was a diagnostic spell. If it bit—and it would bite on most users of magic—it was harmless, even when it worked. If it didn't bite, and the candles went out, the victim was vulnerable but protected. If the candles didn't go out, the victim was not vulnerable. Either immune to warts, or a non-user of magic, or some sort of special case. "How interesting," he said at last. "Why do *you* think the candles didn't go out?"

"I have no idea. The victim was, perhaps, truly virtuous? Whom did you get the hair from?"

The patriarch took a sip of tea. "You don't need to know."

"Really?" Darussis smiled cherubically. The morning after the coronation ball, he mused, you give me one dark hair and say: ask thus and so. Also your fancy dress glove, with which, so you tell me, you embraced the lady from whom the single hair was taken, while you were dancing. A romantic intrigue? Not terribly likely. Power moves you, Gorabani my old friend, not the tender warm bodies of lovely ladies, so whom would you have been dancing with? Duchesses, perhaps, all having longer hair than the one you gave me. In that case the glove would have only revealed the hair as belonging to one of the several ladies it had encountered. Not an unambiguous yes. So the glove had held only one hand. If only one, which one? Removing the diptych from his pocket, he inscribed a single name in the soft wax and handed it to the patriarch.

Gorabani opened it to read: SHAIA. Snapping the diptych shut, he handed it back and nodded. I should have done the investigation myself, he thought sadly, but I've been so damned busy.

The order of battle of the Royal Army that set out from Cymdulock under the gonfalon of Princess Marjia was as follows: fifteen hundred light cavalry under Archdeacon Viluji; the Tarelians, sixty-one hundred strong; the baggage train, which Duke Fadel had furnished, along with twelve hundred mercenaries, mostly infantry, under Nick Sejenics; and finally twenty-five hundred heavy cavalry and forty-five hundred infantry under Duke Bedirny.

They left Cymdulock one morning as the autumn mists were rising and marched thirty miles a day to Rosano, where they picked up remounts for the cavalry and extra supplies for the winter campaign as well as a company of one thousand mercenaries hired by the city of Rosano.

"Rosano could have afforded us more than a thousand men," Princess Marjia said, riding an easy-gaited mare beside Wizenbeak's tall blue mule.

"They had to repair the damage Prince Gatsack did in the late civil war," the wizard replied. "They're still putting stone to mortar on the city wall, so they're short of money."

"Then they should have given us a levy of citizens."

"Civilians?" Wizenbeak asked. "They hired the mercenaries for us, gave us a mess of salt meat, and paid for our horses. What do you want?"

"More soldiers," Marjia conceded.

"No general ever has enough," the wizard said. "Where would you put the ones we have?"

"Murado's plan is pretty good," she said. "Tarelians in the center, Bedirny on the right, the odds and sods under Sejenics on the left with Viluji's light horse. Assuming we have to fight. Will we?"

"At two to one against? I hope not, I really do. Still, one does what one must."

"War is very tiresome," Marjia said, shifting her weight in the saddle.

"No effort should be spared to secure your brother on the throne of Guhland, Your Highness."

"Tell me about it," the little girl said, ignoring the somewhat heavy-handed attempt at irony. "What am I going to get out of all this?"

"Your hand in marriage given to some politically expedient suitor, I expect," Wizenbeak replied, and then, as her eyes unexpectedly teared over, he hastily added, "Fortunately none appears to be in sight."

"Sorry," she said after a moment, "the old implacable spirit was momentarily overcome by the romantic sentimentality of the flesh."

A forced march brought them across the arches of the old stone bridge below Sibetio. Camping on the far side of the Kalyswash, for the first time within the Eastern Marches, they marched through rolling hills and small farms curiously devoid of livestock. The next morning the army started up the old military road, following the southeastern side of the ridge.

At midmorning they made their first contact with the enemy. Viluji's light horse encountered a small cavalry patrol, returning with six extra horses and two prisoners wearing the sable and green of Lagualia. Archdeacon Viluji brought them to Captain Murado, who took them to Wizenbeak.

"I thought you, yourself, might want to question them, Master Wizenbeak," the captain-general said.

"Thank you," Wizenbeak said, pushing his emerald glasses back on his nose to study the prisoners. One was very young, the other was wounded; both seemed nervous. "I am a wizard," he said unnecessarily as Branka and Mischka settled themselves on his shoulders, "and usually I can tell when someone is lying. But my troll-bats, they *know*." The day was cold but both men were sweating, a good sign. Intimidation accomplished. "I am going to talk to each of you separately, asking the same questions. Tell me the truth and nobody gets hurt."

The truth was simple enough. King Kirndal's main army was laying seige to Sibetio Castle. Kalycas, Baran-Beldon, and Ayondela had all fallen. The wounded man said that Kalycas had been betrayed, and the garrison slain without quarter. The young man had been much impressed that there were piles of heads, taller than he was in front of all the fortresses. They thought Kirndal had about thirty thousand men, including nine thousand cavalry, somewhat higher than the wizard's own estimates.

"That will do," Wizenbeak said at last. "Dress this man's wounds, and set up a prisoners' compound."

"What next?" Murado asked, who was quietly dismayed to hear that three of the four strong points had already fallen.

"We continue up the hill," Wizenbeak said. "From the crest, we can see across to Sibetio."

Sibetio Castle was perched on top of a red sandstone bluff at the junction of the Kalyswash and Sibetswash rivers. Gray granite towers and extensive outworks defended a position of great natural strength. The flag of Guhland waved proudly from the highest pinnacle. At the foot of the outworks the Lagualian army was encamped beneath the gonfalon of Kirndal V.

12

The Witch-Queen's Deceit Discovered!

THE great Sipatu wiped his brushes and returned them to their case. At his studio, an apprentice would clean them with turpentine. He turned at the far side of the patriarch's attic office and looked at the life-sized portrait of King-Patriarch Kahun, which now bore Gorabani's face overpainted on the original.

"After the paint has dried for a week or ten days—a fortnight would be best—I'll send one of my journeymen in to put a thin glaze over the whole painting. The face, and the deleted insignia of royalty, right now they look flat and rough compared to the rest of the picture. Don't worry about it. The glaze will unify the texture. Your fellow Orunjan knows about that, of course," Sipatu remarked, looking around the room. "Usually he makes it a point to watch me working. Where is he?"

"Doctor Orunjan is no longer with us, unfortunately," Gorabani said diffidently.

"Pity," the artist grunted. "He was a wretched colorist, but might have been a passable draftsman, if he'd only applied himself. Where is he now?"

"We buried him a few days ago," Kurjima said. "In unsanctified ground. He was apparently involved in a plot against one of the royal ministers and committed suicide when captured."

"I hadn't heard," Sipatu said. "Now artists, an artist *ought* to be involved with the great passions of his own day." A pause. "I suppose that might also be true for a critic." He closed his case with a snap. "Speak well of the dead, I always say. Any art critic that kills himself has done the right thing." He put his floppy hat on his head, bowed politely to his patron, and went clumping down the stairs.

The patriarch returned the formal vestments he had been wearing to the wardrobe. "That takes care of the politically awkward masterpiece,'' he said. "The other thing is, how are we going to get the Tarelian Order through the door?"

"A little repainting won't do it, sir," Kurjima replied. "I checked the book on Pardus Murado to see what might turn up. He was tried and sentenced quite arbitrarily by our old friend Anezkva. Probably one of Fadel's directed verdicts. And his wife, Marya Murado, was sent to the stake at the very end of the witch-burning."

"That isn't very encouraging."

"Not if you need to depend on Murado's undying loyalty to the Church," his assistant agreed. "I went a little further and talked to some of the department functionaries. A bottle of wine and a roast chicken will get you a whole *lot* of stale gossip. In this case, it appears that Anezkva was infatuated with Marya, and had kept her as his mistress for a time. When she left him, he put her name in the mouth of the lion."

Gorabani composed his black-gloved hands. "Ah, indeed. Does Murado know of this?"

"I think so," the other replied. "At the special meeting of the Congregation, do you remember when Anezkva choked up? Murado had just stepped out from behind Doctor Wizenbeak to get a better view of the proceedings."

That's interesting, thought the patriarch. If we ever need Murado *badly*, we can offer him the head of Archdeacon Anezkva. But all he said was: "That's interesting."

"As far as Murado's faith goes," Kurjima went on, "it seems to be rock solid. He believes what the Church preaches. But he has also become something of an anti-clerisiarch."

"I can't imagine why, Doctor Kurjima. What else do we have that requires our consideration?"

"Darussis has been spreading a rather remarkable story about Queen Mother Shaia, sir."

Gorabani shook his head. "Wizards gossip worse than women," he said sadly. "How long do you think it will be before we have to take some sort of official notice?"

His assistant sat down on the soft leather sofa. "A week, ten days, not long. Is there anything to it?"

"At the coronation ball we danced with Her Majesty and recovered a hair from her sleeve. We gave the hair, and the glove that held her, to Archdeacon Darussis for analysis. Without telling him the source."

"You had him do the actual conjuring, sir?" his assistant asked. "Perfectly reasonable, I suppose. Darussis is good.

Maybe not as good as the late Heiby, but good enough. How did he guess it was the regent?''

"Oh, he asked who it was, and instead of lying to him straight off, I said he didn't need to know. It took him about one minute to figure it out, grinning and staring at the ceiling as if he was reading something no one else could see.'' The patriarch walked over to look out the gabled window, clasping his hands behind him. "Then he knew, and lying was of no use. Never lie when you won't be believed.''

"So you have this magical assertion that the regent isn't really Shaia," Kurjima said, sniffing. The room smelled faintly of linseed oil and paint thinner, not unpleasant, but a little strange. "Go set it alongside those similar magical assertions that say she isn't alive and the ones that say she isn't dead. So what? A few more contradictions from the assorted schools of magic around Cymdulock is no big deal.''

"You don't understand.'' The patriarch sounded tired. "The Witch-Queen, Shaia herself, should have died when the mob stormed the Royal Palace. Probably she did. But because she was one hell of a sorceress, or maybe because she was just unnaturally neat, we never got a tissue sample like the one we brought home from the coronation ball. No hairs, no nail parings, no nothing. With the result that we couldn't make a positive identification of the head we thought was hers.''

"Ah, indeed," Kurjima said, composing his long slender hands in an attitude of prayer. "The regent might be a False Shaia, you think?''

That's what we've been *telling* you! thought the patriarch with a flash of temper held tightly in check. "Probably so. Given some young woman playing the rôle, some little bitch that Wizenbeak or Braley picked up for her chance resemblance to the late—'' He checked himself. "—the missing Shaia, proving that *she* isn't Shaia ought to be no problem at all. Do you remember the first thing she did after the coronation?''

"What, sir?''

"She gave up her troll-bat! Probably she couldn't use the damned thing, she was just keeping it as a sort of stage prop to convince the world at large that she was what she claimed to be. And she must have been scared silly of the little monster!''

"So Andesinas' malediction didn't bite on her because she wasn't a user of magic?'' Kurjima looked thoughtful. "Now that could be. What's your point, sir?''

"Why, that we have some silly, weak girl holding the reins

of government, and the Mambrinistas are going to use this to bring her down!" the patriarch said. "The civil war, it's on the verge of starting up all over again!"

"Gently, gently," Kurjima cautioned, holding up one finely molded hand. "Don't upset yourself, sir. Just because the regent may be an impostor, a Shadow Shaia, it doesn't follow that she's a silly, weak girl, does it? She sat on the hill at Sifoty Field and watched the battle unfolding like a true monarch, after all."

"What do you mean?"

"Who do you think is running the other side, Your Holiness? Wizenbeak? A second-rate water wizard, an aging mountebank. Genzari? A mercenary. A good, solid soldier perhaps, but utterly unimaginative. The too, too handsome Count Braley? A master fencer, undoubtedly, maybe something of a strategist, but unsteady. He lacks character, even more than the others. Somehow, Your Holiness, *they* are on top. If the Shadow Shaia were just a pretty face . . ."

"Duke Falenda, the Vilujis—"

"Came on board after the war was already over, after Shaia's side had won."

"The Shadow Shaia's side."

"Understood, sir," Kurjima agreed. "How much did the so-called Shadow Shaia contribute to the victory?"

"Her face, and Shaia's name, and, I'll grant you, a certain poise at the coronation."

"We have imagined that Shaia made a comeback with the poor crooked sticks she was able to gather, Your Holiness. Wrong. A fundamental misreading of the enemy's leadership. The Shadow Shaia must have made some contribution, possibly a substantial one. She constitutes an unknown quantity . . ." A long pause. "I'd let matters ride."

Gorabani frowned. "Explain yourself, please."

"The True Shaia was deeply hated in many quarters, and she was universally unloved."

"Except in the north," the patriarch amended, "among the Orthodox and witches."

"They hated her enemies, sir. She was unloved, even there." Kurjima extricated himself from the couch and walked over to the other side of the room, where he could study the painting.

"I think the question Your Holiness needs to ask is: how would Obuskaia and the rest of the Mambrinista intransigents react when word filters round that the regent is really a Shadow Shaia? Some of them will believe it because they want to. My own guess is that there would be a draining of the black bile in their collective gorge.'' He composed his beautiful hands. ''Let matters ride. It ought to be very difficult for the Mambrinistas to agree on any sort of action, here.''

''Do nothing at all?''

''No sir. We wait for someone to make a mistake.''

''You *may* be right, Doctor Kurjima.'' The patriarch nodded. ''The Shadow Shaia just *has* to be more popular than the real one.'' He composed his hands before him. ''And as regent, such a revelation would not impair her legitimacy. Now if she were impersonating the queen . . .''

''*Then* perhaps the information would pry loose her grip on Guhland's throne,'' Kurjima agreed. ''As it is, Your Holiness, the pros and cons of propagating the report would seem to be pretty much a wash.''

13

Kalycas Province

"Now what, Master Wizenbeak?" Pardus Murado asked. Across the river the Lagualian army lay seige to the last Guhlish stronghold in the Eastern Marches. The wizard sat on his mule and contemplated the vista before him, considering his possible choices.

"How far is it to Baran-Beldon from here?" he asked at last.

"From here?" Murado considered. "At the foot of the ridge is a spur from the New Military Road . . . see it?" The wizard nodded. "From that junction, Baran-Beldon is forty-one miles."

"And we've already marched fifteen or sixteen miles?

"I'd make it sixteen," replied his captain-general. Wizenbeak pulled at his nose. They'd had an early start, and he already was feeling the poisons of fatigue in his muscles. A troll-bat nuzzled his cheek and he absently rubbed the long, soft ears. Well, there was no help for it.

"Half a normal day's march, already. Yes. If we lay quiet on the back side of the ridge here, could we escape detection until after nightfall?"

"Eh, maybe . . . maybe not. The patrol we caught would be due back, likely they'd send somebody out to take a look for them. If they didn't find us, what then?"

"Make a stealthy night march to within striking distance of Baran-Beldon."

"Without being spotted? Ah, sir, I'd have to say the odds were against it. And it's only even money that we'd stay hidden until sundown."

"Hunh-hunh." Wizenbeak nodded. "Well, in that case, I want a forced march. From here to there, nonstop. The men can have anything except sleep. You understand?"

"Yes sir." The order seemed stupid, but the master of the

order was clear in his own mind about what he wanted. "What will we do when we get there, sir?"

"Retake it from the Lagualians, of course."

"Yes sir," Pardus Murado said. "As you know, Baran-Beldon is a really strong fortress, and as you also know, we don't have any seige equipment."

"Kirndal took it by treachery. We'll have the advantage of surprise. And the forced march will give us two or three days before Kirndal is within striking distance of us—assuming that he'll lift the seige and come after us immediately."

"I would expect him to do that, sir," Murado agreed. "Do you have a plan for taking the fortress?"

Wizenbeak nodded. This was a possible contingency he had anticipated. "It's cockeyed, but it just might work."

"Good enough, sir." Murado saluted, satisfied, and rode off to arrange the march. The Old Man had a plan, and all he had to do was execute it.

Extending the rest break for a fireless lunch, the Guhlish Army marched off about an hour past noon. A small vanguard of light cavalry, the Tarelians, Bedirny's foot, then the mercenaries under Sejenics, and finally the rest of the Viluji's horse, with Bedirny's cavalry, who had been held in reserve to counter any possible sortie from the Lagualians across the river.

As it was, King Kirndal watched them march up the Old Military Road and ordered the seige lifted. It took the whole afternoon to dismantle the seige engines and strike camp. In the end, the Lagualians chose to remain on the northern side of the Kalyswash and marched down the River Road. Though running essentially parallel, the River Road meandered with the river and took longer to traverse. On the other hand, they didn't have to cross the partly ruined bridge at Sibetio with the seige engines. Kirndal briefly considered burning them, the better to engage in swift pursuit, but they had cost too much money. That day they made about three miles and camped under the cold, starry skies beside the river.

Wizenbeak's army made seventeen miles by dusk, twenty more by dawn, and were camped a few miles from Baran-Beldon by first light. Murado posted sentries and set a watch for messengers riding up the River Road. For the rest of the morning, he let the men sleep.

Three miles from the fortress and out of sight in the scrubby forest along the ridge, the wizard had a rope strung up the hillside—a heavy, two-inch rope, of the sort used for towing barges on a canal. It was set taut, about four feet off the ground, at an angle approximately ten degrees from the horizontal. Wizenbeak borrowed a spear, kicked off his slippers, and started to walk the rope from the lower end. After a few faltering steps, he jumped off.

"This is harder than I remembered," he told the sergeant who was heading up his work detail. "What I need is a training pole, something like this." He laid the spear on the ground, crossed it with a second spear near the butt end, and used a tent pole to make a very flat A. When they had been lashed together to his satisfaction, he picked up the improvised balance pole and proceeded up the hillside on the rope. Awkward at first, his balance improved rapidly with practice as long-forgotten skills were rehearsed, and the cumbersome training pole was discarded in favor of a simple spear.

"Where'd you learn to do that, Master Wizenbeak?" asked one of the Tarelians who had been rigging the towline for him.

"In my youth," the wizard said, "I was a mountebank, performing such stunts at fairs for a few coppers and the cheers of the crowd. Eventually, I outgrew such foolishness to become the respected member of society and pillar of the community which you see before you."

There was a ripple of laughter, and the sergeant looked irked. "All right, you men," he said, "knock it off!"

"Gently, Sergeant," Wizenbeak said, "another part of being a mountebank was making the audience laugh, and both skills seem to have returned together. Now comes the hard part."

As the men took down the long tow rope and wound it back on its wooden drum, the wizard walked through the woods to where Marjia was working with Mischka.

"How's it going," he asked.

"Not terribly well," she replied. "The little son of a bitch knows what to do, I think, but he doesn't want to do it."

"Typical," the wizard said. "Let's see how he does against Branka, here, who hasn't the foggiest notion of what needs to be done."

Up the hillside were two trees growing side by side, about thirty feet tall. About twenty feet up, a wooden battlement had been improvised, carefully cut saplings nailed to a pair of heavier saplings that had been lashed to the twin trees. Each tree had the edge of one battlement, and there was a single battlement between them, at the approximate height and distance as would be encountered at the fortress.

Wizenbeak took Branka in his hands and pointed to the little wooden battlement. ''See there, baby? Papa wants you to take this skinny piece of string . . .'' He held up one end of the long slender cord Marjia had been working with, and the troll-bat took it in his teeth. ''Good Branka, good baby,'' said the wizard. ''Now, take that piece of string and fly up, and over, and around, and come back to me. All right?''

Branka flew up and over and around, but he dropped the string on over.

''That's a whole lot better than Mischka did,'' Marjia said. She held up the other bat as the wizard reeled in the cord. ''Want to try it again, you little fathead?''

Mischka flew the pattern as neatly as Branka, but dropped the string on around.

Wizenbeak tugged the string. There was a lot of play, but it didn't seem to be caught, and he reeled it back in.

''The string tugs when you make the turn,'' Marjia said, ''I saw it.'' When the end of the line reached the reel, she took a small green twig and fastened it with a square knot. ''Who wants it?'' Mischka looked at Branka, then took the end of the line in his long, mobile fingers, holding it up to his eyes, turning it over, and finally taking the twig, not in his mouth, but in his hind claws.

Marjia launched him in the air, and the reel sang as he flew the pattern over the battlement. This time, there was a palpable jerk as Mischka started back, but he held on, and Wizenbeak could feel the pull in his arm and finger muscles as the troll-bat drew extra strength from his master.

Branka looked disdainfully at his returned cohort and took the twig in his hind claws without any examination whatever. He made a wide sweep and came around at full speed. The string encountered resistance, and Wizenbeak felt a tug in his lower back muscles as Branka exerted extra force. The string broke, and a somewhat crestfallen troll-bat returned with the twig and about twenty feet of line.

''That's not too good, Branka,'' the wizard said as he reeled in the line. He spliced the ends together and finished reeling it in. ''You want to let Mischka show you how?''

Branka took the twig in his hind claws and again executed the maneuver, this time without the flash. The line went smoothly around and over and as it came back, Branka gently kept it moving until he returned the end of the line to his master with a bit of a flourish. ''Very good, Branka,'' the wizard said, fishing a dried avricod out of his pocket as a benison. Branka accepted it as his due, and the wizard offered the line to Mischka, who disdained it, coming directly over for his reward. Wizenbeak smiled and found an avricod for little Mischka. Once troll-bats had mastered a trick, they didn't much care to waste time rehearsing it.

"Now what?" Princess Marjia said.

"Now we wait until dark," he said. "I, for one, am going to catch up on some much-needed sleep."

14

The Teeth-gnashing of Her Enemies

THE Mambrinista leadership caucussed in the Stag's Head Dining Room on the ground floor of Syncretisty Hall, pushing a couple of tables together before the unlit fireplace with its carved marble boar's head, and pulling chairs two deep around the tables for a kind of seminar.

They began slowly, as was their wont, rehearsing old injuries and raging at old insults. At first these were almost casual, but soon the unbanked fires of their passion generated the head of emotional steam that had moved them in the past. Archdeacon Nayatis, red of hair, red of face, and markedly overfed, finally came to the point.

"I've heard this from a couple different sources," he said. "That son of a bitch Darussis has found out the regent is a devil-spawned fake! Now by God, we ought to be able to take that and bend things out of shape with it!"

"Hear, hear!" said several voices.

"Go for the throat," Nayatis said. "I say grab the bitch by the throat and shake her to pieces!"

"Amen, brother!" someone shouted.

"God has given this truth into our hands to deliver us from our enemies!" replied Redhead fervently. "Where the will lacketh not, neither will God withhold the means!"

"Use the tools that come to hand," a voice intoned. "Raise the mob against her," another cried.

"It brought her down before," Nayatis said. "I say it's worth another try!"

Obuskaia knocked on the table with his gold signet ring. "With all due respect," he said mildly, "raising the mob seems to be a bad idea. It won't work."

"Why the devil *won't* it work?" Anezkva demanded.

The big archdeacon sighed. "Two reasons," he said, raising two fingers, "either one conclusive. First, our mob must deal not only with the Palace Guard, but also with the army."

"They did it before!" Nayatis shouted.

"Wrong, sir," Obuskaia growled, "Prince Kahun and the Tarelians together kept the army out of the picture. Without them, our mob hasn't a prayer."

"Plus the Witch-Queen misread the situation," said someone sitting at the rear. The last-minute maneuvering inside the Royal Palace was known in some detail, a subject of continuing fascination to the cognoscenti.

"So she did," Obuskaia agreed, "but *then* it made no difference. You play differently, you lose differently." He blotted his big, bald head with a handkerchief. "The second reason is that storming the palace with a mob is fresh in the minds of everybody. You may be sure that Genzari and Braley have given the matter a lot of thought, that it is anticipated if not expected."

"How are we going to lose if we call out the mob?" Anezkva demanded, his blue eyes blazing.

"I just told you," the big archdeacon said patiently. "Shaia is back and she may not have an iron grip on things, but she is relatively stronger than before. She may now be weaker, but we are *much* weaker. If she sends the so-called Royal Army against our rioters, Doctor Anezkva, we have nobody and nothing to support the poor sons of bitches."

"So?" Anezkva was openly contemptuous.

"So," Obuskaia replied in obvious exasperation, "the Royal Army that Braley and Genzari are putting together may not be much good yet, because the individuals haven't shaken down into a unit. But are you going to send an unarmed mob against trained soldiers?"

"Yes!" Nayatis shouted. "Shaia will drown in the blood of martyrs!"

"Hey, no!" cried a voice from the rear. "These are our own people, for God's sake!" Obuskaia looked back. It might have been the younger Fermin.

"Use your head, Nayatis." The burly archdeacon sighed. "You incite a bloodbath, it won't be the Shadow Shaia that drowns in the blood of martyrs, it'll be YOU!"

The red-faced man opened his mouth, then shut it. "What do you mean, Shadow Shaia?" he said at last.

"The rumor that has you taking the bit in your teeth, the rumor that has set you all raging at your collective fates—the same rumor which I checked to the source—was that the regent is not Shaia, our late well-beloved Witch-Queen. What Darussis found, using a single hair and traces in cloth, was that the Shadow Shaia is *not* a mother, *probably* not a widow, and either a non-magic user or immune to warts.'' The chair creaked as Obuskaia twisted to look around the room. ''So you're going to raise a bloody riot against some poor silly female because she *isn't* Shaia to get *rid* of Shaia? What in heaven's name do you all want!?''

Nayatis looked puzzled for a moment; the argument was almost more complicated than he could follow. Then his jaw set. ''I don't care,'' he said, running his hand through his red hair. ''I don't care whether the rumor is true and I don't care if Darussis found out by black magic! I want That Woman off the throne of Guhland!''

''Any stick to beat a dog with, eh?'' Obuskaia sneered.

''Listen, Buska,'' Anezkva said, ''at least Nats has the right end of the stick. So times are tough. Sitting around with your fat thumb stuck in your big mouth isn't going to help! Don't be so negative about a riot if you can't suggest anything better, for God's sake!''

''Right on!'' shouted two or three voices.

''Look,'' Obuskaia said softly, ''either the rumor is true, or it isn't. What you boys are saying is that it doesn't make any difference. Right, Archdeacon Nayatis?''

The red-faced clerisiarch hesitated a moment over the question. ''That's right, Buska,'' he said at last. ''I'll bring That Woman down any way I can.''

The big archdeacon blotted his forehead with his handkerchief. ''Excuse me,'' he said. ''I had imagined that we were meeting to discuss how to respond to an opportunity. The lot of you sound like you were whipping up enthusiasm for a witch fire. Go. Go! *Go!* Go!''

''We're going to—'' began Nayatis, when Obuskaia stood up and put his hands on the other's shoulders.

''Sit down,'' the big man said, pushing; and Nayatis sat, his mouth open with astonishment. ''I'm not finished.'' He looked around the room. ''What, for God's sake, is different today than it was yesterday? Only that we have found out the Witch-Queen is, just maybe, a pretender, a Shadow Shaia. That is absolutely *all*. It doesn't make any difference to us; we still want her out. It doesn't make any difference to anybody!'' As he spoke Obuskaia suddenly realized that what he was saying was untrue.

He still wanted the Shadow Shaia out, yes, but the old intensity was gone. His cold hatred was fading to cordial dislike, his black malice to pallid pique. "So nothing has changed. Only today, today you get all lathered up and you're going to call out the mob! It wouldn't work yesterday, it won't work today, and if it works tomorrow it will be because something has turned up."

"Nattering nabob of negativism," Nayatis mumbled.

"Face it, boys," Obuskaia said, "we lost the war. It's pretty obtuse of y'all to have forgotten, but that's what happened and you have to face up to it."

"We have an opportunity," Anezkva said, his blue eyes sullen. "Are you just going to let it trickle away?"

"Such an opportunity, old fellow. A magic-derived rumor that changes nothing." The big archdeacon stepped back from the table, knocking over his chair. "You know the maxim, 'Guard on rumor, strike on fact!' I say we'd better be on our guard!"

"Hear, hear!" the younger Fermin shouted. "I say: Let's confirm the rumor and *then* decide what to do!"

Obuskaia picked up his chair and slid it under the table. "Sure, sure, confirm the rumor," he growled. "See what it gets you. Against the regent, nothing at all! But"—he glared around the room—"if she ever sets herself up to be queen, it will knock her flat."

15

The Fall of Baran-Beldon

BARAN-BELDON loomed dark and menacing in the early evening. As the prisoner had reported, there was a pyramid of human heads set outside the main gate on the far side of a dry ditch at the foot of the wall. The sloping sides of the ditch were studded with sharpened wood stakes to deter assault, but because of the terrain it fronted only about two-thirds of the fortress's perimeter. Beyond the southeast corner, the ditch entered a ravine substantially broader and deeper than any man-made obstacle, and on the eastern wall was a massive tower set out from the wall with a sally port facing due south. There was a short, cobbled road leading from the sally port to the ditch, one side flush against the wall, the other dropping off into the ravine. At the ditch, there was a stone bridge, positioned to receive oblique fire from archers on both the southern and eastern walls, and from the grim towers as well.

Thirty feet above these carefully landscaped defenses, a sentry's head slid from one battlement to the next as he made his rounds.

"How many heads, d'ye think?" Captain-General Murado asked. Wizenbeak studied the pile. It looked to be about ten heads high.

"Figure about four hundred," he said after a moment.

"Maybe the whole garrison," Murado said. "Did any escape, d'ye think?"

"We didn't find any strays in the woods," Wizenbeak said. "Maybe they went home, if they got out."

"Or to Sibetio," Murado said softly. "If they got out, of course." He hesitated. "I had friends here, a couple of cousins, even."

The wizard shrugged. The thought of checking through that

pile of heads for friends and relatives . . . "Let's go," he said, and the column of Tarelians moved quietly through the sparse grass.

Following around the east side of the fortress, they came to where the dry ditch entered the ravine. They followed the far side of the ravine, until they stood opposite the sally port tower, now perhaps fifty yards away. The road came flush with the tower, and on the far side, the tower and the curtain walls beyond it were built flush with the living rock.

"So here we are," Wizenbeak mused softly, "probably a little too close for what we want to do." He walked backward about ten paces, then another ten, studying the angle to the top of the wall. "This should do," he decided finally, and one of the Tarelians waved over the detachment carrying a drum wound with tow rope, to set it in place.

Pardus Murado peered into the gloom. The fortress was just as the model had appeared in the tent, so far as he could see, except, except . . .

"The model had a man door in the sally port," he said. "I can't tell from here."

The wizard pushed his glasses back on his nose and repeated the mantra against darkness. What he saw was disconcerting; not the familiar daytime view, but the bare outline of what he was seeking. Gray upon darker gray, the rectangular outline of the sally port with a smaller rectangle set at one edge. With some effort he could make out the ground, and the outline of the tower as well.

"It's there," he said. "Let's get started."

The man on his right handed him a kite reel. A small wooden peg swung at the end of the string. Both troll-bats were sitting on his shoulders, fully alert. The wizard took the peg and offered it to Mischka, who ignored it. He shrugged and offered it to Branka. The troll-bat took it in one hind claw, and Wizenbeak pointed to the battlement at the foot of the tower. No need to go any higher than necessary, he decided. Branka studied the wall for a moment, then took the peg in his other claw, and vanished.

After what seemed like an interminable length of time, he returned with the end of the line.

"Good Branka, good little fella," the wizard said, giving him a dried avricod. Mischka tugged at his sleeve, so the wizard gave him a piece of dried fruit, also.

The man who'd given him the reel took the end of the line

that Branka had brought back and tied it to a cord on a somewhat larger reel. The wizard stood aside and watched as it went from a line to a cord to a light rope to finally—after carefully timing the passage of the sentry—the tow rope. The tow rope, being on a drum instead of a reel, took some manhandling. And mindful of the possibility of unseating the battlement, a corporal was carefully greasing the rope as it went out, until Wizenbeak saw what he was doing and made him stop.

Once the tow rope had been secured at two of the three points, the reel, and a stout tree, the wizard proclaimed it ready. The crew had tested the strength of the third point, the battlement, quite strenuously and he only hoped that they hadn't strained it.

After the sentry had passed once more, Wizenbeak picked up the spear he was using as a balance pole, stuffed his slippers in a pocket, and climbed on to the drum holding the tow rope taut. He paused dramatically, looked around, then grinned as he realized he was waiting for the drumroll, and started up the tow rope.

Thanks to the mantra against darkness, the tow rope glowed before him like a living thing. In a way, working with the limited visibility of his emerald spectacles was a blessing; it kept him from the distraction of what must be a—he hastily shifted his line of thought—"terrifying drop" came as a sort of afterimage. Mischka and Branka shifted on his shoulders, perhaps sensing his unease, but the wizard never paused. How could two hundred feet be so long, he wondered.

Then the battlement was before him. Now was the beginning of the hard part, sneaking downstairs to open up the gate. He rested one arm on the cool, rough stone of the battlement, and then, one swift skip, and he was standing on top of the wall, balance pole converted to a spear. Murado had urged him to carry his swords, which he couldn't use. The sash at his waist had to support his thief's lantern; he couldn't be bothered with swords. The spear, at least, helped him keep his balance.

So. The stairs were to his right, the sentry on his way back from the left, so far so good. As he started toward the stairs, five armed men appeared, the corporal of the guard and the four relief sentries!

The shock hit him like a physical blow—not fear, he had already decided what he'd do and how it would be done, but surprise, sheer startlement. Branka slipped off his shoulder, fol-

lowed a fraction of a second later by Mischka. Branka was drawing on the back muscles, as if he was lifting something heavy,
Mischka he couldn't feel at all. He rehearsed the mantra against
darkness again and saw the five soldiers, pale green outlined
against the deep black background that was marked with gray
lines showing the battlements, machicolations, and walkway in
a sketchy outline. The troll-bats weren't there!

He took a deep breath to calm himself and grasped his pointed
balancing pole. Branka was still drawing on his back muscles,
and the effort, the prolonged effort, was painful. The corporal
of the guard and one of the soldiers started toward him—thinking
perhaps he was the man they were to relieve if they could see
him at all—when from between the battlements behind them
appeared two tiny red figures, materializing not as an outline,
but as a blurred streak. Branka took the corporal, and Mischka
took the sentry.

The corporal gave a kind of a jerk, as it struck a sudden blow,
the sentry simply started to fall, and for an awful second every
muscle in the wizard's body was straining to lower them to the
walkway without making a sound. The other three sentries gaped
for a second, and Mischka leaped at them. Two fell without a
sound; the third was just turning around, perhaps to run, when
Mischka landed on his back, and his knees buckled. Again,
Wizenbeak felt the strain of lowering a body at a distance.
Quickly he went over to them; all the sentries were dead. Stepping over them, he went racing down the stairs, adrenaline pouring through his system to lend swiftness to his feet.

So. There was the sally port, and there was the man gate,
held closed by a blind lock that could be worked only from the
inside and a massive beam. The beam he removed with a single
heave—it was much lighter than he'd expected—and turned his
attention to the lock. He took a troll-bat from his shoulder—it
felt like Branka—and tried to remember how he'd opened locks
with good old Gruchka, back in the old days. Mischka slipped
off into the night, drawing a little push from the wizard's leg
muscles. Slowly, slowly Branka examined the lock, probing it
with his long, slender fingers, taking an interminable length of
time, taking forever, if not even longer. Wizenbeak wiped the
sweat off his forehead with the back of his hand and just when
he thought dawn would break and the black cock of night start
crowing, he felt a tugging in his thumb muscles, and the lock
clicked open. He opened the man door, and, as he did so, felt
a troll-bat, Mischka most likely, drawing on his back muscles

in a major exertion. Then it was gone, and he lifted the shade on his lamp, blew the smoldering fuse into a red glow and touched it to the wick. After a second it caught, and he saw an answering flash from the stone bridge crossing the ditch, as the Tarelians started up the cobblestone road toward the now-breached sally port.

· They covered the ground pretty quietly, he thought, all things considered. As the first squad of the first platoon approached the door, Mischka returned to him, settling in on his shoulder as if well pleased with himself.

"Where's the sentry?" the sergeant asked.

"There's five dead at the head of the stairs," Wizenbeak said urgently. "I don't know where the other one is, the one we were watching." More Tarelians came in, swords drawn, running swiftly, swiftly across the barren ground, and these opened the sally port, lighting torches to guide the first company. The wizard stood in a corner of the wall, out of the way as his men poured into Baran-Beldon, recovering his breath and putting his slippers back on.

After what seemed to be a very long time, there was an outcry, as someone tried to raise the defenders, and here and there lights started to come on. He heard Murado yell something, the cry was passed on, and from outside the walls he heard the drums beating "No Quarter."

They'd discussed it a long time back. The two cavalrymen they'd taken near Sibetio he'd ordered released, so as not to have to order them killed. A sign of weakness, the wrong thing to do in a war, but he'd never pretended to be a warrior—even his troll-bats were fiercer than he was. And Murado was right. Any army on the move, that had to be fast on the march and quick to strike camp, that army couldn't afford to encumber itself with prisoners. Tomorrow there'd be a new pyramid of heads out front. The thought chilled him. No pyramid, he decided.

The sergeant that had led the first squad through the man door came up. "Nice piece of work, begging your pardon, sir. We found the guard at the head of the stairs, just like you said. And we found the other sentry you were worried about."

"The troll-bats got them," Wizenbeak said sadly. "How did they die?"

"The corporal, he had a hole in the middle of his back you could stick your fist into," the sergeant replied. "The others, they were just dead. No blood, no nothing." He hesitated. "The captain, he said to give you his regards. Your batman ought to have your tent set up by now. I'll tell off someone to escort you back there, if you think you're finished here.''

Wizenbeak felt drained and very tired. "That might be the thing to do, Sergeant," he said. "It's been a long day."

16

Witch-Queen's Solution

THE plant room was rather dank and chilly, the sun being long down, and the kitchen beneath it long since closed. The condensation clouding the inside of the glass was made somehow sinister by the cold night sky outside, and the dark green plants seemed almost black by the soft light of the hanging lanterns. Duke Falenda leaned back in his chair as Count Braley accepted a cup of coffee from the liveried servant.

"So I approached Syncretisty Hall about a loan to support raising the new Royal Army," the duke said, holding his unopened diptych in one hand. "Gorabani said he couldn't help, it was up to the individual archdeacons. The ones with banking houses, of course."

"And you approached them?"

"As Her Majesty ordered. Archdeacon Nayatis, the fat redhead, was quite rude. The big one, Obuskaia, offered us rotten terms, really awful, just short of totally unacceptable. The rest, well, they fell somewhere in between." He opened the diptych. "Mostly, they were a bit more civil than Nayatis, but less help than the other fellow."

Count Braley took a sip of coffee. "That's too bad," he said at last. "The news from the Eastern Marches is alarming, to say the very least. Ayondela gone, Kalycas gone, Baran-Beldon gone, Sibetio under seige." He set the cup on its saucer with a slight clatter and looked at his hand as if annoyed. Putting a totally inexperienced wizard in command of a totally inadequate relief force couldn't be counted a plus, either, he decided. "We have to raise and train the Royal Army soonest, we absodamnlutely *must*! But first off we need the money with which to do it."

Duke Viluji walked in, handing his scarlet-lined cloak to the servant. "One might almost say that money is a political necessity," he observed, taking his seat. A second servant poured him a cup of his own particular floral tea and set a tray of little shell-shaped cakes beside him.

"If one was prone to understatement," Braley agreed.

"No money, no army," said Falenda, who, being chancellor of the exchequer, naturally took money very seriously indeed.

"Now, in time of war, no army is a genuine misfortune," Viluji said, stirring honey into his tea and picking up one of the little cakes. "No money, by way of contrast, is a genuine misfortune anytime."

"You can run a war on credit," Braley said. "I know how bankers hate it, but it can be done."

Viluji dipped the cake into his tea and bit into it. "Ahh," he said softly, "the flood of memories this brings back . . ."

"Her Majesty the Regent," said a servant. They rose as Jankura entered, her riding boots clicking on the floor. She wore mauve and silver under a hooded mantle of charcoal gray wool with glossy black piping, the sole touch of color being the Kirndal Ruby at her throat. Lasco Genzari was with her, wearing a general's dress tunic worn open over a plain dark hauberk, twin swords thrust into sash. Jankura took her seat at the head of the table, and the men reseated themselves.

"We are given to understand that Syncretisty Hall has refused us a loan?" she said.

Falenda nodded. He had been given a fool's errand that he had done his best to run. "That seems to be the case, Your Majesty," he said smoothly. "We argued that money was needed for the prosecution of the war, but to no avail."

"We rather expected it," she said. "In the Hall of Mirrors, when the mob sacked the palace, there was a suite of exquisitely wrought silver furniture, about eight hundred fifty pounds as I recall. Chairs, tables, divans, candelabra . . . It would come in handy for melting down if we could lay hands on it."

"It's gone, Your Majesty," Braley said mournfully. "We have a better chance of recovering the fortresses in the Eastern Marches."

"Have we announced their loss?" Viluji asked.

"Enough people know about it," Genzari said, fingering his closely clipped mustache. "By now it should be all over the city. We'll have to make a formal proclamation tomorrow, I suppose."

"With no money there isn't going to be much we can do about the 'state of impending crisis,' is there?" Jankura said. When nobody answered, she looked around the table. "Duke Falenda?"

"No, Your Majesty."

"Duke Viluji?"

The little man dipped another cake in his tea and looked at the table. "I'm afraid not, Your Majesty."

"Then we ought to do something about it," Jankura said softly. "Lasco, the army is on alert and ready to move out when we give the word?"

"As you ordered, Your Majesty."

"What we propose to do then is to take the army—immediately, tonight—to Cymdulock Cathedral and to the other great churches in the city and seize the gold and silver plate amassed therein." Jankura said. "Please advise me as to the wisdom of this course of action, gentlemen."

There was a dead silence, broken by Viluji coughing as he swallowed wrong. "I agree," Count Braley said at last. "If Syncretisty Hall won't lend us the money, we'll take it by force."

"I, also," Genzari said. "There'll be some awful problems, long term, but they can hardly be worse than the short-term problems we face if we just sit."

"Don't do it, Your Majesty!" Duke Falenda implored. "For God's sake, don't do it!"

Jankura looked at him for a moment. "A cry from the heart," she said softly. "Why not, please?"

"You'll restart the civil war, you *will*! We'll lose everything we fought for. There'll be riots in the streets!"

"Not at this hour," Jankura said. "We'll be in and out before the clerisy can raise the mob in any serious number."

Falenda blotted his forehead with a lace handkerchief. "What about restarting the civil war, then?"

"We aren't restarting it," she replied. "Those fires weren't out, only banked. They'd have smoldered for a generation. You know that."

"There'll still be riots," the sleek duke said unhappily, "if not tonight, then tomorrow or the day after. The clerisy will raise the mob like some great hydra-headed monster to bring us down."

Jankura turned to her general. "Lasco?"

"The way to grasp a nettle is firmly, Your Majesty," Genzari replied. "Once you show yourself resolved to cut through a mob, they get out of the way with amazing speed."

"We are resolved," she said. "The lay preachers calling for treason will be hung on the spot. Duke Falenda?"

The sleek duke sat with his head in his hands. This woman is not the True Shaia, he thought, and that knowledge ought to give me power over her, but it can't be done before Viluji and Braley because they don't know.

"May we discuss the matter apart, Your Majesty?"

Jankura stood up and they all rose. She must have had an idea of his intent, because she nodded to Genzari and the three of them went into her sleeping chamber.

"Your Majesty is an impostor," Falenda said as Genzari closed the heavy oak door behind him. "An upstart peasant girl pretending to be queen! Move against the Church, and I will disclose this secret and bring you down!"

Genzari laid his hand on the hilt of his sword, but Jankura shook her head. "I pretended to be queen," she said, "but I was crowned regent in Cymdulock Cathedral. Me, not anyone else. And I will do what I must to set m—" She had been about to say "my son" but corrected herself in mind of present company. "—Prince Dervian on the throne."

"I beg you," Falenda whispered, "don't do this thing."

"Or you will tell my secret?" Jankura shook her head. "I did what had to be done. Shaia was, still is, for that matter, a very hated woman. Tell the people that I am 'Janko' Jankura, a peasant girl pretending to be Shaia, if you want. It can only make me less hated."

"Besides," Genzari said, his hand still on the hilt of his sword, "if you knew, you ought to have made the matter public before the coronation. Break with us, where can you go?"

Falenda looked utterly woebegone, and the corners of his mouth dropped down. "Don't do it," he said in a tiny voice.

"Crying doesn't help," Jankura said. "I cried myself to sleep in the witchfinder's dungeon and I was still there when I woke up." The duke made an effort and got control of himself.

"I suppose you're right," he sighed. "I hate it, but I have to go along with you."

They went back into the plant room and resumed their places. "We have reached consensus," Jankura said. "Right, Duke Falenda?"

"Except on the question of whether we are borrowing or stealing Church property, Your Majesty."

"We're taking it to fight the war," she replied. "I don't expect to give it back, so we're stealing."

"It might be useful to fuzz the matter over, though," he said at last. "If we weigh what we take and keep a record of sorts before we melt it into coinage, we can plausibly pretend we're going to pay it back." He looked distressed. "I am appalled that we must do this, Your Majesty."

" 'Must' brooks no argument, sir," she said quietly. "Viluji?"

The little man shook his head. "I'm sorry I signed on, Your Majesty, I really am, and we *will* regret this night's deed, but 'must' is the word. Let's go, before thought sickens over what resolve you have managed to muster in us."

"If it were done, 'twere best done quickly." Jankura nodded. She stood up and drew her mantle about her. "Let's go, Lasco. Count Braley, attend me. Viluji, Falenda," she grinned, showing strong white teeth, "sweet dreams, gentlemen."

17

Wizard's Solution

THE sun was not yet risen at Baran-Beldon when Wizenbeak summoned his commanders to his tent.

Wizenbeak seated himself on the canvas chair by his travel desk. Duke Bedirny, tall and straight, pulled up the other chair and sat down. Pardus Murado, his armor bloody and soiled from recent fighting, pulled over the footlocker. Archdeacon Viluji and Nick Sejenics sat down on the wizard's cot.

"The fortress is secured, Pardus?" Wizenbeak asked.

"Yes sir," replied his captain. "We'll dispose of the dead at the first light."

"A good night's work," the wizard said, handing the young Viluji a leather case. "Anticipating the outcome, I wrote it in the dispatches, but it's good to hear."

"This will go out at the first light of dawn, sir," Viluji said. "Along with several carrier pigeons."

"Good enough," Wizenbeak said, pulling at his long nose. "Our labors, however, have just begun. We have no time to play at stacking heads. Duke Bedirny, would you be so kind as to have your men gather firewood around the ridge for a funeral pyre?"

"My pleasure," Bedirny said. If he resented being kept out of the assault that took the fortress, he gave no sign. "When do you want it?"

Wizenbeak pushed his glasses back on his nose. "I would expect King Kirndal to come storming up the River Road about noon," he said. 'I'd like the pyre ready to light by then, sir, so we can show him what we've been up to."

There was a ripple of laughter. Bedirny looked pleased.

"So much for the Lagualian garrison. Did any escape?"

"Some of the officers got out the postern gate," Murado said.

"They rode off in a fright toward Ayondela. We'd have chased 'em, but it's kind of hard on a dark night."

The wizard smiled at the thought of the Tarelian infantry running in the dark after the flying horsemen. "Good," he said, "panic is contagious. Mister Murado, can you give me an idea of our casualties?"

"Pretty light, sir," Murado said, "maybe a dozen dead, thirty or forty hurt. That's a pure guess. I'll have the figures later today."

"Yes." The wizard's smile faded. "We now have to furnish a garrison for Baran-Beldon. Start with the wounded. Duke Bedirny?"

"Yes sir?"

"We need three hundred fifty archers for garrison duty."

"Isn't that a little light on the garrison, sir?"

"Hunh-hunh. We're short-handed all around, but with the wounded it's about what you ought to have. I don't expect them to stand a seige, if that's what you're worried about."

"Very good, sir," Bedirny said, making a note in his diptych.

"You're welcome," the wizard said, covering a yawn. "The next thing is our marching orders. When Kirndal shows up on the River Road, we light the pyre and start marching for Kalycas. The cavalry, again, will be held as a rear guard to oppose a river crossing."

"What if he makes a crossing anyway?" Sejenics asked. The bridge on the New Military Road linking Baran-Beldon and Ayondela had been destroyed, but the river was fordable a few hundred yards upstream.

"Bring the foot back, and when he gets about a third of his force across, charge across the floodplain at the son of a bitch. We'll be fighting him in detail with the Kalyswash splitting his army, and with a friendly fortress at our back we can disengage." Wizenbeak looked around the tent. "Questions?"

"Do you expect him to cross?" Bedirny asked.

"Not really, sir," the wizard replied. "I'd expect him to follow us on the other side of the river. He arrives a day late because we stole a march on him, to find Baran-Beldon fallen and us heading for Kalycas. Will he let us steal *another* march on him?" He shook his head. "No, no, a thousand times no."

"I agree," Sejenics said from the cot, "Kirndal must follow. Then what?"

"We took one fort as if by magic," Wizenbeak said, "and I hope to take a second the same way. That's the good news. The bad news is: we have another night march in prospect, gentlemen.''

Expecting the late night call, the sergeants fell the regent's Royal Army out onto the streets of Cymdulock quickly and relatively efficiently. There were no drums or bugles, the tread of marching feet was the loudest sound to be heard, and except for a few lanterns alongside the guidons there was no display of banners or gonfalons. Each unit had its assigned cathedral. Jankura, Count Braley, and Genzari rode at the head of the column going to the great Cymdulock Cathedral itself.

Surprise, when achieved, results in rich rewards. Cymdulock Cathedral was open and unguarded, except for a small squad of watchmen who quickly laid down their arms.

Jankura looked around. In the dark, cavernous interior votive candles provided a host of tiny lights that reflected off the opulent gilding. "Lasco," she said, "put up lanterns, and start loading the carts. Make sure the clerks keep a proper tally of what we're taking. Count Braley, you and the second company and the wizards follow me.''

She walked over to an alcove on the side, opened an unlocked wooden door behind a cloth drape, and followed the count down a stone spiral staircase into the depths of the cathedral, one of the wizards carrying a pale yellow globe lantern to light the way.

The lower level, below the crypt church, was a maze of passages, but Jankura, faced with choice after choice of musty byways, never hesitated, posting a pair of sentries with globe lanterns at each divergence. At last she came to the curtain door, simple wooden planks nailed together, secured with a wrought-iron latch that had been closed with a rather large brass rivet. One of the wizards looked at the rivet and cut it with a cold chisel and hammer. The door slid back on a ceiling-mounted track to reveal the vault door, which the curtain door had concealed.

The vault door was studded with iron bolts and bound with massive bronze hinges that had been reversed so that the hinge pins were inside the vault. A formidable barrier, its natural strength had been enhanced by magic. Charms of great potency were written in red across the dark oak. She motioned for one of the wizards who wasn't holding a light.

"The charms," she said, "can you neutralize them?''

The wizard leaned forward, peering over his glasses. "Oh

yes," he said, taking a piece of chalk out of his pocket. "This is pretty much what we were told to expect, even the word reversals." He wrote a line in yellow above the red, and a second line below it, and recited the lines as a couplet. The red writing began to glow softly, and if one studied it closely, the words seemed to writhe and twist, as if seeking to avert themselves from human gaze.

The wizard took a dagger with an ornate handle out of its sheath, and a fat, sluggish troll-bat out of an inner pocket. He raised them before him, and repeated the couplet twice more, ending with a final ten-syllable line, after which he carefully pushed the dagger point into one of the glowing red characters. Muttering, he placed the troll-bat on top of the hand that held the dagger, and the little animal blinked and yawned and gripped his fist in long, webbed fingers.

Suddenly the wizard grunted and staggered as the knife sank an inch deep into the tough wooden door with a sharp *thwock*. There was a hiss, and the aromatic smell of burning wood, and thin blue flames began to run down the knife blade. These followed the glowing red lines of the protective door-spell, extinguishing the glow one letter at a time.

"If you knew the password, of course, this would simply swing open for you," the wizard said, watching the change of color intently.

"Shit," said Jankura. "If I knew the password, you could be doing something useful like mopping the palace floor."

When the last of the glowing red characters had faded, the wizard slipped the troll-bat back in his pocket, took the dagger in his gloved hand, and worked it loose from the door. On the other side of the door, a bolt slid back with a metallic rattle, bronze hinges groaned, and the door slowly opened. In the distance, an alarm bell began to clang.

There was a subdued cheer from the soldiers behind them. The wizard with the globe lamp stepped inside. In the light, there was displayed an amazing collection of treasures, including, well to the front of the room, the suite of silver furniture that had graced the Hall of Mirrors in the Royal Palace.

"This is safe enough," the second wizard said, kicking a steel wedge under the door, "but we'd better move quickly. Breaking the spell like that is going to set off all sorts of alarms, and probably counterspells as well."

Jankura laughed. "Right," she said, "they might not have noticed the army going in upstairs, but they won't miss this!"

She turned to the company commander. "All right, I want that moved out into the hall, I want it all, and I want it now! Do it!"

The officer hitched the swords in his sash. "You heard Her Majesty," he drawled. "Move it on out, Sergeant!"

The sergeant and his men went in and started lugging the treasure out of the vault, first the silver furniture, stacked in the hallway on the far side of the door, then the twenty-two-pound bars of gold.

The accountant was scribbling away in his diptych, singing a cheerful little song: "Lifo, lifo, lifo-fo, lifo-fo, lifo-fo. Lifo, lifo, lifo-fo, lifo, lifo-fo!"

Finally the sergeant formed his men into a human chain, to hand the gold bars from man to man down the corridor.

Within the vault were jammed rolled-up carpets and racks of heirloom swords, unique, priceless treasures. Some of them had their pedigrees bound to them with silk ribbon; others, possibly given as security for loans, had only a wooden chip tied on with string. The soldiers took them out as the accountant started on a second diptych.

A suit of royal armor hung on a wooden rack, with a pair of royal swords sitting on a box at the foot of it. It bore the device of King Grathnys, and Jankura recognized it from descriptions as the armor he had been laid out in after his death. She handed the swords to Braley and opened the box. Inside was the missing Crown of Guhland, the one Grathnys was to have worn as he laid in state.

"Well," said Jankura softly, closing the box. "This I will carry with my own hands. This is even better than the furniture."

The last item in the room was a tall cabinet, marked with spells of its own. The wizards studied it for a bit, muttering and shaking their heads.

"Ah, Your Majesty," said the one holding the globe lamp, "this might be risky to open without adequate preparation. Maybe we ought to leave it."

"I agree," said the one who had opened the door. "There is a feeling of malevolence, of—of hidden dread here. It makes me terribly uneasy."

"Then leave it, for God's sake," Jankura growled, shifting the crown case under her arm. "Let's get out of this place!"

A sergeant shoved a priceless carpet under the cabinet and poured lamp oil over it. Jankura, Count Braley, and the wizards left the room as he set fire to the carpet, coming out just ahead of the rear guard that was bringing up the massive silver furniture. Despite the dread of the cognoscenti, the fire burned quietly for as long as they could hear it.

"What an incredible lot of stuff," Count Braley said, cradling the royal swords in his arms. "It makes the silver furniture look like trash by comparison."

"That it does," Jankura agreed. "The crown and swords especially. But it was the silver furniture we knew about. No question, that was ours, and it legitimized the whole operation, providing the pretext that we needed to have. You understand?"

This was pretty much what he'd told her, Braley thought, but he nodded and smiled. "Please continue, Your Majesty."

"The point is, the silver furniture was stuff we're stealing back. Therefore, maybe *all* the stuff is being stolen back, including the gold plate from upstairs. That's what decided me on going in. I didn't know about the crown and swords, the armor, the Great Seal of Guhland . . . The Church has lost the high moral position it needs to make a really killing riot."

"I see what you mean. How did you know about this place, the vault, I mean?" They were moving toward the torches of the men they'd posted, going out a lot faster than they'd gone in, despite the heavy load.

Jankura smiled. "Tell you back in the palace," she said. The men holding the lanterns were at the foot of the spiral staircase taking them into the cathedral proper, and Jankura suddenly felt very elated.

"Right. But why did Your Majesty have me along, then?" Count Braley asked. "I didn't do anything."

"Now *that* I can tell you," said Jankura. "Going down here just scared me to death. The whole staff of wizards and the whole second company didn't make any difference. I needed a friend, somebody I trusted for moral support."

18

Arrivals and Departures

UPON waking rather late the following morning after considerably less than sufficient sleep, Wizenbeak found to his surprise that he felt pretty good. Across the river, the first Lagualian cavalry patrols had appeared, riding up to Ayondela, then galloping back with the bad news. He permitted his batman, a young but crafty-looking fellow who catered to the wizard's comfort as a means of securing his own, to help him dress. The hauberk he accepted as a stiff, chafing necessity, and the swords and the scarlet general's sash that held them. The archdeacon's vestments he declined to wear, save only the embroidered skullcap. Breakfast, several courses, served in copiously ample portions, he ate in his tent. His batman, whose name escaped him, could dispose of the leftovers at his leisure.

When he eventually made his appearance, the vanguard of the Lagualian Royal Army was in view. His captain-general, Pardus Murado, approached and saluted.

"Good morning, sir. Shall we light the pyre?"

Wizenbeak looked over at the enemy army on the other side of the Kalyswash River. They were waiting for something to happen, he decided. It wouldn't do to disappoint them. "You may fire when ready, Pardus," he said.

Murado made a hand signal to someone, and a few seconds later came the sound of tinder crackling in flame.

"Very good, sir. Will we have time to serve the men a hot meal?"

A curious connection, mused the wizard, burning corpses stirring the thought of hot meals. Still, if we *know* we're going in for a night march, we ought to give the men as much of a start on it as we can. "Unless Kirndal decides to cross the river," he said. "Yes, a hot meal by all means. See to it."

Across the river the Lagualian infantry came up, banners flying in the bright fall morning. Overhead, the black smudge from the funeral pyre drifted slowly against the clear blue sky toward Ayondela. Mindful of Sejenics' injunction against exposing himself against the skyline, Wizenbeak took up a position a bit below the crest of the ridge, where he could watch the progress of the enemy army without being excessively obvious. The siege train came up ponderously and with great deliberation, ungreased axles creaking audibly even from across the Kalyswash. Behind them came the rear guard, pikemen, and cavalry, walking their horses. Ahead, the cook fires had been started.

Wizenbeak glanced at the sun. A bit after noon, he decided. His men should have finished eating. "Mister Murado."

"Yes sir?"

"Move the army down the road!"

"Yes sir!"

Nothing like a little cheap success to generate enthusiasm among one's subordinates, decided the wizard. The previous night march had been regarded as an unspeakable imposition and prelude to catastrophe.

He remained on the hillside, perched sidesaddle on his big blue mule, looking over the river. A cluster of staff officers sat their mounts at a discreet distance, and after a while Princess Marjia rode over beside him.

"Everybody is on the march again," she said. "Aren't we going off with them?"

"In due time, Your Highness," the wizard replied. "I want to see what Kirndal does. Riding, I can easily catch up with my little army."

She sat her bay mare beside him, looking across the river at the enemy forces. "They can see us, too, can't they?"

"Hunh-hunh," he said, "you can depend on it. Look, they've spotted us starting down the Ridge Road." On the other side of the valley, men were pointing and waving their arms, and soldiers sitting down and waiting for their lunch were suddenly rousted out and formed up by their sergeants. Hopes of a hot meal dashed, the Lagualians marched down the gently meandering River Road, hastily scarfing up flatbread and water as they went.

"I thought they were going to chase us," Marjia said.

"They *are* chasing us," Wizenbeak replied, "the roads run parallel, until the river bends at Kalycas. The River Road, bending with the Kalyswash, joins the Ridge Road there. The noble

King Kirndal hastens to the rendezvous, that appointment with destiny, burning with all the ardor of his misspent youth."

"So why are *you* sitting here like a bump on a log, then?"

"Because I want to see what our man does with his siege train," the wizard said, smoothing his long white beard with one hand. "It will slow him down considerably if he takes it."

"And if he doesn't take it?"

"Then I want to see where he puts it, Your Highness." Mischka came out on his shoulder to help him watch, and the wizard gently stroked the long, soft ears. "The siege train is kind of a key to the castle," he explained. "If I spot Kirndal hiding it under the doormat . . ." Marjia giggled.

They sat on the hillside, talking about troll-bats as the Lagualian army moved out. Kirndal's siege train was left at Ayondela, moved laboriously up the slope and parked at the edge of the moat, under the protecting shadow of the walls. After the teamsters started unhitching the horses and mules and taking them into the barn inside the castle, Wizenbeak and Marjia rode up to the Ridge Road. There Duke Bedirny provided them an honor guard until they rejoined the Tarelians.

19

Confrontation in the Cathedral

JANKURA returned to the nave of Cymdulock Cathedral to find Patriarch Gorabani and a delegation of archdeacons confronting Genzari as his soldiers paused in their task of loading sacred treasure into secular wagons. Well, she thought grimly, Gorabani has his nerve coming in on us like this. And the son of a bitch might, just might, be able to use his moral authority to turn the army around. She walked over to where they were standing.

"Address your complaints to Her Majesty the Regent," Genzari said. His relief was muted, but Jankura had been with him long enough to see it clearly. So they had Lasco worried, did they? This might be worse than the riots Falenda was so fearful about. The riots would have been bloody, but she'd win . . . at least Genzari thought she'd win. Then she grinned. No more time to think it over, she was going to have to win with what she had!

"What seems to be the problem, Your Holiness?" she said, shifting her grip on the box under her arm.

"This outrageous attack on the Church!" Gorabani said, turning to face her. "Madame, this is totally unacceptable, *totally* unacceptable!"

"You provoked it," Jankura said coldly, anger edging her voice. "Did you think we would meekly accept the insolence of Syncretisty Hall's archbankers when the survival of the dynasty hung in the balance?"

"A slur," Obuskaia said, "a gratuitous slur on the archdeacons of the Church! We do not call *you* Witch-Queen, though you have richly deserved the epithet!"

"As regent, we should consider it constitutionally inaccurate," Jankura replied coolly. "Do you think that you serve your country's interests by offering us the same terms you'd offer starving sharecroppers?'' She turned to the patriarch. ''And Obuskaia, here, was the only one of you tight-fisted sons of bitches that would agree to loan us money on any terms at all, Your Holiness! We're fighting a war with Lagualia, and you won't lend us money to defend Guhland, *your* country!''

''Don't try to change the subject, woman,'' Gorabani grated. ''Nothing that has gone between us in the past can justify this unholy violation of the sanctuaries of the Church. For God's sake, unload these sacrilegious wagons!''

Jankura exhaled slowly, as she recalled the mantra for serenity that Wizenbeak had taught her. ''Don't try to change the subject, *what*?'' she snapped. ''You mealy-mouthed hypocrite, I am your ruler, de facto, and de-fucking-jure! What did you call me!?''

The patriarch hesitated; he had gambled on being able to daunt a simple peasant girl, but she'd raised the stakes on him. Genzari, with the soldier's faith in simple solutions, was resting one hand on his long sword. Would the Shadow Shaia push matters to their conclusion? Very probably she might. The Church could use martyrs, and the little fool didn't realize what a catastrophic mistake she was about to make . . . which meant martyrdom was his for the taking. He swallowed, and long years of habit and training took hold.

''Your Majesty,'' he said smoothly, ''if, in the heat of the moment we have overlooked the courtesies due you, excuse it as an unfortunate manifestation of our human frailty.'' Was martyrdom to slip through his fingers? For a moment, it seemed like every cell in his being was casting a vote, and the overwhelming majority of heart and mind came out against. No martyrdom, he was what he was. Afterward, he never regretted the decision, regarding it as a moment when he came to better understand his limitations. ''We ask you not to plunder the Church like the barbarians of old.''

''We have no such intent, Your Holiness. We are, in fact, doing our utmost to ensure the mutual preservation of Church and State in the face of . . .'' She hesitated a moment, choosing her words. ''. . . the profound, even treasonous, hostility of some of the clerisy.''

''Treasonous'' threw Gorabani off stride. As he debated the respective merits of answer or countercharge, Obuskaia stepped forward and laid one hand on the wagon Genzari's men had been loading. ''Your Majesty,'' he said, ''we ask only that you not steal what is ours, that the State not lay hands on what belongs to the Church. We pray you, do not do this thing!''

That could be an opening, Jankura thought, we'll give it a shot. "Ah, Father,'' she said shifting the box under her arm, "you're telling us that what belongs to the Church belongs to the Church, and what belongs to the State belongs to the State, and we shouldn't be taking from one another, right?''

Obuskaia hesitated, perhaps guessing where he was being led, but the red-faced, red-haired archdeacon behind him plunged in without hesitation. "It is the word of God,'' he intoned. "Thou shalt not steal!''

"Indeed, Father?'' Jankura replied. "We just now came up from the understories of this cathedral, where we found . . . well, I'll show you!'' She turned to where the second company was standing beside the pile of loot they'd brought up the stairs. "Mister Sejenics!'' Nick Sejenics looked up to see what was wanted and she caught his eye. "Bring over the furniture from the Hall of Mirrors!''

They came over, three men to a chair, four on the loveseat, one on each end of the tall candelabra, setting the suite of silver furniture before Jankura and the clerisiarchs for their consideration.

"This was in the Hall of Mirrors when the Royal Palace was sacked by a mob,'' Jankura said. "It belongs to the House of Grathnys, Clerisiarchs, and we found it locked up in the basement of Cymdulock Cathedral!''

"A few paltry chairs,'' Gorabani sneered. "Pretty work, but commercial. They could have come from anywhere. And there is no telling how they got where you say you found them, if, indeed, Your Majesty didn't bring them in with you.''

"Fencing stolen property, Your Holiness?'' Jankura grinned, showing strong white teeth. "The old moral superiority is a bit smutted, isn't it!''

"You can't prove that those chairs came from the palace!'' yelled the red-faced Nayatis.

"They bear the Grathnys coat of arms, Father,'' she said, pointing. "Maybe they didn't come straight from the Hall of Mirrors, but we are here stealing back our own property!''

"Now by God, you are not!'' he shouted. "You have laid impious hands, *blasphemous* hands on the property of the Most Holy Syncretist Church, and you must put it back or face instant and eternal damnation!'' He raised one hand, as if in a malediction, but when he started forward as if moved by the spirit,

Obuskaia grabbed Archdeacon Nayatis by the collar and hauled him backward, choking and spluttering.

Well, thought Jankura, this asshole has delivered the whole flaming lot into my hands. She set the box she was holding on one of the silver chairs, opened it, and removed the royal crown. "Church property, Father?" she said, raising it up to eye level. "This is the crown that my late husband wore when he lay in state, just before the sacking! The little wooden tag someone ever so thoughtfully put on it even says so!" She held the crown in one hand and wiggled the little chip at them with the other.

"Well," said Genzari. His voice wasn't loud, but it carried. "We seem to have one thief complaining that a bigger thief has stolen his stuff. Come on, boys, move it on out!"

20

Wizardly Sleight of Foot

THEY rode side by side at the head of the Tarelians: Dr. Wizenbeak, master of the Tarelian Order, and Princess Marjia, his deputy commander; he on his big blue mule, she on her smooth-gaited bay mare. The view from the ridge was commanding: looking into the clear fall air across the Kalyswash Valley, they could see Kirndal's army moving down the road on the opposite side of the river, the cavalry in the lead, keeping pace with the enemy; the infantry following swiftly behind, doubtless cursing the meanders in the road as it followed the river.

"You say the roads come together after a while?" the princess asked.

"At Kalycas Bridge," the wizard said. "Kalycas was built in the gap in the ridge cut by the Kalyswash, or there was a gap, which the river naturally chose to flow through, depending on which authority you take. The Old Military Road, upon which we are riding, goes along the ridgeline, into the gap, across the bridge, over the River Road, and onto the next ridge, from where it goes toward Lagualia."

"And where does the River Road go?"

"It follows the Kalyswash, which makes a sharp turn at the gap," said the wizard, shifting his weight in the saddle, "and goes about ten or twelve miles upstream from Kalycas to a monastery, Saint Posalanji's, if I remember rightly."

"Alanji of the Flowers?" Marjia asked. "I studied her at the gymnasium. She supposedly made the first great compact with the wizards after the Dragon Wars."

"My own education has great gaps and mysterious lacunae in it," conceded Wizenbeak. "I never heard of the good lady."

"It's been a while," the little girl said, "but basically, she had the same problem that Saint Mambrino did. The magic users in the society were using their powers to oppress the general populace, and she founded an order in the Orthodox Church to accept magic users who wished to reform. A middling useful idea, it let a lot of witches and wizards retire to the contemplative life, and that helped, but it wasn't enough. The reason they made her a saint was that she ended the Curse.''

Wizenbeak twisted a strand of mustache around his finger. "Gaps and lacunae," he said. "The Curse?"

"Infertility. A witch could cause livestock or women to stop conceiving. And release them. The witches didn't do it very much, but the wizards came in with their troll-bats, and it was an easy money-maker they couldn't resist using. A few centuries later, Mambrino was burning them wholesale for a lot less. What Alanji of the Flowers did was talk to the troll-bats themselves.''

"That's tee-totally impossible, Your Highness, meaning no disrespect, of course.''

"She brought all the trives of troll-bats in three counties together, to a great gathering, and she talked to them," the little girl said. "I used to wonder about that, about how she was able to keep control over so many, but the scrolls never explained it; she performed a miracle, and that was that. What happened afterward is that the Curse stopped happening. The wizards couldn't do it by themselves, and the troll-bats had somehow agreed not to do it anymore.''

"So they made her a saint?" Wizenbeak asked.

"She earned it, wouldn't you say?" Marjia replied. "I wanted to follow in her footsteps, so of course I wanted to know how she did it, and trying to find out was what led me into magic. The thing was, I found out later, the Curse didn't stop in just the three counties, it stopped everywhere.''

Captain-General Murado rode up beside them. "Excuse me, Your Highness, Master Wizenbeak, it's getting late in the day. Shall we serve dinner at the next break?''

"Flatbread, cheese, and pickled onions?''

"Yes sir. That's the menu for tonight.''

Wizenbeak looked around. The shadows were already pouring into the river valley, engulfing the Lagualians in darkness, and the sun was low on the horizon. "By all means, Mister Murado. See that the men are fed.''

It was time to move out. Princess Marjia had retired to the cabined comforts of her wagon. The end of the evening meal coincided with the first stars coming out in the clear, cold sky. The sergeants hustled around distributing the pine-knot torches that had been cut that morning. Lit, they gave a yellowish light with a resinous black smoke, and a torchbearer marched at the head of each platoon of each company. From a distance, Wizenbeak's little army looked like a religious procession.

As did the Lagualians. Seeing the enemy setting out on a night march, Kirndal lit his own torches and set out after them. Two processions, marching parallel into the gathering night.

At the first break after supper, it was quite dark, the sunset had faded, the stars were out, the crescent moon had yet to rise. Archdeacon Viluji's light horsemen came up, through the columns of infantry, and upon dismounting they took up the torch-bearer positions through the column. At the end of ten minutes, the torchbearers handed over the burning pine knots, and the Viluji cavalrymen, already carrying extra torches in their saddlebags, walked their horses down the road at platoon intervals.

The cavalry sergeants rode slowly down the column and cantered back to the head to assure that their men maintained the deceptive interval. The infantry, mostly Tarelians, sat quiet in the cooling night and watched them go, grateful for the respite from marching. Wizenbeak sat on his blue mule and looked over the river valley, where the torches of the Lagualians kept pace with his own. He tried the mantra against darkness and watched as a very sketchy line moved down the River Road. Inconclusive as to numbers, hardly suggestive as to what was being watched, all it told him was that, exactly as expected, King Kirndal was marching to meet him at Kalycas Bridge.

As the rear guard of the Lagualian army faded from the sight, he called to Murado, and his men formed up ranks with surprising eagerness to double back to Baran-Beldon.

21

The Patriarch Has a Problem

PATRIARCH Gorabani offered his guest a seat on the cushioned leather couch in his attic office.

"Why, thank you, Your Holiness," the plump-cheeked Darussis said amiably, "but excessively soft chairs are hard on my poor back." He pulled up a ladder-backed wooden chair. "If you don't mind, of course?"

Doctor Kurjima shook his head. "That couch is a sign of Lagualian decadence corrupting our own virile civilization, sir. I would not presume to instruct you on your duties, but if it were me, I'd get rid of the effete and sybaritic thing." The patriarch smiled, and all three of them settled into the high, hard, ladder-backed chairs they were used to.

"So what did you find in the vault?"

"They cleaned it out," Darussis replied. "A bag of silver coins burst—the canvas was rotten—and they left it, but that was all. The door-spell was broken by one of the standard counter-charms."

"Inside information, do you think?" the patriarch asked. The location of the vault was supposed to be secret, but was, in fact, widely known among the clerisy.

"Eh . . ." Darussis shrugged. "Maybe. All three of us knew about it, and so did a lot of other people. Including some that had no business knowing."

"So it would seem," Gorabani said, folding his black-gloved hands in his white-robed lap. "What path did they take?"

"They went in from the east side of the cathedral. Judging by the scratches on the floor they made dragging out the silver furniture, they didn't take any false turns," Darussis replied. "And that's where they were seen coming out afterward."

"You're sure it wasn't inside information?" Gorabani asked.

"How far inside?" the archdeacon asked.

"Look," the patriarch's assistant said, "when the Witch-Queen went in, she must have been expecting to find the stuff from the sack of the Royal Palace, or she wouldn't have come. That's point one. She had a route through the maze. That's point two. Finally, somebody on her staff had the wherewithal to open the door to the vault. Don't tell me it would be easy, and don't tell me 'standard bloody counterspell,' Darussis. You come on it cold, it's the easiest thing in the world to freeze the bolt in place. That's the third point. She had inside information on all three of them. Now, who was it?"

"It might have been more than one person," Darussis said. "Why are you pushing the issue?"

"Because I know it wasn't *me*!" Kurjima said. "And if it wasn't me, who was it? There aren't all that many clerisiarchs who knew the damn details well enough to betray them!"

"It could have been anyone," Gorabani said. "Certainly the maze was hardly a secret after all these years."

"The maze, sir, yes. But the charm on the vault door? The curtain door was there to keep that charm secure from casual inspection. Nobody knew about *that* except you and me and Darussis, here, who inscribed it."

"Hey!" Darussis looked indignant. "If you didn't do it, and the patriarch didn't do it, that doesn't mean *I* did it! *Lots* of people knew about that security charm!"

"So name a few, Doctor Darussis," said the patriarch's assistant, folding his arms. There was a rather long pause.

"Basir Orunjan knew about the silver furniture, because he took the inventory on it," Darussis said at last. "And he'd been through the maze, of course. *Everybody* must have been through the maze. Which leaves the charm on the vault door. He would have seen the charm often enough, running the inventory on the witchgold as it came in." A sigh. "He might even have understood it, if he'd taken the trouble. Orunjan could have been indiscreet with lots of people, but we'll never know because he's dead."

"Did you see the body?" Kurjima asked. The archdeacon shook his head. "Neither did I. How do you know he's dead?"

"Ah, why, ah . . . Archdeacon Wizenbeak made the announcement."

"So he did," Kurjima agreed, "and the Witch-Queen sent back his body. Matters unfolded very naturally. I repeat: How do you know he's dead?"

Darussis shook his head. "I just assumed he was dead. We all did, I think. That way, any investigation into the affair had to end with Orunjan."

"Nobody wanted an investigation, so nobody took more than a casual glance at the poor son of bitch," Kurjima said. "And as a suicide, he'd be buried in unconsecrated ground without any ceremony. But what if that was someone else's corpse they turned over, eh?"

"But why would they play a silly game like . . ." Darussis began, and then the scales fell from his eyes. "So that Basir Orunjan could be questioned at their leisure!"

Gorabani rubbed his strongly hooked nose with one black-gloved finger. "That would tend to support the notion that the Witch-Queen isn't really the Shaia we all knew and loved," he said. "The True Shaia tended to think and ponder interminably before acting. Our Shadow Shaia grabbed the opportunity when it came up and figured what to do with it afterward."

"She acted decisively enough when she found out," Darussis said. "Maybe even rashly."

"We hope so," the patriarch said. "History will write her down as rash or bold depending on who writes the history. The question right now is: Was that Orunjan we buried the other day?"

"Maybe," Kurjima said, "maybe not. We'll have to exhume old Basir to make sure we weren't slipped a ringer."

Gorabani walked over to his desk and hit the froe on his wooden writing block with the little wooden mallet, splitting off a perfectly cut three-by-five inch wooden chip about a sixteenth of an inch thick. He advanced the block of wood and cut off a second chip. Taking pen in hand he wrote out the exhumation order, tied the two chips together with a ribbon, and sealed the ribbon with hot wax.

"Your suggestion is most persuasive, Doctor Kurjima," he said, handing the order to his assistant. "Do it now!"

Late that afternoon Kurjima and Darussis stood warming their hands at a small bonfire by the far edge of the cemetery and watched as the gravediggers hoisted up the coffin allegedly containing Basir Orunjan. One of the workers used a pry-bar to open the lid and stepped back. The two archdeacons looked in. There was a body about Orunjan's size, wrapped in the unbleached linen winding sheet, but when Darussis pulled the sheet back, the face was covered with a whitish, aspiclike substance. The archdeacon took two carved wooden sticks out of his bag and carefully removed the dead mask from the dead face it covered.

"What's that?" Kurjima asked.

"A mask," the little archdeacon said. "If this poor sod had lain in state, we wouldn't have known it wasn't Orunjan himself."

He held the flabby, whitish stuff up for a moment, studying it. Then he dropped the mask into the fire and wiped off the sticks with a rag. The mask began to writhe in the flames.

Darussis looked down into the coffin. "Well, stranger," he murmured, "what are we going to do with you?"

The mask melted and burned with a sputtering, yellow flame. "I wonder what else Orunjan told the Witch-Queen?" Kurjima mused softly.

"I expect a lot of people will be asking that very same question," said the little archdeacon. "What should we do now for when they ask us?"

"We take an affidavit that he isn't Basir Orunjan, for one thing," Kurjima said making a note in his diptych. "You, me, and the gravediggers will have to sign it."

"The gravediggers wouldn't know Orunjan."

"Yes, yes. Have them take a look and describe the corpse. That should be sufficient. It looked like half of one ear had been bitten off, for one thing. And there may be other scars. If there's an inquest, we want to be together with our stories."

Darussis took his sticks and moved the shroud back. Besides the bitten ear, there was a dragon tattoo on the chest, and beneath the drawn lips, the left upper incisors and canine teeth were missing. Kurjima wrote it all down, along with the names of the gravediggers.

"This fellow, nobody knows him, nobody will miss him," Darussis said. "But he doesn't belong here. Can you put him with the paupers on the other side of the wall?"

"In the consecrated ground?" one of the gravediggers asked, leaning on his spade. "You'd need a plot assignment, sir. They don't let just anybody in, you know."

"Of course." The little archdeacon sighed. "I should have remembered. Well, nail him up and stick him back in his hole." When the resealed coffin had been lowered into the ground, Darussis picked up a clod of earth and pronounced a blessing on it. He dropped it onto the coffin with a hollow thud, and the gravediggers went to work with the unsanctified dirt.

"Why didn't you just bless the pile they're shoveling on?" Kurjima asked.

"It's my training in magic," the other replied. "I learned always to use the minimum effort for the effect I wanted."

22

The Taking of Ayondela

"You saw the seige train sitting in front of Ayondela," Wizenbeak said. "How long do you think it would take them to get it inside?"

"Twenty minutes," Duke Bedirny replied, sitting at ease on his mount. "Half an hour, at the outside."

They were on the side of the ridge a mile or so northeast of Ayondela, as the light of dawn was just starting to drive the stars from the sky. Sitting at the head of Bedirny's cavalry, they spoke softly so the sentries on the wall and posted around the siege train would not be alerted.

"Half an hour after they got the horses hitched up, I'd think," the wizard said softly. "Maybe an hour or more would be a better estimate. There's no question we can fire the siege train."

"No sir," the duke said.

At the ford, upstream from the ruined bridge on the New Military Road, the Tarelians were crossing silently and without lights, a considerable display of discipline. Looking for them, even with the mantra against darkness, required a considerable effort, but they were forming up along the River Road, and maybe half of them were across.

"We can always fire the siege train," Wizenbeak mused, "but the art of victory is to give one's enemy the chance to make a mistake. Your Grace knows the plan?" A rhetorical flourish. He and Bedirny and Murado had gone over it extensively on the long march they had stolen from Kirndal, as the king followed the will-o'-the-wisp they had conjured up for him.

Duke Bedirny smiled. "Intimately," he said.

"Then go to it," the wizard said.

Bedirny signaled, and a single squad detached itself from the main body of his heavy cavalry and went galloping across the hillside to form up in a scattered line between the castle and the Tarelians forming up on the River Road, facing away from Ayondela. Then a second squad joined the first, with someone calling out a warning in Lagualian to the men on watch. Inside the castle, there was at first no sign that anyone had heard, but then lights began to come on, and presently torches could be seen moving along the walls.

The Tarelians, on being detected, lit their own torches and formed up before starting across the five miles uphill that would take them to the siege train—even for the Tarelians, a long hour's march. More of Bedirny's horse came trotting across the hillside, to form a second line behind the first, acting for all the world like friendly cavalry.

Inside the castle, someone took the decision to try to save the siege train from being put to the torch. The drawbridge was lowered, and teams of horses and mules were hurried out into the dark and chill of the morning, to haul the war engines into the safety of the castle. Even with torches, they seemed to be having trouble finding their own particularly assigned piece of equipment, milling around in noisy confusion as they got in each other's way. Nevertheless, the siege train soon began to make its way across the drawbridge, lurching and staggering, and cursing so they could be heard across the river in Baran-Beldon. A third line of cavalry formed up behind the first two, really quite close to the drawbridge. However, since they were clearly identified by their actions as friendly, the Lagualians paid them no attention.

Wizenbeak had been counting the siege engines making their laborious way into the castle. When he figured that they were blocking the gates in the inner keep, which he couldn't see, as well as the outer one that he was watching, he gave the signal, and the trumpets sounded. All three lines of cavalry turned around and charged for the drawbridge, which was weighted down with the traffic it had to bear.

The Lagualians, taken by surprise, and at first imagining that the cavalry was friendly, offered no resistance. Someone in the castle, however, retained sufficient wit to drop the portcullis at the inner gate, which unfortunately for the defense lodged itself on a catapult, leaving an ample gap for attackers to enter.

Duke Bedirny, tall and straight as in the days of his youth, went in with the second squad, shouting his name as a battle cry and offering quarter for those who would take it. The teamsters, outside and in, rousted from bed and concerned with their horses, at once threw down their arms and called for mercy. Panic being contagious, most of the garrison laid down their arms. Those few preferring death before dishonor were accommodated, and the Fortress of Ayondela was secured before the Tarelians made it to the front gate.

23

Kirndal Cuts Bait

KING Kirndal pulled his cloak about him and sat in the meager comfort of his tent. The cold made his teeth hurt, he had saddle sores from prolonged riding, and the war had gone unexpectedly sour. His valet came in from the cook tent with a large black kettle and poured steaming hot water into a well-polished brass shaving basin. The royal barber then applied a hot towel to the king's face, as Count Osmet, currently lieutenant general of the Royal Lagualian Army, stood by attentively.

"Well, Count Osmet," Kirndal said, leaning back in the canvas chair, "what should we be doing today?" A standard conversational gambit.

"Engage the Tarelians and crush them, Your Majesty." A standard reply, bellicose in tone and void of detail. "We outnumber them more than two to one." A meaningless truism uttered mainly for the sound of the words.

"Yes, yes. However, we are tired of marching up and down Kalyswa Valley only to find them on the other side of the river." A specific complaint. Kirndal relaxed a little as the heat and moisture from the towel softened his beard. After breakfast, he might even be able to accomplish something.

"Then perhaps we should divide our army into two parts and go down the valley on both sides of the river, sir." This was an old argument, thoroughly chewed over. It addressed the complaint without breaking new ground.

"A good way to lose half the army, you fool." The Tarelians were formidable, the wizard was tricky, and Kirndal had very little confidence in Count Osmet, who would be in command of the second army group. He wasn't going to split his command if he could help it, but this morning his rebuttal lacked passion.

"Yes sir. We might perhaps lay siege to one of the castles the

159

wizard recaptured and force him to come to us." This also was a familiar argument. With the loss of the siege train, the only way to take the castle would be to starve it into submission. If they tried, the wizard would cut their supply lines, and they would starve before the defenders did.

"Bah! What with? Try to starve the bastards out, the wizard will go down the road to Kalycas and take it like he took the others." This was the other argument against the move. The wizard had, somehow, taken Baran-Beldon and then exploited a blunder in the defense of Ayondela to take that castle, also. If the Lagualian army strayed very far from Kalycas, the last of the three castles they had taken, there was the unpleasant possibility that the Guhlish son of a bitch might recapture that one as well.

"That's very possible, sir," the count agreed pleasantly. Usually the king didn't discuss strategy before breakfast. Perhaps he was in a bad mood. He did sound unusually tentative, but a courtier learns to cope with mood swings. "If we aren't going to split our forces, and we can't make him come to us, then we really have no choice but to follow after him and try to give battle."

"Shit," said the king. "Marching and countermarching in the middle of winter isn't even sport for peasants." He shivered. "You read Gyasi's dispatches from Cymdulock?"

"Yes, sir." This question, like the others, was largely rhetorical. Gyasi had reported that the regent of Guhland had raided the churches in Cymdulock to recover an unspecified but large amount of treasure. Said treasure was being minted into coinage to pay for the main army that the regent was in the process of raising. "In his early ones, he was very hopeful that the Church would react to the regent's ferocious provocation by resuming the civil war. This is still a possibility, he thinks, but we shouldn't depend on it."

The barber removed the hot towel from the king's face and applied warm and well-lathered soap. "Guhland won't fight no civil war," the barber said, "not while we're holding part of their country, begging your pardon, sir."

"Quite all right," the king said. "Your point is well taken."

"Your Majesty," Count Osmet said, indignant at the barber's usurpation of a courtier's prerogatives, "are you going to trust your *barber* before you trust Archdeacon Gyasi?"

"His advice, perhaps, we take with a grain of salt," Kirndal said, as the barber began stropping his razor. "But trust? Who would *you* trust before the man who daily holds a knife to your throat?''

Osmet laughed politely. It was disconcerting. Sometimes the king was genuinely funny, but to laugh immoderately tended to devalue the courtier as an audience. Unless one was prepared to not laugh at all, sometimes. ''But what do you think of Gyasi's conclusions, sir?''

''He embellishes his reports with all sorts of baroque gossip,'' Kirndal said, ''but the gist of the matter is that he agrees with the barber, when you come right down to it. Come spring, we'll have a major war on our hands when all we were looking for was to nip off a province on the sly.''

The sentry stepped into the relative warmth of the tent and saluted. ''Sir,'' he said, ''Captain Bertino has been sent back.'' Bertino had been captured on a foraging expedition a few days before. ''He says he has a message for you.''

''Send him in,'' the king said.

Captain Bertino entered and saluted. The king lifted a hand in acknowledgment. ''What do you have for us, Captain?''

''Your Majesty. After I was taken, I was brought before the master of the Tarelian Order, Doctor Wizenbeak, who ordered my wounds treated and conversed with me for a considerable length of time before giving me a message to bring to you, sir.''

''What did you find to talk about?'' the king asked.

''About Sifoty Field, when he beat Kahun's army. He told me how King Kahun died—''

''Let us *not* tell sad stories of the deaths of kings,'' Osmet said. ''What was the message for His Majesty?''

''Yes sir. Doctor Wizenbeak, he put it differently, very smoothly, so it sounded perfectly reasonable. What he said was that he wanted to parley. He said he wanted to arrange a meeting between you and him, Your Majesty.''

''He could do that anytime,'' Kirndal said, as the barber finished the left side of his face. ''Send a man out with a flag of truce. What else was there?''

''Sir, it kind of sticks in my craw to say it,'' Bertino replied. ''But what old Wizenbeak said was, they *could* beat us, and they were *going* to beat us, but he didn't want to wait around until spring for it to happen. And he wants *you* to send out the herald.''

At that time, the armies were facing each other about ten miles south of Kalycas, Wizenbeak's Tarelians on the New Mil-

itary Road that ran along the ridge behind Kalycas, the Lagualians encamped on the other side of the Kalyswash. Both sides
had observed the neutrality of Saint Posalanji's Monastery, a
natural strong point in a strategically insignificant location.
Kirndal's herald proposed that the meeting be held there, and
Wizenbeak agreed, setting the time at noon the following day.

The monastery was a complex of several buildings, barns,
dormitories, a library, school, kitchen, refectory, and guest
house. These were arranged around the periphery of the acre of
flat land on top of the ancient volcanic pipe that thrust upward
from the plain, in a great surge of basalt boulders. This was
excepting only the guest house, which sat at the foot of the
narrow path that made its way around the living rock to the
monastery entrance. The guest house, where the meeting was
to take place, was also easily accessible from the River Road. It
was a one-story building of whitewashed fieldstone with a steep
thatched roof, and a wooden stable behind it. A light snowfall
from the night before lay white and untrampled in the fields
around the building.

At noon, Kirndal, the Lagualian herald, and Count Osmet
forded the Kalyswash and approached the guest house at the
head of a ten-man honor guard. From a tent pitched near the
foot of the ridge, Wizenbeak, Princess Marjia, the Tarelian herald, and Pardus Murado rode out at the head of ten men from
Duke Bedirny's cavalry. They came within a bowshot of each
other and stopped.

Kirndal's herald rode over. "Good day, Doctor Wizenbeak,"
he said. "My master wishes to know how it happens that you
have one more person in your party than we do?"

The wizard pushed his glasses back on his nose. "In our
party, Princess Marjia here does not command. I, in turn, am
not of royal blood. Please convey my regrets to your master."
The herald rode back to report. Then both heralds went into the
guest house to inspect it for an ambush.

After they returned, the principals left their honor guards in
place and rode over to the guest house, where monks took their
horses into the stable. The guest house, which provided travelers
with food and drink as well as lodging, had several small bed-
rooms on one end, a kitchen and a bar at the other, and a common room with a fireplace in between. Kirndal's party entered
at the bedroom side, Wizenbeak's by the bar, and both entered
the common room with a certain amount of wariness.

"You wished to negotiate, Doctor Wizenbeak?" Count Osmet asked condescendingly. The five of them stood rather stiffly on the opposite sides of the room.

"I had rather thought to do that thing," the wizard said. "Permit me to introduce our party. On my right is Her Highness, Princess Marjia; and beside her, Pardus Murado, captain-general of the Tarelian Order; of which I, Archdeacon Wizenbeak, have the honor to be master."

"Oh, well." The wizard had some semblance of manners at least. "I am Count Osmet, lieutenant general to His Majesty King Kirndal, here, who has asked me to dispense with the formal recitation of his titles. What have you to say to us, wizard?"

Wizenbeak walked over to the table between them that was opposite the fireplace and sat down. "Won't you join me, Your Majesty?" Kirndal glanced at Osmet, shrugged, and sat down, followed by the others.

"Very good," the wizard said. "A warm fire is a blessing on a cold day. Now then, as you may know, Count Braley and General Genzari are raising an army back in Guhland. They will begin the march here in about a month."

"Six to eight weeks," Kirndal said. "We also have begun raising another army, in Lagualia."

"Ah, indeed. Then I'm sure you have a keen appreciation of the delays we are encountering," Wizenbeak replied. "As you must also know, without your siege train your army is unable to make any real threat against Sibetio, Ayondela, or Baran-Beldon. And by now you should be satisfied that even without the encumbrance of the siege train, your army cannot force a decisive battle."

"You slip around like a cake of soap in a shaving basin," complained the king.

"The mission of the soap is to prepare the royal throat for the razor," Wizenbeak said. "The razor will be here in a month or two. When do you expect your second Lagualian army?"

"Soon enough," Count Osmet said. "What did you have in mind, asking for a parley?"

"We propose the return of the status quo ante, cousin," Princess Marjia said. "You withdraw from Kalycas and the Eastern Marches, and we will sign a peace treaty with you, ending the war."

"The child can talk!" Osmet said in feigned amazement.

"If the courtier could fight, he might have commanded half the Lagualian army against us," Marjia said.

Kirndal laughed. "She scored on you, Osmet. A point for the princess!"

"Your Majesty, it is disgraceful to be defeated in battle by a child, and a girl child at that!"

"We aren't engaged in battle," she said. "We are engaged in negotiations with our cousin." She turned to her tutor. "They don't want to hear it from me, Doctor Wizenbeak. You tell them."

"Yes, Your Highness," he replied. "The question is simply this, Your Majesty. Are you better off making peace or continuing to fight? I submit that making peace is the better choice for both of us."

"You think so, eh? What will you give us?"

"Nothing. I'm too old to be running around on the ridges and in the valleys, especially in the wintertime; otherwise I'd carry matters through to the bitter end. Due to the infirmities of my flesh, I offer you this unprecedented opportunity. You want off the hook, you have the chance."

"Excuse us for a moment," Kirndal said, and he went with Count Osmet to the other side of the common room.

"What do you think?" the king asked softly.

"I'd be inclined to take it," the count said. "The only question is, will the regent honor a peace treaty signed by her daughter, who has to be under the age of consent?"

"Lagualia and Guhland can have a war anytime we want," Kirndal said. "That's what neighbors are for. But once you start that war, getting a peace isn't always so easy." He fingered the tiny gold earring he wore to keep his earlobe pierced while campaigning. "Their relief army is almost certain to get here before ours does, so we stand to lose Kalycas in any event."

"Yes sir." The plan had been to retreat into the Lagualian heartland, leaving Kalycas to stand alone as best it might.

"And we don't really like fighting in the winter without the prospect of some signal victory."

"The winter campaign hasn't been terribly popular among the men," said Osmet, who had hated it. "A Guhlish invasion in the spring, after we signed a peace treaty, that ought to rouse all sorts of enthusiasm."

"Yes, yes. Plus the regent has trouble at home with the Church," Kirndal said, looking back at the fireplace. "That might push her to declare war, but we'd be in better shape if we weren't the ones who started it."

"Yes sir," the count said, "and the civil war in Guhland might begin again, anyway, if she chose to invade us."

"You think we ought to take the offer, Count Osmet?"

"Yes sir. Even with that little girl signing the treaty."

"She's the one that makes it a Royal Army," the king said, fingering his mustache. "We'd have to have her signature. What's our losses to date?"

"The siege train, the garrison at Baran-Beldon, and we're just beginning to run into winter sickness, flu, dysentery and the like. Maybe two thousand dead and disabled, so far."

"What a waste." The king sighed. It figured to get worse before it got better, too. The final figures might be ten times as high if they tried to stay in the field.

"Plus supplies have been troublesome," the count added.

Kirndal nodded. "A high price for a winter's sport, but cheap for a war. At least so far. All right, we'll do it."

At the table, Murado adjusted his sword sash. "You don't have to offer them a peace treaty, Master Wizenbeak," he said softly. "Also, we don't have to wait for reinforcements to beat them in the field."

"You think the Tarelians are back in their old form?" the wizard asked.

"Sir, that's what I've been telling you for some time."

Wizenbeak sighed. "It does seem a shame to waste all that conditioning," he said. "How would you take Kirndal?"

"Set up an ambush on the left flank. Count Osmet is an imbecile. I've been watching him for weeks. He'd bite, and we'd smash the left flank before the right flank knows what hit them!"

"Tactically sound," the wizard replied, "but we don't have the strategic reserves to finish them off. You'd rout perhaps a third of the Lagualian army and have to fight the other two-thirds, and Kirndal might promote someone competent to take Osmet's place."

"It would be a gamble, Captain Murado" the princess said. "This is a sure thing, if it works."

"There is no glory without risk," Murado said.

"We can do without glory if we get the real estate," Wizenbeak said. "The greatest victory is to destroy the enemy's will to win without actually fighting."

King Kirndal and Count Osmet returned to their places at the table.

"A mildly interesting idea," Osmet said. "Might you have a draft of the treaty handy, perhaps?"

Wizenbeak reached into his pocket and took out his diptych, which he snapped open. The king and count read it through.

"This seems pretty straightforward," the count said. "What does Your Majesty think?"

"It will do," Kirndal conceded grudgingly. "Put it on parchment, and I'll sign it."

Murado reached into a leather pouch he was carrying and produced two copies of the document, already signed. The king read them and signed them. They each took a copy and went back to their respective honor guard.

As the master of the Tarelian Order settled himself into his sidesaddle, Murado watched the Lagualians cantering off. "Now what, sir?" he said.

"Now we wait for them to leave," the wizard said. "I would expect to see them pulling out of Kalycas by tomorrow morning at the very latest."

"And what if they don't?" Marjia asked.

A shrug. "Then things go on the way they were before, Your Highness," he said. "No problem. But when they leave, if they leave, *then* maybe a problem could develop. We'll send word home and hope that Her Majesty will excuse her field commander's usurpation of the royal prerogative."

"You mean you just went and signed a peace treaty without going through proper channels?" Murado was scandalized.

"The question never came up," Wizenbeak said.

24

The Patriarch Decides to Fish

ARCHDEACON Anezkva walked into the Stag's Head Dining Room to find a long-handled coffee pot sitting over a heating candle and a couple of logs burning on the fire under the marble boar's head. A basket of sweet rolls was on the spotless linen tablecloth, and Dr. Kurjima sat warming himself in front of the fireplace.

"What is it?" the archdeacon asked. "It's about that bastard Wizenbeak winning the war in the Eastern Marches, isn't it?"

"That might be on the patriarch's agenda," Kurjima replied calmly. "Sit down and have a cup of coffee."

Anezkva sat down and took a clean cup, but made no move to fill it. "It was a mistake making Wizenbeak an archdeacon," he said, "and then we compounded it by making him master of the Tarelian Order. Look what he's done since he's turned his hand to military affairs! He smashed the Tarelians under Fadel in the Semeryan. He defeated King-Patriarch Kahun—killed him, in fact, at Sifoty Field. He put the Witch-Queen back on the throne. And in the Eastern Marches, my God! He retook the great fortresses of Baran-Beldon and Ayondela as if they were nothing, and recovered Kalycas without fighting more than a few piddling skirmishes!"

The archdeacon picked up the copper coffee pot and set it down again, looked at the cup he'd taken and put it back in its place. "*He* was the one that was running the revolution! *He* was the one that was plotting their strategy, the long-nosed son of a bitch! Next thing you know, he'll want to be patriarch, and who's going to stop him?"

"He's done pretty good for a country boy," Kurjima agreed. "I imagine we might want to consider inviting him back to Cymdulock for a victory parade."

Archdeacon Darussis came in and seated himself on the other side of the table across from Anezkva.

"Do *you* think we ought to give Master Wizenbeak a triumph?"

Darussis looked up, shrugged. "If he wants one, I don't see how we can refuse."

"We've created a monster," Anezkva said morosely. "Whoever it was tried to kill him, they had the right idea. It's just a pity that they tried to put the blame on poor old Orunjan."

Patriarch Gorabani entered with Archdeacon Obuskaia and took their seats at the end of the table.

"You think Orunjan was unjustly accused?" the patriarch asked. Anezkva looked up to make a reply and saw Obuskaia's face. Oh shit, he thought, his heart sinking, I wonder how much Buska told?

"He took poison," Anezkva said, trying to avoid an outright lie without admitting anything. "One supposes there must have been a reason."

"He didn't take poison," the patriarch said.

"He was murdered?"

Gorabani sighed. "He may not even be dead, Doctor Anezkva. Kurjima and Darussis here exhumed the corpse for examination, and this is the report of their findings." He reached into an inner pocket and took out a roll of parchment, holding it between the tips of velvet-gloved fingers. "Doctor Basir Orunjan was my colleague, friend, and assistant for many years," he continued, "and he was exceptionally well informed about all sorts of arcana in the administration of the Church. It was only after the Witch-Queen's raid on the vault in the maze that we thought to ask how she could have learned our secrets in such detail. That led us to wonder if Basir was really dead, which is what led to the exhumation order."

He pushed the parchment across the table to Anezkva, who read it, then covered his face with his hands.

"If the Witch-Queen learned about the vault in the maze," Kurjima said, "what do you think she knows about *you*? About poor Basir's hitherto unindicted coconspirators, I should say?"

"Oh, shut up," Obuskaia growled. "He's dead meat and he knows it, but it takes a little time to adjust to the fact."

Kurjima poured the patriarch a cup of coffee, a second for himself. "Take your time," he said agreeably, "as long as you're quick about it."

"Well," Anezkva said after a few seconds, "the question is: If Orunjan is still alive, how do we get him out?"

"We just go up to the Witch-Queen and say, 'Oh, ma'am, you made a mistake when you gave us the body of good old Basir Orunjan and won't you please check out your bloody dungeons to see if you haven't got him stashed away somewhere?' " Obuskaia said.

"That's about all we can do," the patriarch agreed. "We could forgive the plunder of Church treasure more easily than this monstrous deception, this . . . this ghoulish masquerade perpetrated on a fellow clerisiarch!"

"I would expect he's dead by this time," Darussis said. "The man was, after all, guilty of high treason and he's already been buried. Forget about him. What are we going to do about us?"

"What do you mean?" Anezkva asked.

"We have two choices," the patriarch said patiently. "Either we take what we have so freshly uncovered and turn you over to the Witch-Queen as traitors, craving in return the humble boon of a proper burial for the late brother . . ."

"Which might be a bit of an embarrassment," Kurjima said, "especially if your execution was made a public spectacle. On the other hand, it would square us with the secular authorities."

"Who would then be emboldened to demand something like land reform," Obuskaia growled. "What's your other choice?"

"If we don't cast you out, why then we must embrace your cause, if not your learned selves," the patriarch said. "Your treason becomes our treason, and the institution of the Church itself is put at risk."

"Desperate times call for desperate measures," Anezkva said, his blue eyes flashing.

"Perhaps." Gorabani took a sip of the Lagualian coffee from his tiny cup and set it back on the saucer. "We ask you to step outside of yourself, to truly seek what is best for the Church."

"Surely boldness offers a better chance of survival than craven surrender!"

Patriarch Gorabani sighed and composed his gloved hands in front of him. "Think in terms of the survival of the Church, Doctor Anezkva. We have given the matter of bold strokes some careful thought and we must tell you that your own personal survival, and that of Archdeacon Obuskaia here, is . . . what was the word you used, Kurjima?"

"Contraindicated."

"Contraindicated, yes. Exactly. So much more elegant than

Buska's formulation of 'dead meat,' but in essence the same thing."

"What do you want us to do?" Obuskaia asked.

"Think of the good of the Church," Darussis said, picking up a sweet roll and breaking it in half. He took a delicate nibble. "You might wish to retire to the chapel and pray for divine guidance."

"The Church should fight," the big archdeacon said. "And as for myself, I would choose to die fighting."

"Doctor Anezkva?"

"I suppose . . ." There was a long hesitation. "This isn't how I had imagined things would end."

"You're in good company," Gorabani observed mildly, "King-Patriarch Kahun must also have been terribly surprised by the way matters turned out. Part of the human condition is that we imagine dying is something that only happens to other people."

"Yes, Your Holiness," Kurjima said politely. "Some of us may even remember that sentiment from Elementary Theology. As a practical matter, however, if we have decided to fight, the first thing that must be done is to return the Tarelians to their barracks in Cymdulock."

25

The Shadow Shaia Seeks Illumination

LASCO Genzari sat in the antechamber before the queen mother's office, studying the ornamentation on the gilt-frame mirrors that decorated the paneled oak walls. After a decently brief interval, a chamberlain led him into the presence. Jankura was sitting at a desk piled high with racks of chips, a male secretary at another desk with a stack of color-coded diptychs, in which he had taken the dictation of assorted correspondence.

"Your Majesty wished to see me?"

"Yes, Lasco. Take a chair, please." She turned to her secretary. "That will do for now. Draft the letters and return them for my signature." The secretary bowed and left with his stack of diptychs. She turned back to Genzari, who was looking for an undecorated handhold on his chair.

"So. You saw the report from the Eastern Marches?"

"Yes, ma'am," he replied, sliding the chair toward the edge of her desk. "Master Wizenbeak has pulled off a real coup, if you'll excuse the expression."

"So it would seem. What ought we to do about him signing a peace treaty on his own initiative?"

"Honor it, of course. We have things back the way they were before Lagualia invaded *and* the fighting is ended." Genzari adjusted his sword sash and seated himself. "Considering the means he had at his disposal, the result is a whole lot better than we might reasonably have expected."

"We're pleased with the result," Jankura conceded, "but Master Wizenbeak has acted with a most unseemly degree of independence. We were not even *consulted*!"

"That's unfortunate," Genzari agreed. All of a sudden, she's the center of the universe, he thought, and nothing is to happen without her say-so. The deference and adulation swirling about the throne have turned wiser heads than hers. "In the event, a verbal reprimand might be warranted, but it would suggest an unbecoming meanness of spirit. Speaking as the commander in chief of your armies, my advice is to rejoice in the victory and take no notice of any imagined lèse majesté."

The regent made a face. "We will rejoice," she said. "And your advice is noted. Still, why do you think he acted as he did?"

Genzari looked pained. "It must have seemed like the thing to do at the time, Your Majesty. Second guessing any general is pointless, except at a court-martial, when you are trying to educate the others. Second guessing a victorious general . . ." He made a dismissive gesture. "He saw an opportunity."

"Of course he saw an opportunity, Lasco. But that isn't what I meant."

"One does not need to seek an ulterior motive to justify a just action, Your Majesty."

Jankura rubbed her eyes. "I expect you're right, Lasco. But dealing with these stiff-necked clerisiarchs is driving me crazy. We should have arrested the Mambrinista leadership when we went in after the Church treasure."

"I cannot agree, Your Majesty."

"Don't be so stiff-necked yourself, Lasco, it was just a thought."

The old warrior shook his head. "No, ma'am. As regent you have the duty, the *obligation* to think clearly. Our survival depends on it. We were barely able to hold Duke Falenda and Duke Viluji as it was. It has *never* been possible to arrest the Mambrinista leadership."

"Even with Orunjan's testimony?"

"Extracted a week after his supposed suicide? Use your head. Your staff of wizards pulled off a tactical brilliancy, putting that magical mask on the other body, but strategically . . ." Genzari folded his arms and made an impolite noise. "You learned about the vault in the maze. That was useful. We needed the money very, very badly. Of the rest, there was nothing you could act on publicly."

"We could have acted on the information without revealing the source."

"That, Your Majesty, would have *guaranteed* restarting the civil war," Genzari said patiently.

A sigh. "Maybe so. At least it would end the suspense of waiting for the other shoe to drop." Jankura rested her elbows on the desk, fingering the great ruby at her throat. "Well, what's done is done. To know there are traitors plotting against you, to know their names, and to be unable to move against them. I don't know about you, Lasco, but it bothers the hell out of me!"

"Your Majesty must do three things," he said. "First, be patient. Second, be patient. And third, be patient. Eventually they will make a mistake, and then we'll have them."

"An outcome devoutly to be desired. Yes. What are we going to do with that army we're raising, now that we don't have a war for it to fight?"

"We'd be needing an army in any event," Genzari replied. "However, I ordered recruiting stopped on the word of Wizenbeak's victory."

"That's good," she said, "but we still have too many soldiers."

"That depends on what you intend to do, ma'am. If you want to go after the traitors in Syncretisty Hall, we don't have enough."

"Right. If I am to be patient, how do we get rid of the excess?"

"I expect that what we'll do is finish their training," he replied, "releasing the lowest rated in a month or so."

"How many?"

"Maybe one in eight, ma'am."

Jankura looked doubtful. "That still leaves too many."

Genzari brushed his mustache with thumb and forefinger to hide his smile. "Perhaps," he conceded. "Normal attrition will take care of most of the problem, I expect. A lot of men get bored with garrison duty."

"You could be right, Lasco, and we do have to regarrison the castles in the Eastern Marches that fell to Kirndal. She nodded to herself. "That's how we'll work it, then. Wizenbeak and the Tarelians will stay posted in the Eastern Marches until we send a relief force in the spring."

"And you'll give him a triumph when he returns?"

"Yes, yes of course. The old fool's earned one, hasn't he?"

26

At Saint Posalanji's Monastery

THE air was crisp and cold, but the sun shone brightly on the snow-covered fields surrounding Saint Posalanji's Monastery. Across the frozen Kalyswash, which meandered to the northeast before reversing itself as it flowed through the gap in the ridge-line, the proud towers of Castle Kalycas were visible. Kirndal had withdrawn, the new garrison was installed, and the Princess Marjia's gonfalon rippled in the morning breeze over the central keep.

"Now look," Wizenbeak said, riding beside his captain-general as they toured the encampment the Tarelians were set-ting up, "a winter bivouac is all very well but you still have to have proper drainage. Put the mess tents upstream from the rest, over there." He gestured toward a small spring that flowed into the Kalyswash.

"Yes sir," Murado said, making a note in his diptych.

"And the squad tents where you had them, but with the la-trine tents downstream and downhill. Over there."

"Yes sir. Are we going to put wooden floors in the tents?"

"Ah, no-o-o, at least not at first," the wizard replied, shifting his weight in the saddle. Wooden floors would be costly and permanent to a degree that didn't seem justified. "Use straw until we find out what our marching orders are, now that the war has been brought to a satisfactory conclusion."

"Straw," Murado said, a feather of wax curling up from his stylus. "We aren't expecting to stay here?"

"Not for long," the wizard replied complacently. "Her Maj-esty doubtless misses my wise counsel, and the soldiers, well, the sooner we get them back to their barracks, the better."

"That depends, sir," said his captain-general. "In the field you get a different sort of cream rising to the top, if you take my meaning. The rough lout who can't keep his footlocker straight may be a hell of a fighter. Well, in the field, it shows. In the garrison, what you see is the messy footlocker belonging to a slob that gets in fights.''

''As master of the order, I would prefer to inspect the troops as little as possible, Pardus. They marched like hell, and by now they ought to fight pretty good, too. You think they could use work with sword or spear, train them up in it.''

''Yes sir. The men we have are pretty much up to the peak of form. Qualitatively, they may be as fit as we were at Mewis Field.''

''Well, the order is a good bit smaller now,'' the wizard conceded, ''but we ought to be able to recruit up to strength without much trouble.''

''We could do it right here in Kalycas Province,'' said Murado, who had in fact been actively recruiting, ''if you gave the word, of course.''

''Hmmm,'' Wizenbeak mused. There had been a subtle reordering of his priorities in the time he had been leading the order. The soldiers had given their loyalty to him, especially after he had gone up the tightrope at Baran-Beldon. The wizard had accepted that loyalty and felt obligated to reciprocate it. Considering what was good for Her Majesty the Regent and King Dervian, he had simultaneously to consider what was good for the Tarelian Order, when the order was in his thoughts constantly. ''With the cadre in place and properly shaken down, we could expand the order rather easily, couldn't we?''

''Yes sir,'' Murado said.

''Let's think about that for a bit,'' Wizenbeak replied cautiously. His natural impulse had been to say go ahead, but he was also aware of a variety of possible complications. It would be easy to do later, very difficult to reverse, once done. ''When we get the bivouac set up, we'll want a training schedule. Keep the men busy until we set off for home. Recruiting isn't really critical, at this point.''

''Yes sir,'' Murado said. If he was disappointed at not getting official approval for what he was doing, it didn't show. But since his boss didn't want to hear it right now, it wouldn't show on the reports, either. He saluted and rode off to execute the orders on tent floors and latrine placement.

Master Wizenbeak turned his mule about and returned to the monastery guest house where he was billeted with Princess Marjia. After the Lagualians had withdrawn from Kalycas Castle, he had toured the place. The great hall was fit for a king, but the rooms were cold and drafty, and he decided to trade splendor for comfort. Handing his mount over to one of his orderlies, he went into the guest house to find Marjia and her nanny in the common room with the abbot of the monastery.

"There you are, Master Wizenbeak," the little girl said. "As my tutor, don't you think I ought to be able to go into the library up on the hill?"

"I have offered to bring Her Highness any suitable books she wishes to read from our poor library," said the abbot, who was uneasily aware of being surrounded by an army of outlanders. "The lives of the saints, the duties of women, that sort of thing. Her wish to browse through the stacks is entirely unacceptable. We have never had a woman enter the monastery in all the time it has existed."

"I understand," the wizard replied, pushing his glasses back on his nose. "Perhaps as a compromise, you could permit *me* to browse through the library, selecting those books I feel most suitable for Her Highness to read?"

The abbot was not enthusiastic about letting stray archdeacons into his library, either. And as for borrowing books, he could almost see Brother Delgos, his librarian, having apoplexy. Still, there *was* an army encamped around his monastery, this peculiar-looking archdeacon *was* the commander, the prepubescent princess *was* the archdeacon's liege. It was better to remain on good terms with them if at all possible, but the idea of removing books from the premises was almost as bad as having a woman entering them. Evil choices are made to be avoided when possible, deferred when not.

"I suppose we could admit the archdeacon, here, to the library," he conceded reluctantly, "but the removal of any material from the premises would have to be agreeable to Brother Delgos, who has been the librarian, man and boy, for close to sixty years."

After a few more pleasantries, the abbot returned to the monastery, riding what amounted to a manually powered one-man lift, set alongside a much larger freight elevator. Wizenbeak, who had an invitation to visit the following morning, sat down with Princess Marjia in front of the common room fire.

"I'm not sure it would be a good idea for you to go up there, anyway," he said. "We'd have a devil of a time getting you down if anything went wrong."

"We couldn't get you out, either," Marjia observed.

"True, but I'm not of the royal line, so nobody would much care," the wizard replied. "Whereas, and whereas, and so forth, I am responsible not only for your education but also for your safety, it therefore behooveth me not to let you go up that rackety-looking elevator."

"I could take a body guard up with me, couldn't I?"

"To protect you from falling? I doubt if the monks would be too happy about letting a girl in the place under any circumstances, judging from what the abbot said." He walked over and warmed his hands at the fire. "Let alone a girl with a gang of rowdy soldiers along for company. Why do you want to go up there, anyway?"

"The library, of course. It's supposed to have books from antiquity. We might be able to find out the truth about troll-bats, for instance."

"Hunh-hunh," Wizenbeak grunted. "We might. More likely we'll find two stories knocked down to be replaced by three others."

The elevator ride was slow and reasonably smooth, and Wizenbeak found himself admiring the view in the bright morning air. The abbot met him at the landing and escorted him over to the library, which was a stone building of great antiquity.

Once inside the library, they were met by Brother Delgos, a tall, lean monk with stooped shoulders and a fringe of white hair around his tonsure. He wore thick glasses in frames of horn. The abbot made the introduction and left in just short of unseemly haste.

"Well, Wizenbeak," the librarian said sourly, "what is it that you think you want?"

The wizard smiled at the omission of his titles. Delgos was clearly enjoying the home-court advantage. "I don't know, exactly," he replied. "What have you got?"

"Books," was the laconic answer.

"That's very helpful, Brother Delgos; perhaps you'd be so kind as to escort me around and tell me what you have?"

They spent that morning going through the stacks on the first floor, and Delgos, under the wizard's apt questioning, grudgingly began to tell a little of how the library had been organized, and how it had come to be. Now and again he would inadvertently reveal small bits of what the library held.

At noon, Wizenbeak had to return to the plain below to attend to the business of the real world, but the place fascinated him and, before leaving, he saw the abbot to make an appointment to return the next morning.

"What did you find?" Marjia asked that evening, as they were exercising Mischka and Branka in the common room.

"A very strange dragon guarding a very strange treasure," replied Wizenbeak. "I must tell you there is no chance whatsoever for you to visit the place. And as for taking anything out, well, probably not. But that old librarian might let me take some notes, and I could show you those."

He went up the next morning and the morning after that, slowly exploring the other floors of the library under the watchful eye of Brother Delgos. The wizard was never trusted, but as he became known, the librarian slowly became a little more forthcoming with the answers to his questions. And on the stern instructions of the abbot, Archdeacon Wizenbeak was even permitted to peruse one scroll at a time in the tiny reading room, though Delgos or one of his apprentices kept a watch on him as he did so.

"Remarkable," Wizenbeak said, feeding Branka a piece of seedcake, "they have books going all the way back to the Dragon-Human Wars, books I've heard of only because they were referenced in other books, that have been lost just about forever!"

"Did you actually read them?" Princess Marjia asked.

"Well, yes and no," he replied. "I looked through the scrolls, right enough, but the language is archaic, and getting two words out of three isn't really good enough."

"Could you get the drift?"

"I think so," the wizard said, eating a piece of seedcake that Branka rejected. "Troll-bats become a trive when they have sixty-four breeding members. And there is an upper limit, which the authors, on what seem to be purely numerological grounds, guess is five hundred twelve. When a trive exceeds that number, 'splitting is obligate.' "

"Obligate? What are they talking about?"

"From context, it appears that at five hundred twelve trives *must* split, and below that number they *may* split. And sixty-four is a magic number, *because*. Nothing they were saying made any sense, so I skimmed over it." He shrugged. "I made all sorts of notes, though."

"We try not to let a trive get bigger than fifty," Marjia mused as she stroked Mischka's long, soft ears, "because the troll-bats get unruly and hard to handle. Something starts to happen about then, I'll bet, and at sixty-four it *does* happen. When you go back, try to find out what."

"Hunh," the wizard grunted. "What happens is that the little beasts start to act independent. They have their own foolish ideas of what they want to do, which is most often to stop making mother-of-glass and get drunk. What you have to do is split the trive, if you can find a buyer, or prune it." He watched Branka sitting on the table, grooming himself, and sighed. "I never liked pruning. The troll-bats you wind up killing are the troublesome juveniles and the less productive old females."

"That figures," the princess said. "So?"

"So that's what the boss wants done," Wizenbeak said. "As if the trive were purely an economic unit. Well, hell, as far as he's concerned, it is. Only it isn't that simple. The troublesome juveniles grow up to be the best workers, if they ever grow up; and the old females that don't produce much, you have to have a few on hand to keep the trive sweet."

"Right. What would happen if you just left the trive alone, going its own merry way?"

"That's happened a few times," he said. "First production goes to hell, and then some fool goes in to try and restore order, and gets himself killed. And then everybody turns out for miles around to kill troll-bats. And after they wipe out the rogue trive, it is months and *months* before the other trives in the area get back to normal."

Princess Marjia nodded. "I understand. What do you suppose would happen if nobody bothered them, the troll-bats?"

"There'd be some sort of ruckus eventually, the neighbors, or the police would get involved . . ." He paused. "Oh. You mean, theoretically, what would the troll-bats do?" He pulled at his whiskers for a moment. "I suppose they'd get organized, wouldn't they?"

"Maybe. A lot of troll-bat husbandry seems to be keeping them from doing that very thing, doesn't it?" Mischka, tired of playing, leaped nimbly from her wrist to the wizard's shoulder and crawled inside his robe to take a nap. "So what would a trive of troll-bats do if it ever got organized?"

"An interesting question," Wizenbeak said. "They'd make all sorts of trouble, I imagine. Probably the reason we don't know is because nobody ever wanted to find out."

"You can look it up when you go back to the library tomorrow morning, then."

"It'll have to be the day after, Princess. Tomorrow I'm going out to negotiate the purchase of some wooden tent floors, Her Majesty having sent orders that we are to remain in the field for at least another three months."

There was a knock at the door, which was opened by one of the sentries posted outside, and a messenger, well muddied from traveling, entered and saluted.

"Archdeacon Wizenbeak?" he said.

"Over here, young trooper."

"Yes sir," the messenger replied, moving stiffly. "I have a message from His Holiness, Patriarch Gorabani." He produced a small leather cylinder, tied with a scarlet ribbon and sealed with the patriarch's seal in crimson wax. Wizenbeak signed the little receipt chip and broke the seal, uncapping the cylinder and removing the little roll of parchment. The letter was written in Gorabani's own hand, all signed and sealed with the utmost formality. It was short and to the point: To Archdeacon Dr. W. W. Wizenbeak, Master of the Tarelian Order. I. Congratulations on a brilliant campaign which ended the Lagualian invasion of the Eastern Marches. The defense of Guhland may, at this point, be properly left in the hands of the secular authorities. II. You are hereby requested and required to return the Tarelian Order to its barracks in Cymdulock, at once.

Wizenbeak looked at the messenger. "Dismissed," he said softly. "Go get yourself something to eat." He reread the message, but it remained the same. Now what do we do? he wondered.

"What is it?" Marjia asked. Wizenbeak handed her the parchment without comment, and she quickly read it. "You say the regent ordered you to stay put?"

A sigh. "That's what I said. She did indeed, yes, order the Tarelians to make camp here for the rest of the season. The problem is, if the patriarch sends a copy of the order to Captain-General Murado, what will happen?"

The little girl sat looking at the glowing embers in the fireplace for a long time. "Six to five he'd march the Tarelian Order back to Cymdulock," she said at last.

"How did you figure the odds?"

Marjia shrugged. "Back at the palace, one of my mute maidservants used to tell me that"—a smooth, two handed gesture—"in human affairs"—she signed "the" and spelled out "odds"—"the odds"—a chopping, one-handed gesture—"were always"—she signed the numbers—"six to five"—and ground the left fist into the right palm—"against."

"That's not terribly helpful, Princess."

Marjia shrugged and tossed her head. "Why don't you ask Murado what he'd do, then?"

"Hunh-hunh. I'd like to. Only I can't." The wizard took off his glasses and rubbed his eyes. "The thing is, I'm in charge. That means I have to tell Murado what to do. If I ask him will he obey my order before I give it, I'd get the order obeyed if he says yes. Only I wouldn't be in charge anymore. I'd be obeying the regent's order because Pardus Murado said it was all right. And if he wouldn't obey me, what could I do about it? Tag along after the order pretending that it's doing what I wanted? I'm supposed to be the master of the order, for God's sake."

"So tell him about the regent's order and the patriarch's order, and tell him what to do. Either he obeys you or he doesn't. If he obeys you, life is beautiful. If he doesn't, you stay here and send a message to the regent post haste."

Wizenbeak rested his chin in one hand. "That has a certain naïve appeal," he said. "I like Murado, and that assumes that he's an honorable man, a trustworthy fellow. Tell the truth and let the chips fall where they may. Yes." He rubbed his nose between thumb and forefinger. "The only thing is . . ."

"You don't want to tell Her Majesty that the order has mutinied?" Marjia asked, brushing a strand of blond hair back from her face.

The wizard got up and put another log on the fire. "That, too," he said. "The only thing is that Murado and his top officers were conspirators. That's how I selected them out of that mob looking for work before the coronation. At the time it was that, or take the people Orunjan picked out for me." He shook his head. "The lesser of two evils, maybe, but now I'm scared to trust the son of a bitch."

"I understand," she said. "You don't trust him, but you just about have to trust him, don't you? Otherwise how are you going to stop the Tarelians from changing sides?"

"Good question," he replied softly. "Probably it can't be done. I might stop it once, the first time the question comes up, but what happens after that?"

"If Murado obeys you the first time, he ought to obey you from there on out, Wizenbeak."

He shook his head and caught his glasses as they slid off his nose. "Wrong. If he obeys me the first time, it'll be with all sorts of serious reservations. And he'll talk it over with his brother officers, debating what ought to be done. The second time, it won't be me getting the word, it'll be Murado—maybe offering to make him master of the order if he goes with the patriarch.''

"You are master of the order for life," Marjia said. "Gorabani put it in writing."

The wizard fumbled around in his capacious pockets and came up with the Ace of Spades with the knife hole in the center. He flipped it across the table to her. "Tell me about it," he said.

She twisted her head sideways to peer at him through the hole in the card. "Are you afraid?"

"Of course. How should I not be afraid? If I obey the regent, the patriarch will kill me. If I obey the patriarch, it's just this side of high treason."

"Or maybe it's just the other side. What will you do?"

"There is a magical technique known as muddling through," he replied. "I'm going to obey the patriarch, write Her Majesty a long letter of explanation, and hope for the best."

"You know, in your own way, you are a bold, bold man, Master Wizenbeak," Princess Marjia said. "I have known big men, strong men, dukes and generals, who in your position would have jumped on their horses and run away. What do you get out of it?"

The wizard smiled sadly. "No, Princess," he said. "You mean, '*How* do you get out of it?' "

27

On Saint Posalanji's Day

KURJIMA hung up his clerisiarch's cloak and entered Gorabani's attic office in Syncretisty Hall after a polite knock. "The Tarelians are back, Your Holiness," he announced politely. "I saw the first companies marching into their barracks about an hour ago."

"Yes, yes," the patriarch agreed testily. "Wizenbeak said they would, and it seems he is a man of his word."

"You aren't exactly pleased."

"We aren't exactly surprised, either," Gorabani replied. " 'It is only proper that an archdeacon obey the lawful order of his patriarch, after all.' "

"His letter to the regent bothers you?"

"Yes, Doctor Kurjima. His emphasis on the lawful nature of the order is more than a little troubling, given the nature of Saint Alanji's Day this year." Saint Alanji of the Flowers, a most remarkable woman, banished the curse of infertility in ancient times and had consequently been imposed on the existing spring fertility festival, to give that pagan celebration a religious coloration. The logic of her selection and the natural energy of the celebrants had combined to make her day one of the major holidays of the year.

The clerisiarch shrugged. "Don't worry about it, sir. Consider his situation at Kalycas, where you have bid him return, and the regent has bade him stay. No matter what he does, he cannot please you both, and in this case, he obeyed you while sending a closely reasoned argument to Her Majesty hoping to justify an action that defied her specific order."

"So he did." Gorabani composed his gloved hands. "Yes," he sat back in his chair. "We also understand his delicate position vis-à-vis the Witch-Queen, but even so, the inference that he might not obey an order of ours which he considered unlawful is distressing.''

"Would you rather he had obeyed the regent?" Kurjima asked.

"Maybe. It would have created a delay, but we would have been certain where he stood, and worked our way around him. This way . . .''

"After the event, all that he has to do is to defend the Church against her enemies. You yourself said it: 'If we are protected against the initial, unthinking reaction, in a few days' time the Royal Armies will disintegrate.' ''

"That's the theory, Doctor Kurjima. But Archdeacon Wizenbeak is the master of the Tarelian Order in fact as well as in name at this point, having led them to victory in what seemed to be a hopeless cause.'' Also, thought Gorabani uneasily, the man has displayed an astonishing aptitude for military affairs. After a lifetime of mastering card tricks and such minor magic as he was capable of, he suddenly turns his hand to war, and presto! the old fool turns out to be a natural. "After the event, what will he do?''

"You didn't worry about what the several dukes affected by the event would do,'' his assistant replied. "Why worry about *him*?''

"In general, the dukes are predictable. All that has to be done is to play them off against each other and back the winner, even if you can't tell which one it will be beforehand. What if Wizenbeak tries to be a kingmaker?''

"What if he does, sir?''

"What if he succeeded? What then?''

Kurjima sighed. "I suppose it depends on what he wants, sir. If he were to succeed, a big 'if,' and if he then wanted to be patriarch, another big 'if,' *then* you might have trouble keeping your hat. But he hasn't shown the usual stigmata of such overweening ambition. At this point Your Holiness can't do anything about it, so stop worrying.''

"So many things could go wrong, how should we not worry?''

"Yes sir,'' his assistant said. "The things that you can do something about, worry about those. The rest is in the hands of God.''

The black-gloved fingers drummed on the desktop for a moment. "So it is. One could wish for a less evil selection of choices, but here we stand.''

"Why all the agitation about Wizenbeak, then? When the

question of the dukes came up, you dismissed it out of hand, as something to be dealt with after the event."

Because I'd hoped for an excuse to pull back at the very brink, thought Gorabani sadly, but no such luck. And Wizenbeak, who comes out of nowhere to command armies, leading one lost cause after another to victory—how can we bear to put him in control of our lives and fortunes at this decisive moment in history? "That was for the dukes," he said. "We couldn't very well invite them in on the planning, could we?"

"No sir. So why is Wizenbeak different? He wasn't in on the planning, either."

"Occasionally one has the misfortune to encounter a man of destiny, Doctor Kurjima. And to deliberately place ourselves in his hands . . ."

"We are in the hands of God, Your Holiness. Trust Him."

General Lasco Genzari was sitting in the plant room in a general's parade tunic, worn open over a plain black and tan hauberk, drinking bittersweet herb tea from a glass. He looked up as Wizenbeak entered.

"Good morning, old friend," he said. "That was a nice piece of work, the Kalycas campaign."

The wizard handed the long sword he was encumbered with to a servant, who put it in a rack, and took his seat at the conference table. "Thank you," he replied, "and happy Posalanji's Day." Saint Alanji of the Flowers was shortened to Posalanji in the vernacular. "What are we meeting about?"

"The parade, of course. Her Majesty . . ." He hesitated. "Her Majesty did not wish to give you a proper triumph, for whatever reason, and had originally thought to exclude you and the Tarelians from the line of march." He studied the cup in his hands. "She was eventually persuaded of the unwisdom of such a self-indulgent decision and asked me to arrange for your participation."

"Hunh. I should pay more attention to court gossip. Has Her Majesty some reason for setting her face against me?"

Genzari shrugged. "Count Braley might be able to tell you, if he would."

"I'd heard Braley was her favorite." She could do a whole lot worse than Braley, thought Wizenbeak resignedly. He's a strategist rather than a bloody courtier, anyway. I wonder why he has it in for me . . . professional jealousy, perhaps? Did I ever ask him if he wore eye shadow? He selected a coffee cup, and a servant filled it from an ornately decorated pot. "Hey, Lasco, what do *you* think?"

"Two things, Doctor Wizenbeak." One "old friend" was sufficient to maintain his self-esteem in the face of Her Majesty's expressed displeasure. Genzari took it for granted that the servants would report the conversation to someone and, having made the point, felt it was unnecessary to emphasize further. He took a sip of coffee and permitted the servant to refill his cup. "She has a staff of wizards, you know. There may be some backbiting there, some pushing and shoving to be number one. They'd tear you down to make themselves a little taller, if you know what I mean."

A sigh. "Yes." The wizards had it in for him, too?

"The other thing . . ." How can I tell him, wondered Genzari. He and I know that Queen Mother Shaia is really "Janko" Jankura, a peasant girl he rescued from burning. She told me she is oathbound to him, about swearing on the witchfinder's silver skull, about how he taught her. And now, now she is regent, her word is law, she is used to being obeyed. She resents her former servitude, the debt of gratitude she owes, and when Master Wizenbeak acts in matters of state without her say-so, she takes that excuse to display her resentment of him, even though he has won her a signal victory in the process. "The other thing, well, Her Majesty has changed a bit since returning to the throne."

"Probably so, Lasco. I wouldn't be surprised." He took a sip of coffee. "Well then, what arrangements do you want to make for the parade this afternoon?"

Genzari took out his diptych. "Rearrangements, actually. If they meet with your approval, of course. We're moving the Tarelians up in the line of march to just behind the House Guards, putting you on the float with the king, and—"

Count Braley entered the room. "Her Majesty," he said and, as the others rose, he stood by his seat at the table. Jankura entered and took the tall seat at the end, and the three men seated themselves.

"We were discussing the parade, Your Majesty," Genzari said.

"We understand. What was your proposed order of march?" He pushed his diptych across the table to her and she studied it for a moment. "This is pretty much as we discussed it, General, but we have been considering the matter at some length."

"What seems to be the problem, Your Majesty?" the wizard asked.

"The problem, Master Wizenbeak, is to honor the Tarelians for the victory won by their valor, without giving you a triumph in the process."

"I could stay home."

"You'd be missed, and tongues would wag. No, you have to be in attendance. But since you usurped our royal prerogatives in signing that peace treaty with Kirndal, we cannot in good conscience give you the triumph to which you would otherwise be entitled."

"As long as the order marches in the place of honor, I have no real objection to whatever Your Majesty decides."

"That's very kind of you, Master Wizenbeak," Count Braley said sarcastically. "The problem is one of selecting the proper nuance, something to show that you are simultaneously admonished and forgiven."

This would be ridiculous if everybody wasn't taking it so damned seriously, thought the wizard. Maybe Braley doesn't wear eye shadow after all. Maybe he's just trying to do the best he can in the difficult situation of looking too pretty to be taken seriously. I wonder if he wears women's undergarments?

They discussed the matter at length, weighing the imponderables of admonition and forgiveness, issuing a final order of march just before lunch. The regent selected Plan A, in which the king, his tutor, Princess Marjia, the regent, and Count Braley would be on the lead float, while Wizenbeak would be on the second float with Genzari and Duke Bedirny.

As the parade was marshaling its units in the square in front of the City Courthouse, Jankura made one last change in the direction of forgiveness. Reverting to Plan B, she and Count Braley moved from the first float to the second. Then the bells in Cymdulock Cathedral sounded the hour, and the parade got under way to the drone of the warpipes and the roll of the kettledrums.

The lead float turned toward Cymdulock Cathedral on Park of Heroes Boulevard. Wizenbeak noted that other people appeared to be having last-minute problems. A school for lay preachers had erected a bandstand coming out to the street, gaily draped with bunting. On top, there were thirty or forty chairs sitting empty except for a couple of trumpeters. The conductor was probably trying to get his band out of some local bar.

As the lead float came abreast of the bandstand, the front face crashed into the empty sidewalk, the trumpeters stood up and sounded "Attack!" and a strong company of death commandos, shouting "Death to the Witch-Queen!" charged out of the concealed sally port. Each of them had been given the Last Rites, and to symbolize their departure from life they wore unbleached linen shrouds over their hauberks. Their faces they had marked in an ancient tradition, a bar of black paint under each eye to symbolize death, and a bar of white under the black to symbolize salvation. Archdeacons Obuskaia and Anezkva led them to death and glory.

The House Guards, taken by surprise, fought to defend themselves as the death commandos cut through their lines.

Seeing what was happening, Jankura never hesitated. "Guards!" she shouted. "Defend your king!" The company of House Guards before the second float hardly needed her orders. They had already drawn steel and begun a counterattack. Both troll-bats popped out of their pocket in the wizard's robe, galvanized by the surge of wizardly adrenaline.

For one brief second King Dervian stood, his sword drawn, his tutor guarding his flank as the surviving guardsmen tried to prevent the death commandos from swarming onto the lead float; and then, as the swiftly running guardsmen from the second company scrambled on the back of the float, one of the guards cut Dervian down from behind!

Jankura saw it, they all saw it. She gave a little cry and went into shock. Wizenbeak grabbed her so she didn't fall.

"Tarelians!" he shouted. "To me! Long live Shaia! Death to traitors!"

Archdeacon Obuskaia and a handful of his strongest swordsmen had cut their way through the disorganized House Guard, and seeing the regent on the second float they charged, shouting, "Death to the Witch-Queen!"

From behind them came an exultant tenor shout "The king is dead!" and Dervian's head was thrust upward on the point of a spear.

Genzari, Bedirny, and Braley drew their swords and stood at the edge of the float to meet the charge. Archdeacon Obuskaia and three of his men leaped onto the float, swords flashing in the sunlight. Genzari and Braley each cut their man, sending them falling back to the street. Duke Bedirny wounded his and was cut down by Obuskaia. The wounded man, bearded, grinning, slashed at Genzari, who parried the stroke as Braley killed him. As he fell, spraying the massed yellow jonquils with his

blood, the two remaining death commandos took his place.
Genzari and Braley retreated to make a stand in front of Jankura,
who was standing quietly with Wizenbeak's arm about her waist.
There was a heeltap's pause, as the wizard frantically wondered
how to direct his troll-bats in some helpful way, and then Obuskaia, a great bear of a man, stepped forward, gripping his
sword in both hands and raising it level with his right shoulder.

"Death to the Witch-Queen," he breathed, and led the charge
against Count Braley. There was a flash of steel, and the archdeacon retreated a step or two, holding his side and bleeding
from the mouth. Genzari had cut left and right, and one of the
death commandos was down. The other pivoted on buckling
knees, making a slow arc with his sword as he fell off the edge.

A second, larger, group of death commandos had formed and
was charging, to the blare of trumpets and the shout of "Death
to the Witch-Queen!" They ran into Pardus Murado and the
Tarelian Order shouting "Shaia!" and went down in a brief
flurry of swordplay.

Obuskaia pushed his sword into the float and, using it as a
cane, eased himself onto the mass of yellow jonquils. He put
his face in the crook of his arm and died, his sword standing
beside him.

Then Tarelians were everywhere. The death commandos were
dead, except for one. Beside the first float, Archdeacon Anezkva,
his blue eyes blazing, was holding Princess Marjia by the hair,
his companion sword at her throat. Nobody moved.

"Give me the Witch-Queen," he said in a high, clear voice.
"Bring her to me that I may kill her, or the princess will die. I
swear it!"

"Braley," Wizenbeak said. "Take Her Majesty and start
walking toward him."

"What?"

"I want the son of a bitch distracted. Now move!"

Count Braley sheathed his blood-wet sword, put Jankura's
arm over his own, and helped her off the float.

Wizenbeak stood perfectly still, and as soon as he saw Archdeacon Anezkva's attention focused on Jankura, he cupped
Mischka and Branka in his two hands, holding them up to his
face. "Save her," he whispered urgently, and both troll-bats
were gone on the word. Mischka took the archdeacon's sword
arm at the wrist, rotating it out and away from Marjia's throat,
the wizard grunting with the effort. Branka landed on the archdeacon's chest, just above the heart, his webbed hands outthrust

before him. Wizenbeak didn't feel a thing, but Anezkva's blue eyes looked suddenly concerned as his heart went into fibrillation. He opened his mouth, dropped his sword, and sank to his knees. Marjia pulled her hair from his loosening grasp and, as he fell to one side, she ran over to Wizenbeak, the troll-bats fluttering a little behind.

The wizard stepped off the float, amazed at all the bodies lying about, and caught her as she jumped into his arms.

"Nice work with those troll-bats," Count Braley said, shifting Jankura's grip on his arm so he could remove his sword from its scabbard and clean it with a piece of silk.

"Thank you." He glanced at a drop of blood running down the count's forehead. "Are you all right?"

"What?" Braley ran his finger along his headband; at one place it was cut half through. He brought the finger down, brushing the tiniest of cuts. "The big fellow at the end, he was pretty good. I'm fine. Now what?"

Genzari stepped stiffly off the float to join them. His parade tunic was cut horizontally across the top, and diagonally across the chest. His hauberk had protected him from the first cut, but the diagonal cut was bleeding freely.

"I need to talk to you," Marjia whispered in the wizard's ear. "Keep me with you, for God's sake!"

"Lasco," Wizenbeak said, "Lasco, are you hurt?"

"Not badly," Genzari said, wiping his sword and sheathing it. "There's no bubbles, no whistling from the chest cut, at any rate."

"The House Guard is pretty badly cut up, sir," Pardus Murado said. "Shall we cancel the parade?"

Wizenbeak sighed. "Cancel the parade by all means, Mister Murado. Count Braley, we'd best get the regent back to the Citadel."

"Shaia isn't the regent anymore," Princess Marjia said. "Dervian is dead!"

A clerisiarch came up and handed Wizenbeak a scroll bearing the patriarch's seal. "His Holiness urgently requires that the Tarelian Order take up a defensive position around Syncretisty Hall, Master Wizenbeak," he said. "Immediately."

28

Saint Posalanji's Night

GENZARI entered the plant room in the Citadel wearing a plum-colored silken robe over his bandages and handed his long sword to the nurse who was attending him. "Over there," he said, pointing, "the sword rack is over there." He took his seat at the table, across from Duke Falenda, whose usually bland face was creased with worry, and an openly agitated Duke Viluji, who was holding his hands in his lap to hide the prayer beads he was twisting. Beside him, Count Braley still wore the headband with the sword cut, but Jankura, at the head of the table, had changed into black, except for a crimson sword sash.

"Thank you for coming, Lasco," she said.

"I'm sorry to have kept you waiting—" he began, but she cut him off.

"Your wounds were incurred in our defense," Jankura said. "In my defense, actually. Thank you very much."

"Yes, Your Majesty," Genzari said, sliding his seat under the table.

"And that's another thing. I'm not royalty. I'm not Shaia. You knew it. Wizenbeak knew it. Falenda knew it and has now felt obliged to bring the matter into the open." A faint smile. "He wishes us to dispense with the masquerade."

"Yes, Your Majesty," Genzari said. "But I took oath to serve *you*, to uphold *you*. And the crown you wear merits the respect I give. What are your orders?"

"That's all very well for you, General," Viluji said, putting his prayer beads on top of the table, "but some of us had sworn to uphold the house of Grathnys!" The beads rattled through his fingers. "What are we to do now? What in *hell* are we going to do?"

"Ride out the storm," Count Braley replied calmly.

"With *what*, for God's sake? Princess Marjia?"

"The army will stand by Her Majesty as long as we meet the payroll," Braley said. Which doesn't really answer Viluji's objection, of course. Without Dervian, we aren't legitimate. If we aren't legitimate, there are maybe half a dozen dukes with a better claim to the throne and potentially bigger armies. If one of them marries Marjia . . . He dismissed the thought. Using Princess Marjia as bait to tease first one duke and then another was a silly, stupid game. In the long run, or maybe not-so-long run, Her Majesty was finished. It might be time to consider seeking a new master. "Whether she rules as Shaia, Queen Revenant, or the Shadow Shaia, or whatever can be decided later. Our enemies also have serious problems, not the least of which is that Her Majesty is still alive. Right now, the question is when and where to strike back."

Duke Falenda nodded glumly. "You may be right." He sighed. "If the army stands by the Shadow Shaia, she has a chance for all her lack of pedigree." The words were uttered with a notable lack of conviction.

"A pity they killed Bedirny," Duke Viluji said. "Bedirny was firm as a rock. I'd feel a whole lot better if Bedirny was here."

Falenda shrugged. "Perhaps. He died defending Her Majesty, thinking her the True Shaia. If he'd only known . . ."

"We don't have time to replay the assassination," Braley said. "What do you suggest we do?"

"You might start by getting Princess Marjia into the Citadel," Viluji said. "Some duke grabs her, he has an iron-fisted claim to the throne once he marries her."

"She freely chose to stay with Master Wizenbeak," Count Braley said. "I put the question to her, and she refused to return to the Citadel with us."

"She is a mere child," Falenda said sourly. "You should have made her come."

Braley laughed. "Sure I should. Just grab old Wizenbeak by that long nose of his and twist until he says 'Take her away, boss,' and that's all there is to it!"

"Wizenbeak wouldn't give her up?"

"He told me to ask her," Braley said. "The wizard said it was her choice, and I took him at his word."

"A good answer," Genzari said, nodding approvingly.

"What do you mean by that?" Duke Viluji asked.

"He isn't holding her himself. Marjia is a royal pain in the ass, but she remains free. We don't have her, but we don't have to snatch her from the wizard, either.''

Duke Falenda upended the tiny coffee cup on his saucer and a servant filled it from a long-handled pot. He watched the aromatic steam rising for a moment. "Princess Marjia is the key to the situation,'' he said at last. "One way or another we have to get her here.''

"Wrong,'' Jankura said. "The key to the situation is to finish the war with the Church before the dukes have to take sides.''

"Yes, Your Majesty,'' Braley said. Finding someone else who took his advice as well wasn't going to be easy.

"What makes you think you have a war with the Church?''

"Oh hell, Viluji,'' she said. "The sally port those death commandos came storming out of was set up on Church property. There were two—count them, T-U-E, two—archdeacons leading the charge. And the blood on the pavement—the flies hadn't even got there when Gorabani orders the Tarelians to defend Syncretisty Hall! *Tell* me we don't have a war with the goddamned Church!''

Viluji sat in his chair, the prayer beads clicking unhappily. "What are you going to do about it?''

"Fight.''

"Good,'' Genzari said. Smash the Church now, we can worry about the dukes later. "We outnumber the Tarelians more than two to one. We'll move into position this evening and take them first thing in the morning.''

"We'll move into position this evening,'' Jankura agreed. "Then we'll see what Master Wizenbeak does. A day or two to let the situation ripen won't hurt a thing. The Tarelians aren't prepared to withstand a siege. And, of course, it would be nice to move Marjia to a place of safety.''

"Her Majesty may be right,'' Braley said. "If we can settle with the Church, the dukes might fall in line. In any event, it looks like our best chance. Or do Your Graces disagree?''

"That depends on how you deal with the Church,'' Falenda said at last. "I, myself, wouldn't be terribly pleased with any wholesale slaughter of clerisy.''

Braley adjusted his sword sash and sighed. The clerisy was connected to the nobility. Bastards and younger sons for whom the various dukes sought to find a place. "If you figure out a way to avoid it, let me know,'' he said at last. "At the very least, we're going to have to hang the Mambrinistas.''

"You'll start the civil war all over again,'' Viluji said.

"You mean it hasn't been restarted already?"

"Lasco is right," Jankura said. "It's time to move out the army and see what happens. The Church has killed one King of Guhland too many."

Archdeacon Doctor William Weird Wizenbeak, master of the Tarelian Order, and Princess Marjia, sole survivor of the House of Grathnys, walked leisurely along the defensive perimeter the Tarelians had thrown up around Syncretisty Hall. Horses, which would have been more appropriate to their station, required stabling and feed that were not available, and so they went about on foot. Here the pavement had been ripped up to form a barricade of cobblestones, there canvas had been hung over a freshly opened sewer to serve as an improvised field latrine.

"What do you think?" Marjia asked.

"We could have done without separate latrines for the officers, probably."

"Don't try to be funny. What do you think?"

"About your plan." It wasn't a question. Marjia had an idea about doing something to keep Guhland from being plunged back into civil war. The fact that he, personally, found it distasteful, dangerous, and more than a little crazy didn't alter the fact that he hadn't been able to come up with any viable alternative. To do nothing, the firm, resolute course of the brave but unimaginative, was to court an utterly predictable disaster. The Royal Army under Genzari and Braley was already taking up positions opposite their barricades. When they decided to move, there would be one hell of a fight, and the Tarelians, lacking room to maneuver, would be wiped out to the last man. There would be negotiations first, of course, about getting Marjia back to the Citadel. But nothing resolved his own personal dilemma, of his loyalty to Jankura and to . . . not the Church, but to the Tarelian Order. The patriarch could go fry his hat, and the clerisy as well, but the Tarelians had fought for *him*, they had died for *him*, and he had to find a way out of this terrible cul-de-sac for *them*. "Yes."

"That's a big help," she said. "Yes, what? Are you going to try to trade me off to some duke for his support?"

The wizard shook his head. "No, no. I don't like your plan, that's all. But to use you as a pawn in Gorabani's game isn't any better." He owed her *some* consideration; in theory he was still oathbound to her as the reincarnation of Queen Shaia. And her plan had a certain crazy audacity . . . "If there were something else we could do, some other way to get out of this awful predicament.''

"You can shave your beard and bug out," Marjia said. "Me, they will be looking for. And once they get me, I don't figure to last very long. Except for a few odds and ends, my magic is lost to me; and sexually—well, hell, I'm not going to bind a duke to my interest *that* way. You, my old tutor, are the only chance I have left. And you don't like my plan.''

"It seems so megalomaniacal," he replied. "It isn't like me at all.''

"So close your eyes and think of Guhland. If it works, you spare them the second installment of the civil war, right? Think of the Tarelians. They'll wind up dead if you insist on being properly humble as befits your lowly station." She sighed. "If you wanted to go with another plan, maybe I could see it, but you haven't got a clue as to what comes next.''

"I have a clue," Wizenbeak protested. "Standing pat, staying put, going the course, has got to be a catastrophe.''

"Are you going to let it happen?''

They stopped in front of Saint Mambro's Church, down the street from Syncretisty Hall. The pews had been taken over as temporary billets for the Tarelians, and the basement had been taken over as general headquarters. Wizenbeak and Marjia were temporarily housed in the vestry behind the church building.

"No, Princess," he said at last. "We'll try it your way. I'll give it my best shot." She gave him a hug, and he stroked her blond hair. "Here." He reached into his pockets and handed her two sleeping troll-bats. "Hold them for me till morning. And go to bed. Nobody will take me seriously if you hang around trying to coach me.''

He watched her as she went with her escort over to the vestry, and after her nanny met her at the door, he went down the stone steps into the basement of Saint Mambro's. He found Pardus Murado and his senior officers standing over an improvised sand table.

"Our order of battle doesn't look all that good, does it, Pardus?" he said conversationally.

"Well, yes, it's a lousy position," Murado replied. "The patriarch says 'Defend Syncretisty Hall,' and we don't blame you for setting up to do it, but the whole thing is going to be street fighting and barricades if it comes to blows.''

"You think we'd lose, don't you.''

"We shouldn't be fighting, Master Wizenbeak! The patriarch

ought to hand over the conspirators to the civil authorities! We never took oath to defend a pack of traitors, for God's sake!"

The wizard leaned over the table to study the disposition of his troops. "Perhaps Patriarch Gorabani is one of the conspirators," he observed, pushing his glasses back on his nose. "What would you do then?"

A long pause. "We swore to defend Guhland and the Syncretist Church," Murado said. "I never imagined I'd have to choose between them."

An officer came up and saluted. "Sir, the Royal Army has taken up positions opposite our barricades on Dyer Street."

Wizenbeak nodded. "That closes the circle, doesn't it?"

Murado put a little red flag opposite the Dyer Street barricade on the sand table and nodded. "Yes. Yes, they seem to have moved out right smartly."

"And if you were in command over there, what would you be doing bright and early tomorrow morning?"

"I'd sit tight, sir. We eat breakfast, they eat breakfast. At noon, they eat lunch, we tighten our belts. That's assuming they don't turn off our water, of course."

"Right," the wizard said. "Time is not on our side, and win or lose, the Tarelians are going to get chewed up pretty badly."

His captain-general laughed. "Win? Are those little troll-bats of yours going to pull something out of your hat for us?"

"Hunh," Wizenbeak grunted. Step one—persuade the Tarelians they ought to go with him—seemed to be pretty well in hand. So try step two. "You've been thinking in terms of Church and state, of loyalty to the patriarch or Queen Shaia. Let old Gorabani do your thinking for you, you and the Tarelians are going to be dead meat in short order. Forget about Gorabani and Shaia, think about the Tarelian Order and Guhland!"

Murado looked at him. "I'm loyal to the Church," he said, "but I'm loyal to Guhland, too. What should we do?"

"Let's take it a little at a time, Pardus. Do you, or anyone here, doubt that Gorabani himself set up the assassination attempt this morning?"

"How do you figure, sir?" asked one of the officers.

Wizenbeak reached into his robe and pulled out the order to defend Syncretisty Hall. "This. All signed, sealed, and delivered into my hand at the very moment the attack ended. I did it, we're in place, but if you start to think about it, Patriarch Gorabani has blood on his hands up to the elbows."

There was a general murmur of assent.

Well, thought the wizard, put the question to them. "So do we wish to die defending a regicide?"

"No sir," Pardus said, "but we don't seem to have a lot of choice."

"We have a choice," Wizenbeak said, amazed at how well this was going. "The Royal Army has us surrounded, but we have Syncretisty Hall in our pocket. All we have to do is go in and tell old Gorabani that he's got to step down. And just so there isn't any room for confusion, he can appoint me as his successor."

"What?" Mouths dropped open. The same reaction he'd had when Marjia sprang it on him.

"Me," the wizard said, with a touch of diffidence. "I, myself, will go in and become patriarch. I am, after all, an archdeacon and a not unworthy master of the Tarelian Order, if I say it myself."

Murado looked very thoughtful. He didn't say, "That's crazy!" He didn't say, "It won't work!" He just stood there looking at the sand table, at the red flags surrounding the outnumbered green flags, for a long, long time. "You've been a good master of the order," he said at last. "What would you do as patriarch?"

Wizenbeak sighed and proceeded to be somewhat less than totally frank in laying out Marjia's grand design. "To tell you the truth, I don't know. Whatever has to be done, I'll try to do it. I'd like to bring Church and Crown into some semblance of harmony."

"We just walk in and tell the patriarch, 'The jig is up'?" said one of the officers.

"Gorabani has to go," Murado said. "He *will* go, one way or another. The only thing is, do we, the Tarelian Order, go with him?"

"Couldn't we sleep on the question?"

"No," Murado replied firmly. The habit of conspiracy dies hard. As the full recognition of the disaster produced by the corrupt and treasonous policies of the Church had sunk in, he had begun to look for a way out. To follow the master of the order was more than he had hoped for. "I don't think Genzari is going to attack at dawn, but we can't depend on it. And time is running out—has run out." He looked around. "Are there any other questions?"

"Let's have a vote," said one of the officers. He opened his knapsack and took out a handful of black beans from one pocket, white beans from another, and put them on the table. "Pardus, do you want to hold the jar?"

Murado nodded, and someone handed him a large earthenware pot that still smelled faintly of herring. The officers gathered around, and he handed each of them a black bean and a white bean. "This white bean," he said holding one up, "stands for loyalty unto death, following the orders of Patriarch Gorabani like good soldiers, regardless of the consequences. The black bean, here, is more of a gamble. A black bean means we go with Doctor Wizenbeak, for good or ill and the possible damnation of our immortal souls. You understand?" There was a murmur of assent, and he walked around with the jar as each officer dropped in his vote.

With each bean, Murado counted the number, ending on thirteen as he cast his own vote. Then he dumped the jar on the table for all to see. Thirteen black beans lay before them.

Pardus Murado adjusted his sword sash. "Good," he said with evident satisfaction. "There's nothing like unanimity when taking a leap in the dark! Let's go, Master Wizenbeak!"

29

Wizenbeak Performs the Old Hat Trick

THE Congregation of Clerisiarchs was gathered in the meeting room of Syncretisty Hall, contemplating their red yesterdays and their glorious tomorrows. Men who had made a career of words, hurling insults like javelins, cutting with the deadly nuance, the poisoned implication, could not now believe that events had overtaken them, that words would no longer bite. And so they sat fretting over plans that would never be executed, debating issues that had already been settled.

"A point of information," Archdeacon Viluji said. "Assuming that we do, in fact, have control of the Princess Marjia, as the patriarch has assured us, have we had any offer from any duke, any duke whatsoever, for her hand?"

"It's still too early," Kurjima said wearily. "The dukes are unsure of how to move, and not yet willing to take any serious risks on our behalf. We have no offer in hand, but it is reasonable to expect that offers will be made."

"When, please?" Viluji asked.

"We expect that offers will be made in a timely fashion," replied Kurjima, begging the question. "Except for Duke Falenda, Duke Viluji, and the young Duke Bedirny who swore fealty to the so-called Witch-Queen immediately upon the death of his father, the remaining dukes are potential suitors. All of them."

"With all due respect," said Archdeacon Darussis, who had been over this ground before, "the dukes are waiting to see the dust settle before they lift a finger to help the Church. The False Shaia cannot maintain herself in power, you tell us—"

"She can't!" Kurjima snapped. "There is no way that wicked woman can hold power!"

"Fine and dandy!" Darussis replied, his white hair bristling.

"It might be true, eventually. But if she moves against us tomorrow, I tell you that she can't be stopped! And when the dust does settle, we *aren't* going to be a whole lot worse off than we are now, we are going to be *dead*! I say the time to make a deal is the present, right now, this very evening, *if* there is a deal to be made!"

"Out of order, Darussis," Patriarch Gorabani said grimly. "We can hardly invite the dukes to submit sealed bids for the hand of the princess. And as for dealing with the Witch-Queen . . ." He shook his head. "At the very minimum, a deal with the so-called Witch-Queen would mean hanging the 'short list' which she submitted before the coronation." He composed his black-gloved hands in front of him. "One assumes that our brethren on the list might reasonably object to such a deal!"

"They were the ones that got us into this mess!"

A messenger crossed swiftly to Gorabani and handed him a pair of wooden chips neatly tied with ribbon and sealed with wax. The patriarch read it and grimaced. "Our cup runneth over," he said. "Archdeacon Wizenbeak has condescended to grace Syncretisty Hall with his presence and even now wishes to speak to us. Everyone else has, why not him? Send the old fool in, by all means."

Wizenbeak strode in, accompanied by Pardus Murado and a company of swordsmen in battle dress. There was a nervous rustle among the assembly.

"Good evening, gentlemen, Your Holiness," the wizard said politely. How am I going to get this started, he wondered uneasily. Patriarch Gorabani has considerable presence, up there on that gilded throne of his. A shrug. "You will be interested to learn that I have had a letter from Her Majesty."

"The so-called Witch-Queen?" Gorabani asked. "She has no claim to the throne of Guhland. She is merely a poor, foolish impostor trading upon her chance resemblance to the late Shaia."

Right, thought Wizenbeak. For what it's worth, it's out in the open. Well, we go from one point to the next as best we can. "Her Majesty was brief and to the point," he replied calmly. "She said that the Church had killed one King of Guhland too many." The Congregation stirred uneasily. This was something they had thought but had not voiced. "The Royal Army agrees with her, seemingly."

"Indeed." The patriarch rubbed his hooked nose. "And is that why you come here with a company of common soldiers?"

"I was fearful of encountering archdeacons wearing their shrouds, Your Holiness." Chew on *that*, you sanctimonious sons of bitches! "This morning, Archdeacon Obuskaia died within six feet of where I was standing."

"The report was that you slew Anezkva with your troll-bats," said a red-faced archdeacon on the right. "Did you?"

"He was the last of the death commandos," the wizard replied, "threatening the life of Princess Marjia. Say rather that I saved the princess."

"We understand," the patriarch said. "What else did the so-called Witch-Queen say in that letter you received?"

"Her Majesty asked me to move the Tarelian Order aside, to stop defending 'the nest of traitors in Syncretisty Hall.' "

"And do you agree with her, Master Wizenbeak?" Kurjima asked.

"That the Church has killed one King of Guhland too many? Yes. Yes, I do."

"In which of your multifarious capacities?"

"In all of them," the wizard replied. "The one which concerns you most, however, is that I am the master of the Tarelian Order."

Gorabani sat impassively, his face cold and stern. "We made you master of the order and we can unmake you. Indeed, it is hardly fitting that such a one as you should even be a member of the Church, let alone an archdeacon. That, too, can be remedied."

"You might wish to burn me as Witchfinder Fadel burned my illustrious predecessor, Archdeacon Nasar-Namatu," Wizenbeak suggested, making a mock bow. "The threat of excommunication is almost excessively modest in your present circumstances."

"Burning can come later," Kurjima said, but the threat was empty, and he knew it.

"No," Wizenbeak said, pushing his spectacles back on his nose. "Nor excommunication, neither." What I have in mind is that Patriarch Gorabani should resign in my favor, but how can I tell him that before all these people? He must yield, but in front of the Congregation of Clerisiarchs, all I can do is kill him. "We have a problem, Your Holiness. It might be advantageous to caucus on it briefly."

Gorabani sighed and rubbed his eyes with thumb and forefinger. The worst case scenario, he thought bitterly, the one that was so bad that we didn't bother to consider it, was that we should kill Prince Dervian while leaving the so-called Witch-Queen alive and in power. Well, that's what we got. And now this mountebank stands here telling me we have a problem. "There will be a brief recess," he said as he got up. "Ten minutes. The Stag's Head Dining Room, Doctor Wizenbeak?"

Sometime near the end of dinner the servants had simply left. The meal had been served and eaten, but the dishes had not been cleared away, and the candles burned themselves down in an empty room. As Murado gathered the plates and stacked them on the sideboard, Gorabani and Wizenbeak seated themselves at the cleared table. The tablecloth was dusted with crumbs and stained with wine, mute testimony to the force of the disaster that was overtaking the Church. Murado stood politely behind the master of the order, as Dr. Kurjima seated himself beside his master. The Tarelian swordsmen waited discreetly outside in the hallway.

"You seem pretty sure that Her Majesty is an impostor," the wizard said. "How much do you know?"

Gorabani shrugged. "That's about it. No name, no history. But without Prince Dervian, she can't rule. Did she offer a deal?"

"No, she only promised to deal *with* you. In the circumstances hardly an offer at all."

"Without Prince Dervian she can't rule," Kurjima said, "and *we* have Princess Marjia."

"The Shadow Shaia might have trouble ruling," Wizenbeak agreed pleasantly, "but not before she sorts out the odds and sods in Syncretisty Hall. And *we* do not have Princess Marjia, Doctor Kurjima. She is with *me*. Which brings us to the point, Your Holiness. Her Majesty won't deal with you; and you, in turn, can no longer deal with her. But me—" He tapped himself on the chest. "*I* can deal with both of you."

"You?" The patriarch composed his black-gloved hands in front of him. "What sort of deal?"

The wizard removed a deck of cards from his pocket and shuffled it three times. "Her Majesty was for a time my apprentice," he said, turning up an ace. "In some circumstances, I might still be able to exercise a measure of control over her." He turned up a second ace. "More control than would seem warranted to an outsider." A third ace lay on the table. "And what I offer is the only deal you're going to get." He turned over the fourth ace.

"You don't know that," Kurjima said. "The dukes will be competing for the hand of Princess Marjia!"

Wizenbeak smiled. "Then they'll approach *me*, won't they?"

"What do you want?" Gorabani asked.

"Your hat. In return, I'll try to get you pious traitors and vile regicides out of this alive. The whole bloody lot of you."

"No. We might let you dispose of Princess Marjia to your own benefit—"

"She isn't yours to give away, Doctor Kurjima."

The patriarch brushed at the crumbs on the soiled tablecloth. "So you said. However, we will not, we cannot, tolerate the continued presence of the Witch-Queen on the throne of Guhland!"

"Make up your mind. Either she *is* the Witch-Queen, or she *isn't*. The 'so-called' Witch-Queen, the 'False' Shaia, is not someone you can't tolerate. Right?"

"Yes. No. I don't know." A grimace. "It would be much easier if she were to step down."

"You can't deal with her, Gorabani? It might also be easier if *you* were to step down."

"She can't maintain herself in power, Master Wizenbeak. You know that, don't you? She's finished."

"Eventually, maybe. What are you going to do tomorrow morning when she asks me to have the Tarelians stand aside to let her march into Syncretisty Hall?" The wizard twisted a strand of whiskers around one gnarled finger. "No sense in getting ourselves killed when we can't stop her, right?"

"We would inflict unacceptable losses upon the Royal Armies," Gorabani said. "After such a victory, she would be easy prey for any coalition of dukes that could get organized. If you stand firm, the False Shaia won't attack."

"That happens not to be the case. It pains me to contradict Your Holiness, but the main question seems to be whether my former apprentice will order the attack after breakfast, or after lunch."

"Your former apprentice, yes." The patriarch sighed and rested his elbows on the table. "I suppose you imagine that you have some idea of how she's going to act?"

Wizenbeak grinned. "Well, yes, actually. Whereas you have this strange and convoluted theory of how some imaginary female *ought* to act." Hope springs eternal, he thought, as he squared the deck. "The reason for all this outlandish theorizing is so that you people don't have to face up to getting hung for treason!''

Hope does cloud the judgment at times, thought Gorabani. ''I suppose you want my decision tonight?''

''If you decide yes. You can decide no by not moving a muscle.'' The wizard put the cards back in his pocket. ''The Tarelians *will* stand aside tomorrow. You know that, don't you?''

''Yes.'' A sigh. ''Yes, I suppose they will. If you assume the patriarch's hat, you say you'll save our lives?'' Wizenbeak nodded assent. ''What about our property?''

''Hunh, I'm not even sure about your lives, but I'll try. You lose a war, bad things can happen, right?''

''Right.'' Gorabani rubbed his eyes with thumb and forefinger. No choice, he thought bitterly, no choice at all. ''Well, when we reconvene the Congregation of Clerisiarchs I'll propose you as the new patriarch. And leave it up to them. If they buy what you're selling, the hat is yours. At which point we go upstairs, Doctor Kurjima drafts the formal transfer, and it's done.''

Wizenbeak returned to his temporary billets in the vestry as the black cock of night was crowing. Saint Mambro's Church was a looming black presence against a sky where the first stars were beginning to fade. And he felt very weary, as if he had personally had to persuade each individual clerisiarch of the rightness of his course of action. Maybe he had. The arguments had been rehashed often enough. The Tarelian guard let him through the kitchen door, and he put a splinter into the banked coals in the stove to light a candle. Marjia, who must have been listening for him, came down the stairs with Mischka and Branka.

''How did it go?'' she asked.

''The threat of hanging concentrates men's minds wonderfully,'' the wizard replied. He reached into his pocket and pulled out the patriarch's hat. ''You may call me 'Your Holiness,' and roust up the cook to fix some toast and coffee by way of showing respect.''

''We're out of coffee,'' Marjia said, ''but you've made a good start.'' She went over and pulled at the bell rope. ''So, Patriarch Wizenbeak, is it now?''

''Yes. Gorabani bought the argument. So did Darussis, and young Viluji, and the Reformers.'' A yawn. ''The others, a lot of them, didn't want to hear it, so we had to repeat everything over and over again. God! What a den of imbecility and fanaticism! That place is encrusted with such a deposit of stupidity as you wouldn't believe."

"I believe it," Marjia said. "The next thing is to set up a meeting with Jankura. Has she sent in an ultimatum, yet?"

Wizenbeak yawned. "Nothing so far. Murado thinks maybe this morning sometime. I could use some sleep, especially if we're out of coffee."

"Right," she said as the cook shuffled in. "Lie down on the bench over there." The bench was a good length, and horizontal, a good direction, and as the wizard lay down, one of the troll-bats came flittering over to rest near his forehead. The cook and the princess were discussing breakfast as the cook put a stick of firewood in the stove, but the sound of their voices grew fainter and fainter.

He awoke with a start. The kitchen was light. Or at least lighter. Marjia was dressed. Breakfast was on the table. Time felt like it was the next morning. Wizenbeak sat up, yawned, and rubbed his face in his hands. He felt pretty good, all things considered. There was a platter of scrambled eggs on the table, and fried potatoes, and toast with apple butter on the side. Good stuff. And a pot of tea, with a jar of preserves beside it, northern style.

The cook held his chair for him. "It's an honor to serve Your Holiness," she said humbly.

Oh yes, he thought. *That's* what I was doing last night. Almost, it took away his appetite. "Bless you, my child," he murmured.

He was stirring preserves into his second cup of tea when Pardus Murado came in with a scroll bearing the royal seal.

The wizard opened and read it. "Shaia of Guhland, Queen Revenant, commands that her loyal subject, Doctor William Weird Wizenbeak, master of the Tarelian Order, remove said order from the position of guard it now holds around Syncretisty Hall by noon today."

"That's the way of the world," he sighed, wiping his mouth with a napkin. "Catch a little nap and events overtake you." He handed the scroll to Murado. "What do you think?"

"It's what we were expecting, sir."

"So it is," Wizenbeak said, blowing on his tea. Good old Pardus, he thought, he doesn't care what I do as long as the order comes out in good shape. "Yes. I'll draft a reply and have it sent over by herald."

"What will you be saying, sir?"

"Nothing specific. I'll simply propose a meeting and sign myself 'Patriarch Wizenbeak.' "

30

Jankura Maintains Her Right

MIDMORNING and a light spring rain was falling. Under a company-sized shield pavilion Jankura stood wrapped in her black cape, looking across the plaza at the barricade the Tarelians had erected where Dyer Street ran into Fenjio's Lane. Several companies of the Royal Army were massed opposite the Tarelian barricade, and others were standing on the side streets, waiting for the order to attack. So far, neither side had made a move.

"What do you think Wizenbeak will do, ma'am?" Genzari asked.

"Pull out," replied Jankura. "Of course I've been wrong about him before."

In human affairs the odds are always six to five against, thought Genzari, but even if the Tarelians pulled out, they'd have evil choices to make. "And if he doesn't?"

"Give the army a hot meal and send them in." Once Jankura had recognized that she was going down, once she accepted it, the decisions had become easier. Everything since she had escaped burning in Huitmire was pure gravy, and if her string was about to run out, well, she was going to go out in style.

"Right," Count Braley said. He didn't like Her Majesty's attitude. Being fatalistic about defeat was one thing, accepting it was something else entirely. "What about Princess Marjia?"

Jankura shrugged. "What about her? If we have to go in, she's the least of our worries. If we don't, I imagine she can be persuaded to come home."

At the barricade, a white flag was displayed, and after a moment the Tarelian herald came out, holding a roll of parchment above his head. He walked across the plaza, toward the shield pavilion, and when he was stopped, an officer and guards escorted him into the presence.

"Good morning, Your Majesty," he said, bowing to Jankura and handing her the scroll. "You may or may not have heard that last night the Congregation of Clerisiarchs accepted the resignation of Patriarch Gorabani from that office, confirming his selection of Archdeacon Wizenbeak as his replacement."

Astonished, Jankura looked to Genzari, who shrugged, and to Count Braley, who looked completely impassive. "We hadn't heard," she said. "Patriarch Wizenbeak?"

"Yes, Your Majesty. He wishes to arrange a meeting with you to discuss a possible settlement of the differences between Church and Crown."

"Old Wizenbeak the new patriarch? We understand." She broke the wax seal and read the scroll. It simply requested a meeting, naming the herald as his agent to arrange it, and was signed and sealed "Patriarch Wizenbeak."

Jankura stepped aside with her generals. "All right," she said. "I was braced to go storming in there and smash the Church flatter than a tromped-on tree frog. I didn't really expect Wizenbeak to come through for me and I certainly didn't expect this. What do we do now?"

"Talk to him," Genzari said, fingering his closely clipped mustache. "We at least owe our old friend the courtesy of listening to what he has to say."

"I agree," Count Braley said. "The situation has changed, possibly for the better, and we would have honored his request for a parley under the previous circumstances."

"Yes, yes. Right. I'll talk to him. I *want* to talk to him. But what am I going to say?"

Genzari and Braley looked at each other, and Braley shrugged. "Don't say anything. Be polite, effusive if you want. Listen to what he says, and ask for time to think about it. Just the fact that we're willing to talk says quite a bit."

She nodded. "Very well. Count Braley, will you arrange the meeting with the herald?"

"Yes, Your Majesty. What time?"

"Right now, if we could." A shrug. "As soon as possible."

Count Braley grinned and nodded. He walked over to the herald, and after a short discussion, a squad from the Royal Army moved into the center of the square with Braley and the herald supervising, and put up a squad-sized shield pavilion. Thrusting spears into the holes left by displaced cobbles, they braced the spears with guy ropes and unfolded the glass-reinforced fabric shields to rest on the overhead connecting ropes. The Tarelians sent out a table and chairs borrowed from the Café Fenjio, setting them up underneath; and the herald returned behind the barricade.

"We're all set, Your Majesty," Braley said. "When Wizenbeak and the captain-general of the Tarelians step out from behind the barricade, you and I and Genzari cross our front line and meet them at the table."

"He agreed to three to two?" asked Genzari.

"The herald thought it would be all right. There are six chairs out there if he wants to bring somebody else." Braley looked up. "Damn. There he is. Let's go."

The five of them walked across the plaza in the cold, misting rain, arriving simultaneously at the table set up under the shield pavilion. The men were wearing battle dress, except Wizenbeak, who simply wore a plain black and tan hauberk under his wizard's robes, and the white patriarch's hat. Jankura wore black, with a crimson sash.

"You're looking well, Your Majesty," the wizard said pleasantly. Uncertain of how to proceed, she offered him her hand. He took it and kissed it, and in return offered his own hand. "You may kiss our ring, Your Majesty; you will, in fact, be the very first."

Jankura looked startled, but following protocol, she made a curtsy and kissed the patriarch's ring. "You've come up in the world," she observed as they seated themselves around the table. "You wanted to talk?"

"Well, no, actually. I wanted to shave off my beard and run away, but the Congregation of Clerisiarchs prevailed upon me to accept this terrible burden for the good of the country." He sighed. "So here I am. One of the things I promised was to secure the life and freedom of the entire Congregation of Clerisiarchs."

"The men who plotted the death of Prince Dervian must die," Jankura said calmly. "I imagine that Gorabani was one of them, but there were surely others."

"Perhaps," Wizenbeak said. "In the event that we are unable to come to an agreement, I do not propose to sit behind these silly barricades defending Syncretisty Hall. We will take the clerisy and make a sortie for the open country."

"Not a bad plan," said Braley, who had rather expected it. "And when do you propose to put it into effect?"

"When I am convinced that further discussion is futile," the new patriarch replied.

"The Church must pay for the crime of regicide," Jankura said grimly.

"I agree," he replied, "but it is impossible that they should consent to pay you, 'Janko' Jankura, the Shadow Shaia, the so-called Witch-Queen. They'd die first."

"That could be arranged, Your Holiness," Genzari said.

"No doubt it could, old friend," the wizard replied, leaning on the table. It rocked on the uneven surface, and he sat back in his chair. "Nevertheless, I have a plan."

Braley looked interested. Strategically, the wizard had a tendency to be somewhat superficial, but he was never dull. "We would be pleased to hear your proposal . . ." He hesitated a moment. ". . . Your Holiness."

"The title falls a bit strangely on my ear, too," Wizenbeak agreed. "Anyway, my plan has good parts and bad parts. First the good parts. In lieu of hanging selected individuals in the clerisy, what I propose is wholesale land reform."

"The Church wouldn't put up with it," Jankura said.

"Ah, but I . . . we . . . am the Church," he replied. "Basically, what I have in mind is first, returning the property of those Orthodox property owners that were burned as witches to their Orthodox heirs—a project presently stalled in the courts, by the way. Second, the present titleholders, the most aggressively devout—not to mention litigious—Syncretists, are to be compensated, not with a refund of the token and totally insufficient monies they paid out, but with title to an equivalent property from the immense landholdings of the Church."

"That isn't a bad idea," Braley conceded. "The land was what they wanted, and mostly they got it at bargain rates, but why not give the Church land directly to the Orthodox?"

"Aha!" Wizenbeak had asked Marjia the same question. "We first return Orthodox land to Orthodox landowners. Very straightforward, very proper, comparatively uncontroversial. But when we simultaneously take land from the Church, we give it to the Church's strongest supporters. Converting them to supporters of the land reform of which they are the beneficiaries."

Braley nodded approval; someone must have been advising the wizard. The plan was altogether too sound for him to have conjured up on his own. "Very good, excellent. Continue, please."

"Having once started land reform, the *rest* of the Church land will be distributed among our friends, not the dukes so much as the smallholders. The main thing is to get the forty percent of Guhland the Church owns back on the tax rolls.''

"You told the clerisy you were going to do this?" Jankura asked.

"No, I told them what they wanted to hear, that I'd do my best to save their miserable hides from being nailed to the barn door. When they asked me how, I said I didn't know."

"So far, I'm willing to go along with the program," Jankura said. "What are the bad parts you mentioned?"

"Well . . ." The wizard rubbed his long nose, seemingly at a loss for words. "Basically, the only way to make a change that drastic is to stabilize the Crown. A strong king is absolutely necessary. And you, Jankura, my dear, are a peasant girl up there pretending to be the universally and passionately hated Witch-Queen. You'll have to step down, I'm afraid."

"I will maintain her right," Genzari said softly.

"Whom did you have in mind as her replacement?" Count Braley asked.

The general scowled at the strategist. "You would presume to discuss Her Majesty stepping down?"

"Gently, Lasco," Jankura said, laying a hand on his arm, "I want to hear what Master Wizenbeak has to propose."

"Prince Kahun made himself king-patriarch," Wizenbeak said. "Having already secured the patriarch's hat, I propose to do the same. To secure my claim to the throne of Guhland, I will marry Princess Marjia!"

There was a moment of stunned silence at the table.

"You want to be king?"

"No, nor patriarch neither, but it's either that or see Guhland plunged into civil war. With the Royal Army and the Tarelians, who are also a Royal Army, incidentally, the dukes had damn well better behave."

"You're serious?" Jankura asked at last.

"Yes, darling."

A long sigh. "I guess you are," she said. "Well, then, Your Holiness, you've given us a lot to think about. Suppose we take a break and meet back here this afternoon?"

"That's agreeable," the wizard said. "One thing."

"Yes?" Genzari asked.

"Can we bring the Tarelian mess wagons through your lines? No sense in the men missing a meal if we aren't going to fight."

Genzari looked at Braley, and Braley looked at Jankura, who looked at Genzari.

Count Braley lifted an eyebrow. This wasn't a standard siege situation, by any manner of means, and if he was going to seek future employment with King-Patriarch Wizenbeak, he didn't want to be excessively hard-nosed here and now. "Suppose we let the noon meal in and meet you back here at two?" he suggested.

"Two o'clock will be fine," the wizard said.

As they walked back to the barricade, Murado looked very thoughtful. "What do you think will happen, sir?"

Wizenbeak shrugged. This was going pretty much as Marjia had predicted, so far. Maybe she was right about the rest of it.

"They'll caucus," he said at last, "and then they'll come back to cut the best deal they can. And Her Majesty will cut it this afternoon, because she's afraid her people will sneak out in the night and make a separate peace if she stalls around."

"That's just amazing, sir. How did you figure it?"

The patriarch sighed. He had asked Marjia the same question, and she had given him the answer one of his professors used to use when asked to explain some particularly difficult thaumaturgical proof. "It just logically follows," he said.

31

Happy Ending, Nice and Tidy

IN due time King-Patriarch Wizenbeak went to Cymdulock Cathedral for his formal investiture as patriarch, and again for his wedding to the white-gowned Princess Marjia, and a third time to be crowned King-Patriarch of Guhland. They lived in interesting times ever after.

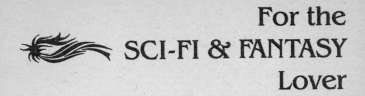